MW01536339

# EYES OF REVENGE

# EYES OF REVENGE

*Sequel to "Eyes of the Innocent"*

G.R.R. Restivo

Copyright © 2008 by G.R.R. Restivo.

Library of Congress Control Number:     2008903586
ISBN:          Hardcover                978-1-4363-3711-3
               Softcover                978-1-4363-3710-6

All rights reserved. No part of this book may be reproduced or transmitted in any form or by any means, electronic or mechanical, including photocopying, recording, or by any information storage and retrieval system, without permission in writing from the copyright owner.

This is a work of fiction. Names, characters, places and incidents either are the product of the author's imagination or are used fictitiously, and any resemblance to any actual persons, living or dead, events, or locales is entirely coincidental.

This book was printed in the United States of America.

**To order additional copies of this book, contact:**
Xlibris Corporation
1-888-795-4274
www.Xlibris.com
Orders@Xlibris.com
45142

To
John Schiro
**In Memoriam**
1955-2005

"On wrongs, swift vengeance awaits"

Alexander Pope

# FOREWORD

The last five years since my first novel, *Eyes of the Innocent*, was published has been an exciting time. My novel was received with great anticipation, and all who read it not only were giving me thumbs-up, but also even quoted from the book. I was nervous at first, thinking people will hate it or not understand my writing. My nervousness went up in smoke after the first calls came to me. It was a hit, and it was then I decided not to end it all there but to continue with the characters and of Caesar, as one of my friends called him, super cat. I wanted to bring out the same theme but in a different vein and environment. If you loved the first book, you might be surprised how far I took the characters. Caesar and his friends get in trouble again, and the humans, well they are always in trouble. Like the first book, I thought up a different way to smuggle drugs into the country; but in this book is an invention of my imagination, but it can be constructed. It would be fantastic to see but who am I, Jules Verne?

My idea for the novel came one day in the Caribbean in Trinidad, and I wrote the first outline coming back on our return trip to New York. I wanted it to be as exciting and fast paced as the first book but had to get all the characters involved and introduce some new characters especially in the animal world. I think the new animal characters will be enjoyable to the reader. I realized I had left out an important type of bird in the first book especially since it took place in New York City. I watched and observed the various birds and their mannerisms to try to capture on paper their thoughts and lives.

In my first book, I was remiss in not naming some people who were instrumental in making the first novel possible. First, of course, my wife, Loretta—or Lori—who typed and typed the first book and this book more than once. Vin Trapani, my talented nephew, who did the first book cover artwork and this book's cover. He is a terrific artist. My sisters, Nancy and Eleanor, and Vicki my niece, who let me use their homes to have a book signing; and my sisters have become my greatest agents for the book. My brother, Alfred, offered to edit the first book since he found mistakes in the grammar. Sorry, Alfred, this time it's to be professionally edited. My friends Marsha and Neil and Hayley, who let me use their home in Long Beach for a book signing. And to all the others I received wonderful accolades from after reading the first book, get yourself ready for a ride with the sequel.

Since the first book was published, we lost our cat, Frisky Beep-Beep, who was the gentlest of cats I had ever had the pleasure to share a home. The great Enew, as Caesar would say, took him into heaven; and I hope he is happy. We miss him a great deal.

I want to thank two special people who influenced me in my early years, and that was my mother and father. I had parents who were direct opposites and gave me each end of the spectrum. My father was from Sicily and was a stern parent with a tough-love attitude. You knew he'd kill for you, but he'd never say it. My mother was saintly, and my life was tied to her; and it was from her saving her pennies and buying me toys that let my imagination run rampant and that gives me these crazy ideas. She had no money, just a Montgomery Ward credit card. She was magic, and I loved her.

Have a great time reading the book, and remember, your imagination can take you anywhere you want.

Enjoy,
G. R. R. Restivo
February 2008

# PROLOGUE

## IT WAS NOT OVER

White was the color of the concrete sidewalk as it shone from the sun while the black muscular animal stretched its frame across the windowsill. The sun made him feel good today, and the summer sun was hot. He could lay in it for hours, staring out the window at humans walking to wherever humans go in the midday. The black cat reached out his paws, and, instinctively, claws came out. Larger claws than other cats that matched his large frame. His claws had killed before and would kill again if need be, but he daydreamed of the past and its pain and of his happiness now; of his mother and her killer, and his travels of almost a lifetime. The memory of the night in the deep water when he saw his mother's killer for the last time gave him chills down his spine. He could still remember the killer's scent like that of the rat; it was slimy and smelled of death. His revenge on the man was complete, but still there was doubt in the cat's mind. A lingering, nagging thought that just wouldn't disappear. Was the human rat dead? Did he go down with the flying machine? There was no sign of the killer, and the humans did look for him in the water. He kept stretching his muscles. No other cat except the legendary Simmark had traveled such as he. He heard the talk of other animals, especially the blabbering blue jay, Fletcher, speak of his exploits and his deeds; but this did not impress him. He was a happy cat now, with all that nasty human business behind him. Still he had dreams, haunting dreams, that the human rat who killed his mother was not dead. He dreamed of the rat's head coming above water again and again smiling that strange human facial expression. In the human rat's hand was his mother's head and in the other was a gun, pointed at him. The more he swam away, the more the human rat was behind him, edging closer at each moment. Then he woke up. The dreams never lasted long, but it bothered him consistently. He knew it's from all he had been through, but he had this bad feeling that just wouldn't go away.

The black cat stretched again, rubbing his head against the windowpane as he did. It has been an easy three moons from that night, and he had lived the life of one of his Egyptian ancestors—or so what his master kept saying. People came and went in this den, taking pictures of him and talking to his mistress. Then there were the people with bright lights that leave white dots in your head for a time. He would shake his head to remove the dots, and the people would laugh at him. He would look at them and think to himself how strange humans are, with their stranger habits. Some things he would never understand. The cat lay back and fell asleep. His body started to shake, and his legs began running quickly. A meow, low and raspy, could be heard. He was in a chase, and he was the hunted. It was not over.

*    *    *

# THE EYE OF DEATH

The ship rocked with the coming and going of the infinite sea. It was pitch-black out on the ocean as a tall man entered into a small rowboat from the shore. He could barely see the ship anchored off the coast, but like a bloodhound he could scent his target.

The tall man started to row, and as he did he thought about the past. Ever since he left New York City, he'd been working down here for the Colombians.

He had one obstacle though, Captain Noble from New Jersey. Noble recognized him from the city, and the tall man needed to fix the situation. The Colombians wouldn't care. All they gave a shit about was their merchandise shipments and their schedules.

The rowboat arched closer to the ship, and the ocean cried as it hit the breakers nearby. It was an eerie gray night with no moon.

Captain Noble was entertaining a young lady from the island, and their clothes were thrown throughout the ship's cabin. The young girl had lied about her age to Noble. She had said she was twenty-one, but she really was seventeen. Her name was Marta, named after her grandma of Mexican descent. She was part-Trinidadian and part-Mexican. Marta figured if she could hook up with an American she could get away from her mother's house, and this man was the most likely candidate to come along in a while. She scoped him out days ago in the local pub in Port of Spain.

He was docked with his ship off the coast and promised her to take her with him to see the rest of the Caribbean. She jumped at the chance—just anything to get away from this island. And he had money, and she didn't care from where it came.

They lay down and started to drink some wine when a noise could be heard aft, and Marta jumped. She was afraid her mother might send the police after him since her cousin was on the police force.

"Don't be scared, it's just the ocean hitting the side of the ship," Noble smiled as he caressed her breasts. They started to kiss, and any noises they heard were now lost in their desires.

The tall man easily rowed the boat alongside the ship and quietly placed his feet on the ship's deck. He knew Noble gave the ships' crew freedom for the night. The tall man figured he had some bimbo in the cabin with him.

He couldn't use a gun since the local police would investigate, and also he didn't want the Colombians to think he did it. He sneaked closer to the long cabin and peered in. Noble was with a girl all right. She was young and pretty. What a waste. They were deep into their lovemaking when he spotted their path to death. They were drinking wine, and the cabin was divided into two rooms. The lovers were in the bedroom, and the forward room was a living room of some sort. The tall man noted wine with glasses half drunk. He slipped into the room, taking out two white pills from his pants pocket and dropping them into the wine. He would wait. The noises in the next room indicated they were almost done, so the tall man slipped out easily onto the deck.

He could hear them laughing as they entered the living room. Noble was speaking, "Ah, that was great, Marta, let's eat. I'm hungry."

With that, the two sat down and had the cheese Noble had prepared along with the wine.

"Captain, I can't wait to see New York City." Marta grinned at him.

"You will love it, baby," Noble said as he started to feel uneasy.

"Boy, I fell on clouds with you, it's exhilarating," she exclaimed and started to get up to dance, but fell to the floor.

"Marta, what—" Noble stood up and fell to the deck.

The tall man came in smiling. Now he will be in charge of the operation, and nobody will recognize him.

He dropped the bodies out onto the deck to make it look as if they were swimming naked and drowned. He tossed them both into the ocean. The police will think just another tragic drowning.

"Ha ha ha," came the laugh. The locals will think it was accidental.

"Hee hee," the tall man laughed as he looked up with his one eye at the dark sky.

*     *     *

Tony Massaro loved downtown Manhattan. He had been working in the area now about five years and knew of every little alley and lane. At lunchtime when he couldn't meet Libby, he would walk the area, investigating new shops and buildings. His favorite hangout was the old fort at Battery Park not far from the Staten Island Ferry. He would sit there and eat lunch or walk the Battery Park promenade at the water's edge. Here the Circle Line took people to the Statue of Liberty and Ellis Island. Tony would watch as tourists, excited by the splendor and grandness of it all, stood in awe of the Statue of Liberty. They would scream and take pictures and have smiles on their faces as the ships departed.

It was here he met Vinnie. At first, Vinnie was dressed somewhat decent and talked like anybody else about the weather or lunch or baseball. Vinnie loved the Yankees like him, so they would sit on those hard benches and talk about the pitching or hitting. Tony never realized the truth about him until another draftsman saw him with the man. It was a shock to him. Vinnie was a homeless man who begged in the park for money or food, but Vinnie never asked Tony for a dime. Tony often wondered where he worked and asked many times, but Vinnie avoided the question. He liked the man and decided to help him out. Tony would give some workers in his office money to give to Vinnie in the park as they passed. He knew the homeless man would be embarrassed if Tony offered him something. Vinnie was just a friend and a noontime bullshitter with Tony, and he wanted to leave it that way.

The two would walk now up and down the shore from the Westside to the East and back again. Vinnie knew everything about downtown New York. Tony guessed he was a laid-off seaman or dockworker. His hands were rough, but it could have been from being outside consistently. He knew the former Governor's Island building workers, the Staten Island Ferry seaman, and the priest at the downtown church. Here Vinnie would go religiously and light a candle every day. He would go in the morning and deposit a quarter or a dime, and light a candle. Here he would stand or kneel for a while and then leave. Tony found out about the homeless man from the priest when they were introduced. Father Spoto told Tony about Vinnie's story when the homeless man wasn't there. He was a dockworker who got laid off because he loved booze too much. He had two grown children who never saw him. It was a sad story.

Tony twice took the Staten Island Ferry during lunch with Vinnie, and they had a great time talking baseball and eating hot dogs while sitting in the wind on the outside deck. Every seaman knew him, and at one time the captain asked him to come up to the bridge. Watching downtown Manhattan on the ferry was great, but it left Tony sad that a man like this was with no house or job. He looked at Manhattan and thought about all that money and of the haves and have-nots.

Vinnie sometimes would not be around for days, totally disappear, and then reappear with no explanation; and Tony asked for none. When Tony told Libby, she offered to help him find a job; but Vinnie was too proud to take charity from Tony, yet he wanted to help the man. If he could get a line on what he wanted to do, then maybe he could.

Tony pressed him one day about his past, and Vinnie reluctantly admitted to being a dockworker, but now he tended bar off and on and that was it. Tony didn't want to get into it then; it seemed to bother him greatly when he mentioned the bar. Something in his voice was a warning not to go further.

Gallo volunteered to put him through the computer to see who he was, but Tony wasn't for it. Even though Libby was still in litigation over the Hollander will, because a cousin contested the will or some such thing, she offered her help; but Tony refused. He wanted to get him work without anybody's help.

One day, Vinnie said he would be gone for about a week but would return, and he would be richer for it. Tony asked if it was dock work.

Vinnie smiled. "Yeah, sure, not with my luck."

"Take care of yourself, Vinnie." Tony smiled and shook his hand.

"You do something for me, Tony?" Vinnie asked meekly.

"Anything you say."

"Would you light my candle in the church for me every day," Vinnie said low and looked into Tony's eyes, saying, "I trust you," as he reached into his pocket for money.

Tony walked back a step. "No, no, I'll take care of it."

"I'll pay you back, when I get back, you know," Vinnie assured him.

Tony smiled. "I trust you too."

They laughed and shook hands again.

"See you soon," Vinnie groaned and walked away down the shoreline.

Tony had an eerie feeling that he would never see his friend again.

\*     \*     \*

An older man sat on the cane chair. He was a dark olive skinned Mediterranean type with a long nose and a longer moustache. A cigar protruded from his mouth, and circles of smoke surrounded his head. He sat in front of a younger man dressed in an exclusive suit and shoes. The younger man's hands were done professionally as he lifted an expensive gold pen and wrote a name on a piece of paper.

"Mark Gallo," he remarked as he wrote; next to the name he wrote "morte."

The old man nodded and spoke, "Don Tremonte would like this taken care of immediately with, of course, Don Cimbari's blessings."

The younger man smiled.

"It can be done, but for a price. Tell Don Tremonte there will be a, a let us say, a future desire."

"Whatever the price, I was told."

The younger man rose and reached out his hand. The two men shook hands, and the older one left as quietly as he came. The young man left the den and descended the stairs to the wine cellars.

When he got to the port wine, he pushed a level on the shelf. The shelves swung out effortlessly, and he entered a carpeted room with a chandelier hanging from the plastered ceiling.

A big robust man nodded, and he entered through a pair of oak doors. Don Cimbari sat, eating pistachio nuts and throwing the shells into a gold ashtray. Two bigger men sat on his left, eyeing the young man.

"Dad, old man Tremonte sent a messenger with a death wish for the summer." The young man laughed as he sat into a leather chair in front of the desk.

"I know he wants that famous cop killed."

A big man on the left woke up. "Isn't that the one who fucked up Hollander and our action?"

Don Cimbari turned his head. "Please don't curse here, yes, he is the one. Tremonte claims he killed his son."

"Let me kill him, Dad. It will give me good practice and besides I'm tired of running the store."

"No, no way. You are too close, and don't act stupid. I don't believe we should do this, but it has to be done. We've been embarrassed too much by this cop and his animal cat. Give the contract to the Dino brothers.

"Now, where's Nino, I need to know how the connection from the general is working. New shipments have been coming in, but I've got no reports on the action. I want to see all the aspects of this movement from beginning to end, and who's handling it on the outside. Give me all the names of our people at each drop-off and pickup. It must be organized to a science."

The son nodded.

"Oh, and, Anthony, don't go out with that Frenchie anymore. She's not for you. They don't understand us. I'll get you someone from Sicily, now go."

Anthony left hurriedly.

"Just like his mother," Cimbari laughed, "smart as a slug."

*     *     *

Mark Gallo pushed his Ford Crown Vic government car through the lanes over the Brooklyn Bridge into New York City. It was Saturday, and he had permission to use the lab at the DEA. Director Rasin had given him carte blanche throughout the department. On the back ledge of the car sat Caesar, who had become his constant companion. Since the Hollander case, the cat was his pet on loan. Libby and Tony had bought the brownstone in Brooklyn Heights and rented the top floor to him. Caesar spent time up and down the stairway. It was a family now. Sam and Arthur would also visit constantly, but it was Caesar that was his closest. The cat had saved his ass several times, and Gallo learned to love an animal he previously had hated.

He steered his car into the parking lot at Federal Plaza, went through security, and took the elevator up. When they got to the lab floor, an agent checked his ID and saw Caesar.

"Hey, isn't that the cat who saved the people on that ship?"

"And he helped catch one of the biggest heroin smugglers in the country," Gallo added. "Look at his collar." Gallo picked up Caesar and showed off the silver medallion.

The agent read it, "Special Honorary Agent, FBI, DEA. The agent's eyes opened wide.

"You must be new here?" Gallo asked.

"Yes sir, from Georgia, assigned last week, but I know the story, and I saw him on David Letterman and in *People* magazine. Imagine that—an agent."

"It was given to him by Director Rasin and Director Gant." Gallo smiled, leaving the man astounded.

Gallo entered the lab and started his experiment. He felt if the DEA and other enforcement agencies could train dogs to sniff drugs, why not cats? Unfortunately, cats do what they want—not what you want—so he maintained a constant repetitive training period, where he would let Caesar smell the heroin, or crack, and then feed him. He would then hide it in a cabinet and set Caesar down. Sometimes Caesar would find drugs, and sometimes he just didn't give a shit. It was frustrating for him, but he kept trying.

The telephone rang, and Gallo answered.

"Mark, is that you?" came a familiar voice. It was Philip Simpson, the director of the New York DEA office.

"Yes, it's me, and Caesar is still trying to be a dog."

"Look, I've got something important to tell you, can you come over to my place?"

"Of course. I'll be right there." Gallo placed the phone in its cradle.

*Why would the director want to see me?*

He gathered up Caesar and left in his car to Kings Point, Long Island. Simpson's house was a sprawling ranch with white stucco exterior on vast acreage, with the usual tennis courts in the rear. The director was sitting by his indoor pool when Gallo arrived.

"Mark, want a drink and one for Caesar?"

"Okay, make mine a scotch sour and my friend some water with ice.

A maid nodded and returned with the drinks. Caesar meowed his approval and remembered another pool from the past moons. He shuddered and let it pass.

"Mark, there's no way to tell you easy, but there's a contract on you. The Organized Crime Bureau of NYPD thinks so. They overheard a discussion about you."

Gallo sat back in his chair, and was not surprised.

"I bet I can guess—Tremonte, right"

"Yes, but its got more muscle than that, it's Cimbari's men, at Tremonte's urging."

Gallo took a swallow. This was not new to him, but he would never get used to this.

"Jesus, I never killed that son-of-a-bitch's son. He was alive. Damn it. Now, Cimbari."

"Look, Mark, we want Cimbari in the worst way. His family is responsible for a majority of the drugs getting into New York City and the surrounding areas. Even though you and the cat put a dent in it. Maybe we can work this in. What if we make it known that you have joined us and were being sent to the Caribbean indefinitely?"

Gallo inched closer.

"We have a strong belief that Cimbari has hooked up somehow with the biggest madman of them all, General Hso Sung-Tang. You know the general who runs the Golden Triangle of drugs in Southeast Asia. We can't find the connection, and we have established several island communication centers throughout the Caribbean. If he finds out you're there and work for us, he may postpone it."

"He gets the shit into New York? How?"

"Would you like to work for us temporarily? I'll give you clearance, and I'm sure Rasin will okay it."

Gallo looked into his glass, thinking, *Oh god, here I go again.* Then he looked at Caesar.

"Can the other agent here go too?"

Simpson smiled and laughed.

"I'm sure Rasin would say if he was here, 'Bring the fucking little demon.' He whipped their ass before and he can do it again."

"Okay, I'll do it, but temporarily."

Gallo shook Simpson's hand and promised to meet Monday on the details.

"I will keep in touch with you only and no one else. Watch your ass."

Gallo left and pulled out of the long driveway and turned to the cat.

"Well, Caesar, we're off again. Let's hope it will be easier this time."

The cat looked at him, and meowed. It was an "I know" meow.

Gallo entered the Long Island Expressway and pushed down the accelerator on his way home, and to what else he didn't know.

*     *     *

Fletcher sat on the limb, teaching his young chicks the ways of the world.

"Trust no one but yourself. Hate the squirrel, especially Perry in the next tree. He loves bread and always takes it from us.

"Watch out for the crows, they are the worst. They'll eat anything in sight, and they rob from your mother, Abigail."

The four young chicks listened intently.

"The magpies are our cousins, but be very wary of them. They are silly and will get you in trouble. Eat berries, but watch out for the tree with the little red berries on the next man's lane. It makes you nutty, like the squirrel.

"Your distant cousin, the cardinal, is a freeloader. He comes in from the north country and expects everything to be given to him. I have to serve him night and day. It's ridiculous, I'm not his albatross. I'm even older than him, the pointed-headed little—"

"Fletcher, what's wrong with you? Don't teach the chicks that." Abigail swooped down onto the perch.

"Every time you try to teach them, it goes into family problems. Just because he's my cousin doesn't mean you can bad-beak him that way."

"He's a pain in my tail."

"Okay, chicks, let's go, you're father has been eating those bad raspberries again." Abigail took the chicks under her wing and flew away into the nest.

Fletcher sat totally perplexed. *Ah well, another satisfying class,* he thought as he flew onto another branch.

From here he could see the whole area. The old human, Lockwood, had thrown some bread out on to the sidewalk, and those little dumb sparrows and blackbirds were eating up the food. Some flew off to their nest with a piece of bread bigger than their body, and others stayed to eat. Fletcher was particular where he ate. Lockwood's bread was usually wet, and he hated wet, soggy bread. The sparrows weren't as particular. They would eat anything, anywhere.

Fletcher watched the sparrow lookouts in the low branches looking for enemies of the birds. He noticed a movement in the lookout's tree, and a chirp. All the sparrows on the ground flew as one into the trees. Something had spooked them, and Fletcher flew nearer.

That's when he noticed the enemy. It was a dark-colored gray cat, and he had the lookout in his mouth. This cat he had never seen before. Fletcher gave out the common birdcall for danger, and a nearby blackbird echoed it. Fletcher checked out his tree for his clutch family and then returned his keen eyes on the cat. He felt sadness in his heart for the sparrow, but he knew it was the natural state of things. Something Fletcher never really got used to about nature.

Having been bestowed the head aviary or head bird, he perched the closest to the gray stranger.

He was a large cat—almost as large as Caesar but not with Caesar's demeanor. He taunted the sparrow as he made a meal of his prize.

"I will catch everyone of your brothers, sisters, and mates until I have feasted on all."

Fletcher laughed at his young boastfulness, and the cat noticed.

"So a large one has come down from the high perch to watch me. Be careful, big jay, I can eat you too," the gray cat meowed.

Fletcher laughed in his face in the common tongue, "So you expect me to fall for your clumsy leaps and noisy movement. It's easy to go after defenseless little birds that are starving for food and will risk their life for a crumb. Your like will never get up here and get the large birds—you're too fat and slow."

Fletcher hoped he got the cat's hair raised so he would jump onto or toward Fletcher. The branch Fletcher perched on was only strong enough for a bird's weight not a cat. It was a long fall to the ground from here. He hoped he would try and a pest would be gone.

The cat spit at him and meowed under her breath, "I am not so silly as to leap to you, Jay, for I would fall. You are smart, but I am smarter. I will wait for my chance, and when that day comes, I pray to Enew that I will have your jay neck in my mouth to snap."

"Ha, enjoy your last meal here, cat, because from now on, I will watch you. If you come anywhere near this territory, all the animals shall know by my call. You shall starve, so do yourself a big cat favor—get lost, go chase your tail in another territory."

The cat looked at him with hate and swore this to him, "You shall surely be my best meal, and when I do, the territory shall know my strength and bring me respect. They will say, 'Bear is the mightiest and the best for even the head aviary could not escape him.'"

The cat crawled down the tree to the ground and strutted off with his sparrow prize.

With that sickening speech thankfully over, Fletcher cawed out to the cat. "I hope you get a large hairball and cough yourself to death," Fletcher wisecracked.

Fletcher flew to a tree to watch him as he walked into an adjacent lane and down to a large human street.

Fletcher sat back on his perch and thought, *Just what I need now—another big pain in the tail, and to be a watch bird for the not too smart sparrows.*

He thought about telling Caesar since he was the head felenex, but he would handle this himself. Besides it's more fun this way. He would think up clever ways to annoy and pester this fish-brained cat.

It would be an interesting summer.

\*      \*      \*

At the same time, Gallo was talking to Simpson at his house at Kings Point among the tennis courts and the million-dollar sunny estates. Vinnie sat in a darkened bar on 146th Street in Harlem. He was the watchman now during the day and was hired for the week. A big shipment was due to arrive by the usual way, and he was to watch the empty bar until Lee came in with Black Madonna. He really didn't like drugs and never used the shit himself, but he needed the money, and they paid very well. More than he could make anywhere else now, and the liquor was free.

The bar was depressing. The front storefront windows were blackened out with paint and a dusty stained red sign hung high above the doors. The bar itself was wood and was used heavily during its heyday, but now it was abandoned and was falling apart. The lights were fluorescent and all broken—except for two lamps, which flickered on and off.

He had brought himself a roast beef sandwich at the greasy spoon next door, and Vinnie was eating it, when the Pill came in. Pill pushed all kinds of uppers, dopers, acid, and coke, even angel dust for the right price. He never liked the name Pill.

"What's up, homeyless?" Pill asked as he sat with his legs spread as far as he could, which was considerable due to his six-foot-five frame.

"Nuthin', just resting, working for Lee."

"Yeah, fucking Lee, he makes too much. That motherfucker. He never tells me about his stuff. I can help, I can fuckin' help. He and that iceberg Madonna don't fuckin' trust me. Fuck, I got this motherfuckin' territory here. Everybody knows. Even the cops leave me alone, the fucks, shit. You got any stuff?"

"No, and don't need any." Vinnie tried to not have any kind of conversation.

"Shit, you're fuckin' stupid, makes you feel great. Fuck. Hey, do you know when the shits coming, tonight or tomorrow?"

"Don't know. Lee doesn't tell me, Pill."

"Fuck him and that stupid ass bitch. Tell him I was here looking for him."

"Okay." Vinnie waved goodbye as Pill slammed the door.

As the Pill left, he walked down the street and touched his ear and then his mouth in an obvious gesture. The two undercover officers nodded slightly and sat in their dark unmarked Ford. It was set.

*       *       *

He perched on a tree branch overlooking the human path with their dirty moving machines. He never understood humans; they were always rushing back and forth and dropping all kinds of food everywhere. They were like the pig family, or so he heard. Everything was left on the ground. It was good for us pigeons, but it was dirty.

Clay never could or would understand them. The whole lot of the human race he had no use for, and he hated every bird too. They are all as nutty as the squirrels.

Clay had no use for anyone. He hated everyone. Left as an orphan one day, he grew up on the human streets fighting for food morsels with the sparrows. He was a fully white pigeon—except for a brown spot on his breast—and was ridiculed for his color among the birds. The birds would complain he drew too much attention to them while they ate. Humans would notice the white pigeon and try to capture him. This would scatter the birds, and all the pigeons would lose their food to the squirrels. To get away, he found a hole on the side of a dead tree to live; and since he was very young and alone, he was always starving. One day, he was walking on a human street, avoiding those big metal things called cars when he was almost hit by one. An old pigeon named Sunny saved him by pushing him out of the way. Sunny had a wry sense of humor and called him Clay because he was dodging cars looking for food. The name stuck, and soon all the birds called him that.

He grew up hating the world and its viciousness. Life was a miserable state of affairs, and he always waited for the next problem. He hoped death would take him like his mother and father but it never did. This area was unbearable with the helpless sparrows and the pigeons unaware of life around them, but he stayed because anywhere else would be just as bad. Sunny showed him the neighborhood and where to go for the best food and where the enemies lurked.

One sorrowful day, Sunny went out for food and never came back. Clay assumed a cat killed him, or worse a car hit him. It made him hate the world more.

As he sat on the branch laughing at the humans and their silly ways, the other birds would fly down and go after crumbs—but not Clay; he refused to as he matured. Clay knew where to go for food. Not fight for food on the street but behind where the humans live as Sunny showed him. There were smelly collection bins that the humans always overfilled. How wasteful the humans are.

Clay would fly down there at any time, and sort through it all. Picking out all the prime pieces, Clay would sit there by himself, content with his loneliness; and knew he put one over on the rest of the world. Getting over on the world made him ecstatic.

It was a rainy day when he was getting on top of the waste bin when he spotted an enemy. It was a local stray dog named Hilton. Clay had heard about him from the other birds, but he never saw him up close. This dog had killed many pigeons in the last year just for fun. Hilton had spotted him, and was ready for a kill. Clay couldn't fly straight up since there was an overhang over the bins. He knew he was dead.

Clay flew to another side of the collection bins to avoid the dog, but it was inevitable. The dog was closer now, and death was in his eyes. The dog growled that death knell he had heard before.

A strange sound could be heard from behind the dog. It was a large cat. The most intense-eyed cat he had ever seen. The cat meowed loudly once and confronted the dog. Clay knew cats were normally no matches for dogs, but this one didn't give off any scent of fear.

"The pigeon is mine, black one," came the bark from the dog, Hilton.

"Not today, go home. A bird will not be harmed in my presence," the black one spit.

"I don't listen to cats," came the bark.

"This cat you will. I am Caesar of the line of Simmark." His eyes glowed, and it seemed the cat grew larger. Clay was in shock.

"I have heard of you and your tale. I know you are friends with the head cur Sam. I will back off out of respect for the head cur." With that, the dog trotted down the alley, not looking back.

The cat sat down and stared at the pigeon.

"Oh, I see, you saved me for your dinner," Clay said cynically.

"No. You can go," came the response.

"I can go? Who and what are you?"

"I once promised never to harm a bird, and I will stick to it," Caesar stated, giving the bird that intense stare.

"I don't believe it," Clay said, shaking his head.

"Ask Fletcher, the blue. He knows the whole story. I have to go now. I will see you again, pigeon." With that, Caesar pranced off.

"The name is Clay, if you don't mind," he chirped out.

Of all the crazy things I have seen, that was the first time anyone ever helped him. Clay would look into this cat and his tale. The pigeon flew off and was convinced he just dreamed it all. There is no such cat.

*     *     *

Gallo was getting ready to leave for the Caribbean when he got a call from his friend at the Organized Crime Bureau of NYPD. Stanley Kufelski was his name, and Gallo met him a month ago after the Hollander case. Stan was constantly on the Cimbari family and their operations, and if Don Cimbari farted he knew it.

Stan sounded strange and wanted to meet. They agreed to meet at the First Precinct.

Gallo rushed there and met Stan, who ushered him quickly into a drab green office with the blinds pulled shut. Stan wasted no time.

"Gallo, I'm in trouble. I can only talk to you. You're not, not with anyone," he was stuttering. "You know I've been following the Cimbari thing a long time. Going to his club and his fucking home," Stan said nervously. His hands started to sweat profusely.

He walked over to the water cooler and turned on the little radio he had placed on a shelf. Stan turned the dial till it was loud and sat down.

"I can only trust you. Someone in this organization is a major leak. I don't know, but it's leaking bad. Cimbari knows our major movements a day in advance, I know." Stan wiped his forehead.

"As you know, we've been working with DEA to get this slime; yet he's one step ahead. We had a big bust planned for Queens. It's some fucking warehouse in Springfield Gardens. We go, and it's empty except for marble tile. Another one we had with DEA in Astoria. It was a laboratory and a shopping area. We had firsthand knowledge of its authenticity. Bust the place—nothing, fucking nothing, nobody's that good. Yet, we get these small operations, one up in Harlem the other day. Busted some selling sleazy bar. We had a snitch, and some homeless guy gets whacked. Some guy named Vinnie Bodanno, who's at the wrong place, at the wrong time. Turns out he was just there to watch the place. You know he was once a cop this guy. Guess what? He had a piece of paper with your friend's cell number."

Gallo was surprised, "Who?"

"Your friend, Messaro. Ask him what he knows about it." Stan showed Gallo the paper with the number on it.

Gallo nodded his head. "I will."

"Anyway, we got the pusher and his entourage, but this is where it dies. Small cheese, not the rat." Stan said quietly and got up again and looked out his office room window.

"And now there's these death threats, because I brought this up to the lieutenant. Someone's been calling my home and talking to my wife." Stan looked into space. The radio blasted louder.

"Wait a minute, you tell your lieutenant, and all of a sudden there're after you? C'mon, why?" Do you have some evidence?

Stan turned and looked at Gallo, and a strange sneer appeared on his face,

"Maybe."

"Go to the captain or higher. You got to do something, or can I help?"

"No, no, I don't want to involve you or anybody else, not even my partner knows."

Stan sat down again and grabbed a pen and jotted down a number.

"Take this number. If anything should happen to me, call it. Someone there will have the evidence, I hope." Stan gave the paper to Gallo.

"If someone asks you about this meeting, tell them it was over your trip to the Caribbean."

"What are you going to do, Stan?" Gallo asked, hoping he could help.

"I don't know. I'm in a dangerous position." Stan stood up to end the meeting.

"Don't worry, I'll figure something out." He was more composed now.

"How long you going to be in the Caribbean?"

Gallo stood up. "About three months, I guess."

"Good luck, Mark." Stan put out his hand. "Watch yourself, and promise you'll take care of the situation, resolve it now."

"I will."

Stan smiled for the first time. "And don't drink the water."

Gallo left with a chilling feeling behind him. *Why did he tell me, of all people?*

He questioned himself all the way home. When he got home, he placed the telephone number Stan gave him in his desk.

Caesar jumped up on the desk and rubbed himself against Gallo.

"Well, cat, you all packed?"

Caesar meowed his yes. Just then a familiar voice yelled from downstairs, and Gallo answered it. It was Tony, his landlord.

"C'mon down for dinner, Mark."

Gallo grabbed Caesar, and they walked down the flight of stairs.

Libby, not used to maids and butlers yet, cooked a veal dinner for the three of them.

Caesar wedged between Sam and Arthur for the plates on the floor filled with goodies. They ate from each other's dishes regularly. Arthur was losing out on his portion, usually because he was the smallest.

Libby asked Gallo why he looked sad. "I mean, you are going to the Caribbean tomorrow."

"Oh, nothing, just some sad news about a friend. He's got himself in a mess. Tony I have to ask you. Do you know a Vinnie Bodanno?"

"Vinnie Bodanno? Wait, I know this guy I meet all the time in the park. His name is Vinnie. He's sort of a homeless character." Tony was confused

"Well he's dead. I found out at NYPD, and he had your cell number on him."

"I gave him my number in case . . . Jeez, the poor guy. How?

"It's the usual. He was the watchman for the drugs and got in the line of fire. Gallo didn't want to drag this on so he changed the subject.

"Just watch out who you make friends with next time."

Tony sat there for a while, pondering the man he met almost every day in the park. It was insane. Poor Vinnie was always looking for the fast buck.

Libby did some small talk, and the mood changed. They ate, and Libby said no more, but she thought about Gallo. She knew this man too well, almost as good as Tony. She felt something for Gallo, but it wasn't love, yet it was more than friendship. It was not easy to explain.

She told Tony that they would visit Gallo once he was set in, but she didn't know where, and Gallo couldn't tell her. Libby would miss him.

They ate dinner, and Gallo said his goodbyes. Libby kissed Caesar goodbye and told him to watch over Gallo; he needed watching. Caesar meowed his understanding of Mistress Libby's request. He would always protect his family to the death.

Gallo went upstairs and after some final packing went to bed. Caesar slept at his feet, his protector.

Mark thought about Stan. He should have insisted Stan give him the information so Gallo could have exposed the leak instead of Stan. He had no ties to anyone in the NYPD.

Gallo fell asleep dreaming of his ex-wife, Gina, and her smile and his kids, as Caesar twitched in his sleep being chased by the black-cloaked man. A bright full moon shone through his blinds and on to the bed, where both slept.

Their leaving tomorrow would be the trigger of coming events that will change many lives.

\*   \*   \*

General Hso-Sung Tang sat in his palace in the deep recesses of the Vietnam jungle. It was raining out and his men were going about their business. His heroin trade was remarkably good this year and his coup of teaming with the American Mafia was a stroke of luck.

He sat throwing darts at an old picture of Ronald Reagan. His George W. Bush poster was already full of holes. The general had built his empire up from the war. He even worked with the American CIA in Cambodia to obtain information for drugs. It was a mutual respect in those days.

He was never a soldier and certainly not a Vietcong. He could give a shit about communism. It was the capitalists and their weaknesses he lived off. He built a fledging trade into a multibillion-dollar international business. He conservatively estimated that he supplied 50 percent of the worlds' heroin from here at the Golden Triangle. He was in good shape for a man in his fifties, wide and muscular but with a nasty scar on his face from the war. *Fuck the Sicilians and to hell with the Afghans. They were nothing*, he thought. He had his own army now. The American Mafia had sent people to discuss the trade among them, and his movement of drugs with the Pacific Rim Airlines was his idea. They helped acquire licensing in the Caribbean for all the airports. It was sweet and now the newest deal was at the threshold of trillions.

His oldest son entered with his usual cursing of the weather.

"Fucking shit rain," he yelled as he shook off his poncho.

"Sit down, my son, I must talk to you about our affairs, and it's good that the weather is bad. No one will interfere with us."

His son, taller and leaner than him, was a hated manager here. The men thought him too hard on them, but he liked it that way and had raised him as such. Unfortunately, his son had wanderlust in him and loved the cursed Western ways. The corrupt lives of the West he experienced in Hong Kong stayed with his son, and his longing to see America was a constant argument between them. He now had the means to solve his dilemma. A stroke of brilliance that even his slut mother would agree was beneficial for both.

"Son, Tao-Tse, I have an assignment for you."

"Father, please don't call me that, I want to be known by my Western name, Tom."

"Yes, well, you know our operations from here are deep and complex to the shores of the fucking USA. I have recently contracted with the Mafia a system that the pigs at the DEA could never discover, and I want you to complete it and oversee its coordination.

"Keep in mind that this coalition is the American Mafia and the Colombians. With this system we shall be the funnels to America of all the drugs in the world. It's foolproof. Everyone will use our system just like Visa card. Our operations now are good but too overt, and they can be too easily hampered. I'm placing in your hands my trust that you will handle this for me. I can't go. I'm too well known. You will have two contacts. One is the son of the Mafia head named Alfredo Cimbari, the other is a tall American, about forty-five and calls himself Mr. Franks.

You are to meet them on the island of Puerto Rico. Franks has a yacht given to him by the Colombians since he runs their coke or crack up the U.S. coast. Be careful of this one."

Tom was excited beyond his dreams to be near America and work for his father. This was fantastic. Money was his god.

"Where is the base, Father?" his son said, licking his lips.

"Through extensive research, we found the best spot near America, an island in the Bahamas called Cat Island. We bought a piece of land through a third party, who mysteriously came down with a bullet. The Mafia took care of that. It's an area in the south of the island, and a ranch house will be your operational headquarters." The general smiled at his son as he spoke.

"Meet with this Mr. Franks and set up the dates for shipments. Once our operation system is completed, it will link Cat Island to mainland America. I cannot show you here how this is laid out, but our scientist genius, Dr. Zine, will explain it to all. We also have a group of politicians and some DEA agents, which we have on our side. Fucking Americans can't refuse dollars. There are other complications, Son. The American Mafia—well, Mr. Franks doesn't get along with them. It is up to you to smooth their feathers and keep the shipments moving. Watch out for the Colombians, the Valli family—they are ruthless."

His father stopped to light a cigarette and picked up the telephone. "Let us take a break, my son. Send in the Filipino."

A small swarthy man came in. Tom recognized him as the scumbag from Manila he always fought with over shipments in their planes.

"My son has trouble with you, why? Have you been skimming off the top?" The general blew smoke toward the man.

"No, no, General, my people and I watch your money carefully at the airport. It all goes out and pays its price, ha heh!"

"My man tells me you had five kilos missing on your ledger last month. Where is the shit?" His voice rose higher.

The Filipino started to sweat.

"No, no, there was no extra five kilos as I told your son."

Tom laughed. The man was right. There was none he knew of. He had marked down five kilos but didn't ship the extra five and blamed the stupid Filipino. He couldn't wait to be the top man when his father was gone.

"We'll, my son doesn't lie to me, and so you must be. I cannot have fucking thieves in my system."

"No, no, I beg you, it is not me. I didn't count wrong. Maybe your son is mistaken."

The general stood up and stared at the man.

"My son is not wrong." He pressed a button, and two military-dressed Cambodians came in armed with AK-47s.

"Execute him," the general said halfheartedly and sat down.

The Filipino begged for his life to no avail. The two large men dragged him out. Tom sat happy; he got rid of the fuck and got a free five kilos, which he sold on the market in Hong Kong. Sweet. His father resumed his conversation as though nothing had happened.

"Dr. Zine has developed a new process that could revolutionize travel, but we are going to use it for another kind of traveling, trafficking. Ha ha ha."

His son laughed with him as the rain hit the windowsills. In the distance, shots could be faintly heard among the rain's clamor.

*     *     *

A warm breeze hit him in the face through an open window while a palm tree beat in the gust.

He lit a cigarette, the first one today, and dragged on it longingly and thought about the job. The DEA had a line on a drug cartel meeting in Puerto Rico in the near future, and since his work here has not been fruitful, they wished him to investigate. The last month had been boring, and Gallo was tired of the research.

He walked over to the refrigerator and pulled out a Coke. This island had two things for sure—beautiful black women and Coke. His partner here took advantage of both. Gallo couldn't either get in the mood or was brooding over Gina and the kids still. The island was a small one in the American Virgin Islands group adjacent to St. Thomas, and the DEA furnished them with all the necessities. Their research really hadn't turned up anything except some natives with tall tales. One native believed the cartel from Colombia was building an underground network. He heard it from his relative in the Bahamas. A drug subway, he called it. Gallo laughed out loud—what a joke.

Many ships here were caught with coke or marijuana going to Florida, but that was it. His belief that he was making a dent in the trade was diminishing.

Caesar walked in through his little trapdoor that John, his partner, had made. Caesar took to the agent John early, and they ate together every night. John was late getting back from his date with Sabrina. The ocean in the distance made its usual roar on the beach, and he had a lousy TV dinner as Caesar looked for John.

It was close to 9:00 PM when John walked in white and pale.

"Mark, listen," he grabbed Gallo and walked over to the couch and sat down.

"Sabrina knows an airport worker at the St. Thomas airport."

"C'mon, she knows everybody everywhere and has had them every time," Gallo laughed.

"No, this is different. She says this guy has seen some strange things being shipped to the Bahamas."

"Such as what, jawbreakers?" Gallo laughed.

"Stop, listen, an airline from the Caribbean named Pacific Rim Airlines based in Nassau has had parts flown in from America for a large tank."

"So?" Gallo sipped the Coke and shook his head.

"This airline is one of the few that covers the South Pacific and from its base in Manila. It also takes flights to Vietnam."

"I repeat, so?"

"So didn't we receive a crash site report the other day from the Filipino that a plane was found with everyone dead and nobody knew for days. No report or crash investigation for days, Mark."

Gallo started to sit up straight.

"Where is this report?"

John got up and went to the computer. He hit three keys and a crash report came up. The picture of the plane was bad, but what was strange is that the fuselage was separated from the wings.

"No report for three days, that is strange," Gallo remarked.

"And now someone talks about a tank supply for the Bahamas. We should look into this, Mark."

"Maybe you're right. Let's see who owns Pacific Rim Airlines."

Gallo punched the white keys, and the dossier on the company appeared on the green screen:

Pacific Rim Airlines
Bases: Manila and Nassau, Bahamas registry
Fleet: DC-3 planes
Cargo: Mostly commercial operations and some passengers.
Owner: HST Group, Manila
Flights to South Pacific islands, Southeast Asia to the Caribbean

It continued, and Gallo got interested the more he read.

"I think we should inform the office about our suspicions, but since they are a cargo company there's nothing wrong with an oil tank shipment."

"Gallo, who said oil tank? It was a gas tank—you know, like propane—but it was in parts for a very large use." John bit into a donut, and the jelly mashed out the side and on to his lap.

"Okay." Gallo was intrigued, and it was the most exciting thing in a month.

"Look, tell Sabrina to be careful. I want to meet this guy at the airport."

John was washing his pants. "Yeah, I'll tell her, but it might be difficult. He went home to Port of Spain in Trinidad. Some family death."

"That makes it easier. I have a friend in Trinidad, a close friend whom I trust. We sailed the seas together."

"Yeah, I heard about your 'cruise,'" John laughed.

Caesar sat on the chair, watching and listening. Ever since he got to this strange land, he's had an uneasiness or foreboding of bad things to come. He enjoyed the different animals here with their strange dialects of the common tongue. This was interesting, and John, Master Gallo's friend, reminded him of Master Tony; yet his fur would stand up at times and his whiskers would sense danger too often. He sensed something in the air. He missed home and his pals. Master Gallo was too busy these days to pay attention to him, so he would go into the countryside.

The insects here were nasty and large, so he steered clear of them; but there wasn't much else. There were many fish to play with at the shore and some sort of weasel with a bad attitude, which hated to talk to cats, he said. The weasel said we were useless animals. Caesar told him that he met rats with more personality. The weasel, of course, turned and ran away. The birds weren't much friendlier. They're brightly colored but bores. Caesar wished Fletcher was here. Boy, could he tell these flying snobs a thing or two. If it weren't for this strange foreboding he felt, this would be a very boring place.

He was still having nightmares of a black-cloaked man grabbing for him, but just out of reach. He was constantly running into darkness, not seeing in front of him, just the human grabbing and laughing. He would wake up meowing loudly, but the two humans never heard him at night. Their ears couldn't pick up a dog bark. Humans do have trouble with their senses.

He closed his eyes and wished for a peaceful dream of his friends back home.

*   *   *

The man sat in a dark smoky room in secluded house in San Juan, Puerto Rico. The people arriving had come from different routes. The Colombians and Mr. Franks came by yacht off some island group, and the American Mafia contingent arrived from the airport. Cimbari sent his second son, Alfredo, and two of his best hit men as guards, Nino and Cinguamani. The third group was his. The general's contingent consisted of him and the three large Chinese bodyguards. It was a meeting to cooperate in their only common goal—drug smuggling.

Tom started it off.

"Gentlemen, my father has sent me here purposefully to guarantee that what all of you have contributed to can be done and with 100 percent assurance of delivery. Our scientist and technicians are presently finishing our project to its completion. As agreed, all standard drug lines will remain open, and it's very important to continue your standard drug operations. We don't want the DEA to feel left out. Let them catch some of your planes, boats, etc. Our route is a foolproof method and will—and I stress this gentlemen—we'll never be caught unless someone here should let it slip out. If any fucking bastard should, the other cartels will take over all the other's action and money in the venture and kill its representative present here. This is our only condition, so it behooves you to police yourselves. You will all sign papers to this effect. Are there any questions or additions to your contracts?"

Alfredo raised his hand and stood up defiantly with a smirk.

"What you are saying is that if someone from our organization should give out information on this so-called 100-percent-proof route then you take us over and kill me." Alfredo was laughing.

"That is right." Tom smiled.

"Ha ha ha ha, you must be fucking kidding. We put a lot of money into this. We could never agree to such a condition. Its un-American, it's a . . . a unconstitutional, it's"

"Pardon me, but when you see this operation you will have no misgivings. Once we take shipments from your agents, we guarantee, time and place, to all your specifications."

"Well, I have to check this with the old man." Alfredo sat down, shaking his head.

"What about your end, Mr. Franks?" Tom asked.

A tall lean man sat straight up and rose from the chair; he was about six feet three and all in black with a black fedora. His face was well hidden as he walked over to the shadows of the room.

His voice was raspy with a touch of a New York accent.

"This is interesting, but before the Colombians can commit to such an agreement, we must see this route as you call it. In this, I agree with the Italians."

"Good"—Tom rose—"in about three weeks we will meet on Paradise Island in Nassau, at the hotel I designate. Please be there. We will then take a charter flight to the island."

Alfredo rose. "Are the terms still the same, 40 percent cut of all our merchandise shipped through here?"

"Yes, and it's a bargain, you will see. Good night, gentlemen."

They parted as easily as they came. Alfredo thought Mr. Franks was familiar, in his manner; he had seen him before somewhere. It would come to him.

\*     \*     \*

Tony Messaro sat at his desk in downtown NYC and thought about the job he was about to undertake. He had never worked on any Caribbean residences, but Furness was adamant.

"Tony, you got to come down here and help me. I'm opening up an advertising agency, and I need you to design my office." Furness talked in his usual Trinidadian accent.

It would be a challenge and an experience to design and build on an international level, but what to do about Libby. She's stuck on that television soap, and has been too busy with the accountants and lawyers from the Hollander's estate. He wanted to go, but then another part of him didn't. Their wedding date was to be in the spring of next year, but they had set no actual date.

He sort of agreed to Furness's request when he told him of other pending jobs in Port of Spain. Libby was excited for him and urged him to go and assured him everything was all right.

"I have Sam and Arthur to watch over me. Don't worry. What could happen to me? Besides, I'm too busy to get into trouble."

He agreed, but it still bothered him that with Gallo on some island in the Caribbean, there would be an empty house here. Maybe he would call Gallo when he arrived through his office in the city.

He placed a call to the DEA office and gave the extension Gallo told him to use, and after going through three people, the last voice was helpful but disinterested.

"Yeah, I know who you are. You're the architect who helped at the airport," the dry voice answered.

"Right, right. Get a message to Gallo, tell him I'm on my way to Trinidad to see a friend and do drawings."

"Okay, I will."

The receiver went dead, and Tony placed it in its cradle. "Well, looks like I'm Trinidad bound."

He looked out the window at Manhattan and the New York skyline, and wondered how he would do.

*   *   *

The three animals lay in the shade, taking in the breeze. They talked about Caesar and his bravery and fortitude.

Sam raised his head to look up. That pesky jay wasn't around to butt into the conversation.

"Where's Fletcher, he's been gone all day? Some bird clutch meeting?" Arthur asked.

"Don't know, I am just thankful. He's been chirping about some renegade cat he wants me to take care of. I'm too tired, and I'm still not totally over that wound at that man's lake."

"It's a pool, Sam, a pool," Missy yelled at him.

"A pool, good, silly names, it even smelled bad and humans swim in it too, ugh."

"I can get rid of that cat. Caesar put me in charge when he left," Arthur meowed as he stood up and stretched.

"I've seen that cat, Arthur, but he's too big for you," Missy barked.

Just then Fletcher arrived with Max the seagull.

"Hey, ugly, put your talons here." Fletcher pointed for Max to perch. "See my friends. I want you to meet them. That red cat is Arthur, the big half shepherd is Sam, and the slightly pregnant one is Missy."

"Oh no, now he's bringing seagulls to shore to talk to us," Sam complained.

"Watch your jaw, canine, breathe; this is the gull who helped me with Caesar. He's nothing to look at, but he's smart. It keeps me awing of what's going on at the shore, and when you know about your territory you can fight them on the land, the sea, and everywhere. We will fight them to the last breath, and—"

"Shut up with the television messages and stop hanging around old man Lockwood's window. You're like a parrot, you repeat everything," Sam barked up at the tree.

"Okay, but I've been gliding with Max learning the air currents. You never know when I may need it. My little wings hold up pretty good. Right, Max?"

Max nodded as he grabbed a leaf with his large beak and bit down.

"By the way, Fletcher, I can get rid of that mutt cat that's been bothering your birds," Arthur noted as he looked up.

"No, no, Art, please wait for Caesar. This stray is too big, and he's got the killer instinct you don't have."

"Who doesn't? I'll scratch him on his face." Arthur made a sideswipe with his paw and hit a low bush branch that bent back and hit him in the face.

Missy and Sam laughed, "Listen to bird seed head up there, Arthur. For once, he's right." Sam shook his head.

"I don't eat bird seed, it's too dry and it tastes like old feathers, but listen only Caesar could handle this. I wonder how he's doing. Everybody asks about him. In fact, when I tell them I'm his friend and once saved the famous cat, they can't wait to meet me. I like to appease the masses."

"Oh, Roeko, help us," Missy yelped.

"They came from the great river upstream to touch my wing and the young ones want a feather from me—it's amazing," Fletcher beamed.

"I sing the songs of the legend of Sam the Firebreather and of Caesar, the black cat in the line of Simmark. Anyway, got to go, my adoring clutch beckons, parting is such sweet potatoes." With that Fletcher and Max flew into the sky.

"It's a bird, it's a plane, its Fletcher, see you soon," The jay chirped as he flew off as Sam put his head down in disbelief.

"Maybe old man Lockwood will shut his window and his television soon, I can only hope." They all nodded and fell asleep.

*   *   *

The black girl raised her shirt to show off her large breasts to the seated man. He grabbed them as if they would disappear and sucked on them lovingly. She lowered her mini skirt and revealed her bare crotch. The man, half nude, picked her up easily and placed her on the bed.

He removed his trousers and lay on top of her. At first, she responded to his motions until his intentions were clear to her. Common sex was not his intent, but pain and degradation of her body was his goal. He started to bite her hand and slap her repeatedly. She was not a big girl, so her efforts to get away were fruitless and was not appreciated by the man. She managed to get off the bed, but he grabbed for his waist belt from his pants and started to beat her with it. He pulled her back on to the bed.

Welts appeared on her chest, and no one heard her screaming. The man had rented the penthouse level and bribed the hotel desk and manager for a no-disturb night. The Colombians were into their own thing on the same floor and paid no attention to screams.

He turned her around onto her stomach and started to beat her on her back, and as he did he screamed as loud as she did. He yelled one more time loudly and had an orgasm.

He collapsed on top of her, totally relieved for minutes. She was crying and yelling in a Caribbean dialect.

He reached for his wallet and peeled off five one-hundred-dollar bills and threw them into her face.

"Get the fuck out," the man yelled.

She grabbed the bills and ran to her clothes and out the door.

The tall man lay nude except for a black patch over one eye. He was never able to make normal love since the black demon and the cop took his eye from him. He hated everyone and trusted no one. He adopted black as his color in remembrance of that day. The man rose and opened the closet door. There hung a shoulder holster with a

Browning 9mm pistol. He reached for it lovingly and stroked it ever so lightly. He checked the magazine for its contents. It was fully loaded. This made him happy. He returned the magazine into its cradle in the pistol.

"I'm going to kill that fucking mongrel cat. They made them heroes with pictures in the papers and the television."

He pointed the pistol into the air and swore his vengeance.

"You're dead heroes, soon."

*     *     *

Sabrina lay in her apartment in St. Thomas overlooking the bay. A large cruise ship was docked in the harbor where the American tourists downloaded daily to spend their dollars. Sabrina wished she could go to America and spend some of this money she's been earning. The Colombians had been keeping her on tap to control the American agents here. They told her what to say, and she got U.S. dollars in return. It was lucrative. In another six months, she could leave this island and go to Miami or even New York City. She wanted to see a Broadway play and go to the top of the Empire State Building, but something in the last two months had changed her mind. It was the American agent John. She had fallen for him in a hard way and now her emotions were all confused. The Colombians were suspicious since he came to the nearby island. Sabrina just didn't act the same as with the other agents. Passing out bad information and erroneous tips was easy, except now.

It was somehow different because John occupied her mind constantly. The tip about the airport worker was true, and the Colombians would kill her if they knew she had told the American. She must tell John the truth before anything else happens. He was coming here today with his partner to go over about Robie, the Trinidadian.

Sabrina heard a knock at the door and she rushed to see John, but a fist greeted her at the opening of the door. It was Mendes, her contact with another Colombian. Mendes grabbed her as she was about to fall. He was an expert in keeping people alive and punching them at the same time.

"Fucking slut," he yelled as he hit her on her mouth again. "Tell me what have you told the American, tell me quick and I'll make it a painless death. Carlos here will put a bullet in your brain, and it will be all over. If not, you will beg for the bullet before I'm through."

He grabbed her and threw her onto the couch.

"I didn't tell him anything," Sabrina yelled as she wiped blood off her mouth. "Only the things you told me to say."

"I don't think so. Some of our men saw you with that fucking Trinidadian two days ago. He flew to Port of Spain, and you have both Americans coming here. They can't help you. It is true. If I kill them, it would cause me more pain, but a pig like you is of no meaning.

Just to make sure I think I will change my mind, Carlos, get me my bag."

The tall Colombian retrieved a black bag, and Mendes took out a packet of white powder.

"This is heroin, my heaven, for you. No bullet for you, just ecstasy in a little bag. Who will care about an overdosed cokehead? You see this is the real thing, not cut down or diluted, and I saved it for you. Now did you tell them about the airport worker, and what else?"

Sabrina was terrified, but she knew John was coming, so she tried to stall the Colombian.

"So what if I met a Trini, I fucked him, so what does it have to do with us and the Americans?" Sabrina tried to hold back tears.

"Oh, my little slut, well he happens to work for a particular airline that we keep tabs on. There are no coincidences in this business. Go on."

He started to take out the powder onto the coffee table. Sabrina looked down and prayed.

\* \* \*

"I want you to meet her, she is beautiful and there's a feeling there." John was smiling.

"Don't tell me you're in love. Oh god, with a native. She's using you to get to America, come on, John," Gallo urged him.

Caesar sat in his usual place on the rear windowsill of the car as they drove down the dusty road to Sabrina's house. Caesar started to get used to the smells of this land. It was fresher and had strange animal scents.

"It's not like that. I think its different, Mark," John exclaimed forcefully, and Gallo stopped his dissent; he didn't want to alienate John.

As they approached the apartment townhouses, there were some cars parked in the private lot. Sabrina lived at the top floor, and John noticed something.

"Mark, usually Sabrina waits for me on the balcony and comes down. Her door's closed."

"Oh, don't worry she's probably in the can doing her face for you."

They parked, and Gallo grabbed Caesar.

"Remember, Mark, you're my brother-in-law down for a vacation. Say you brought Caesar for a ride"

They climbed the concrete steps, and Gallo noticed the architecture. It was a Spanish design with clay tile roofs and stucco walls in pinkish beige. Balconies lined every apartment with white rails.

As they approached the top floor, Caesar started to get edgy. Gallo never saw him like this except for one time. It was when there was trouble.

John was at the door about to knock when Gallo pushed him aside and dropped Caesar behind him. Instantly, two bullets came through the door where John was standing. Gallo fired into the window where a shadow stood behind drapes. He placed three rounds into the area. The shadow disappeared.

Silence followed. The apartment was still, and John had regained his footing under the other window. Caesar sat behind Gallo, remembering that sound of gunfire. It was a bad memory.

"Whoever you are, come out hands up, DEA," John yelled out.

"Fuck you, American, your girlfriend is here and I want out. If not, I kill her now. Let me get into my car with her, and I'll let her go at the airport."

"No dice," Mark yelled out.

John was sick. This job was clear, but his heart was gone. He shook his head.

Gallo saw his partner's anxiety and tried to think of a way out. Above the balcony walk was a roof overhang, a sort of trellis. He had an idea, but Caesar would have to cooperate. Gallo lifted Caesar above to the trellis over the door, hoping he will remember what to do. They had practiced this trick in the lab.

He motioned to John.

"Okay, okay, you got your deal. Come on out, we won't shoot."

Mendes opened the door and stepped out with a gun to Sabrina's head.

"Don't do anything," Mendes spit out. "She's dead, let me pass. You wasted Carlos, but I have no tears." He laughed, walking and pushing Sabrina. The girl's face had a mess of blood and bruises. Her shirt was torn to reveal a breast. Mendes was clutching the torn shirt.

Gallo looked up easily at Caesar, who was eyeing the stranger. He hoped the cat remembered the training these past weeks. *Please, Caesar,* Gallo prayed, *do it now.* Gallo motioned to the cat with his hand on his head.

Caesar looked down. It was a strange man, and Master Gallo and John were holding their guns toward him. The stranger talked in a mean, hard tone, which he disliked, but there was something else. There was a gun in the stranger's hand pointed to the female. It was a death gun. He had smelled this before, and then he remembered something Gallo taught him—to be like a dog and to protect the helpless. He sensed danger, and he reacted like a dog. His claws came to their full extent, and his mouth opened to reveal large teeth.

Mendes was smiling as he came closer to Gallo, tormenting him as he did.

"Back off, pig."

In an instant his smile turned to a scream, releasing his girl and reaching for his back. He started to yell out to get a demon off him. Gallo reached for Sabrina and pulled her away as John put his gun into Mendes's face.

"Drop the gun," John yelled.

"Fuck man, agh, get him off me, shit, ahh."

Blood was on his neck and back as Caesar had buried his claws deep into the stranger.

"Off him, now," Gallo yelled as Caesar took his sweet time getting off Mendes's back. Gallo thought Caesar enjoyed it too much. Mendes was in pain as he handed John his gun.

Sabrina was crying, and Gallo signaled to John his partner to go to her. John picked her up in his arms and brought her down to the car.

Maybe he was wrong, Gallo thought, maybe it was love. He was envious.

"Fucking gatto. Where you get him man? Shit. He tore my fucking back. What is he a fucking leopard or something? Get me to a damn fucking doctor."

"Just sit down with your hands on your head and bleed, shit head, or I'll let the el gatto go after you again."

Mendes sat down with hands above his head obediently.

Caesar jumped on to the balcony rail and looked down. John was hugging the female. *This must be John's mate*, he thought. He was glad to have stopped the stranger from killing her.

Sabrina hugged John and looked up teary eyed. The cat she had heard about these past weeks had saved her. He glared down at her with knowing eyes as she looked at him in amazement.

Each knew the other's feeling without any language.

*     *     *

William Shakespeare Furness sat on his balcony off his Diego Martin home in Trinidad, as the northerly wind came over the mountain. A black bird with an orange eye sat on a nearby roof calling out for her mate. Two other black birds joined in the love calls and chirping could be heard in the distance answering them. Two dogs, a rottweiler named Bruno and a mix breed terrier named Colby, ran up the front steps to their master and sat by his side. They loved their master.

Furness couldn't wait for Tony's arrival. He had pulled some strings with the ministry office and with Caribbean Air officials to get his guest to come to Trinidad. He was owed many favors and since his seafaring days were over, networking his past acquaintances and friends was easy.

Since his travels with the famous cat, he had returned to his mother's house that had been left basically empty these last two years. When his mother passed on, he decided to go the sailor's way, but this last trip changed his mind. He wanted to live in Trinidad and grow here and maybe raise a family. The latest trendy crime in Trinidad was kidnapping rich people for money, and he had to watch out since he was famous now.

Renovations to his house were underway, and the contractor was stupid so Furness had to watch every damn thing. That's where Tony would come in, besides other projects he had in mind

The telephone broke his daydreams.

"Billy, Billy it's me," came a very excited voice.

Furness only knew one person who called him that from the old days.

"Robie, when did you get in?"

"Oh, last couple of days, been living with some family, just called to see if you want to go party."

"Yeah, man. When?" Furness was happy to hear from his childhood friend.

"At the boatyard, you know that bar we once set on fire." Robie laughed loud.

"Tuesday night is good about 7:00 PM. I got a friend flying in from NYC and do you mind if he joins us?"

"No problem, Billy, see you then." Robie hung up.

Furness put the phone in its holder and wondered where Robie had been. Last he heard he was working at some airport. Well, he got up to get the house ready for Tony.

Bruno started to wag his tail as the man approached the front door. The big dog barked and the man turned and threw him a treat.

"Well, Bruno, get ready for some company."

*   *   *

Big Al Dino sat on the couch in the living room of a modest two-story house in Staten Island. The house was a safe house of the Cimbari family and was a favorite of the Dino brothers. Frank was cooking a marinara sauce—their usual Sunday meal—and Big Al was watching the Yankees on television.

"Hey, Frank, when do we leave for the Caribbean to do in this fed?"

Frank Dino walked in with a pot in his hand dressed in an apron with a lit cigarette in his mouth.

"In two or three days, Cimbari's son has to get us the tickets. He's a real stupid ass."

Al nodded and joked, "Remember when he couldn't find the muke who lived in the Bronx. Ha ha, he got lost and we had to find him for the old man."

"Yeah, yeah, the asshole. He couldn't find his bed in his bedroom."

They both laughed, and Frank went back into the kitchen and stirred the marinara sauce as he cut up some basil leaves.

Frank Dino was the oldest and had red hair and green eyes which is unusual for a Sicilian, but it ran in the genes. His mother and sister were both redheads. He was born with overly large feet compared to his height which was five feet six. His feet were size 11 ½ shoe, hence his nickname, Frankie the Foot. He was the deadlier of the two with a cold calculating personality. He always got his mark in the last thirty or so years.

Alfonso Dino was the same height as his brother but outweighed him by one hundred pounds. Al had pneumonia as a baby, so his mother, after Alfonso was healthy, compensated by feeding him twice as much as Frank. Even so, Alfonso was rotund but deadly with guns, so they called him Big Al.

Both were content to stay single and really never got involved with women. Frank one time had gone through a semiserious fling with a woman in Manhattan, but it faded when she mentioned marriage. She wanted Frank to quit the business and do some desk job with her father. He said his goodbyes while she cried one night in a Little Italy restaurant. He always thought what would it had been if he did listen to her. He thought about her on and off, but was happy in his life now.

Al was the smarter of the two, having actually gone to college, and was going to be an insurance agent when one night Frank needed help with a job in the Bronx. He wanted Al to watch his back with a dangerous mark. Al killed his first man that night to save Frank, and that's when they became known as the Dino brothers.

The two had killed many a mark for the Cimbari family in the following years, but it was getting to them. It wasn't as easy as it was years ago. They were in their late 60s now and wanted to retire and live the simple life. The family wouldn't let them because they were reliable.

Frank called out, "Al, here's the pasta. Get the wine."

"Okay, okay, coming." Al grabbed a chianti and sat down.

The two sat around the small round table slurping up their spaghetti. Frank was a good cook. Al loaded up the spaghetti with parmesan cheese.

They had already packed for the Caribbean trip for their flight.

"Frankie," Big Al noted, "this should be an easy one."

"Yeah, we get it done, and we can spend some time in the sun."

Both nodded as a drop of marinara sauce stained Big Al's white shirt, while he sucked linguini into his mouth.

*   *   *

Tony Massaro sat on the Caribbean Air flight 1011 as it arrived into Port of Spain. He grabbed his carry on bags and exited the plane into intense heat. It was raining as it often does in the afternoon in

Trinidad, and Tony noticed Furness at the gate after he went through Trinidadian Customs.

Furness hugged him and grabbed his bags.

"Welcome to Trinidad. I've got everyone anxious to meet you on these office buildings in Woodbrook."

Furness looked at ease to Tony since he saw him last. They got into Furness's SUV and drove north to Diego Martin.

Tony noticed they drove on the wrong side of the road and the steering wheel is on the opposite side of the cars.

"Yeah," Furness laughed, "we had the British here for years, and they influenced this country almost too much."

Tony smelled the native odors and the green of everything. Palm trees everywhere, poinsettias and fruit trees were in every yard. Peddlers sold their wares at every intersection just like in Brooklyn, and Tony noticed the people walked slower than New York.

He felt as if someone had lifted a great stone from his head, and the stress he always felt in New York City was disappearing.

Furness was talking,

"And this is the Savannah, on top of the hill is the Hilton, the upside down hotel."

Furness directed the SUV around the Savannah, pointing out offices and government buildings as he did.

"My cousin is in the regiment there, and I will introduce you to him later. I've also got a friend coming, a surprise visitor. I haven't seen him in years. I thought he worked at the airport in St. Thomas. I guess he quit and decided to come home."

Furness guided the SUV around the big field called Savannah and continued, "We'll see him tomorrow. Anyway, I'll take you to my house and you can clean up, and tonight we'll meet the developers on this project."

Tony nodded his okay, taking in all the sights and sounds.

He thought of Libby, and he was worried about her. He wished she could have come with him, but she had a job too. Then he thought of Sam and Arthur and then he hoped Caesar and Gallo were all right.

He prayed they were all well, and safe. Tony felt far removed from all his friends and family, but he would enjoy himself while he was here. This would be an easy trip. He couldn't guess what was going to happen.

*　　*　　*

She glided through the air currents, glancing down ever so slightly as she turned to get closer to landfall. Her eyes were sharp, and all the humans and the animals below never noticed her. The air up at this height was cold and crisp, but the bird never let it bother her. She loved the open sky and its exhilarating temperature.

She had left her clutch due to an argument with the aerie heads. Her brother, Peregrines, was in charge now, and told her to be his right wing and defender of the clutch. As a female, she would attend to the nest now keeping it safe for the new nestlings coming. Ketvel would have none of that. She wanted to see the world not sit in a nest watching other families' chicks.

Ketvel daydreamed about adventures and focused beneath her. She had flown and glided some time now and wasn't sure where she was.

Below, the land had the human nests with their usual noise and smells. This was something Ketvel couldn't take. The humans destroying the land they inhabit with their moving nests on land and on water. Humans have been such a sad breed.

Ketvel noticed a tall structure near the main river and alit on the top post. From here she could see the world and hear its sounds.

She was enjoying her day and sat and noticed the sloppy noisy gulls fighting over a piece of flesh from an animal.

They were beneath her in the avian class structure, as her mother had taught her.

"Now don't associate with the other birds, they are lower in the bird kingdom then us. We are the kings and queens of the skies. Remember well," her mother would beat into her.

Ketvel never forgot and never talked to any other birds outside the clutch. Today would change her life. Ketvel, with her keen eyesight, spotted a white pigeon by itself in the woods to the south walking alone. An easy prey and she had not eaten all day. Ketvel swooped down off the bridge and hit top speed in about two seconds.

The pigeon, unaware of the danger, walked beneath a human bench, noting a scrap of a piece of popcorn. He was hungry and had been depressed all day.

Just as he walked under the bench, a noisy wing passed over him and into the trees. The pigeon looked up and got a glimpse of the pigeons' worst enemy. It was a falcon, and she was after him. He knew if he flew off, it would be over in a second. The old pigeon had warned him of such birds, but he never saw one before. He decided to sit it out; maybe the falcon will give up.

Ketvel was mad. How could he have seen her, or was it just plain luck? She edged closer to the ground, trying to scare the pigeon to fly off. It didn't work. This pigeon was nobody's fool. This would take some doing.

She swooped again within inches of the bench, trying to scare her prey. No movement from the pigeon so Ketval decided to angle a different downward approach.

Ketvel, in her enthusiasm, swooped down and glanced a branch on a low-lying tree knocking her down to the ground, dazed.

When the pigeon had seen the errant flight of the killer, he took off, leaving the falcon on the ground. He flew to the head aviary, Fletcher, to tell of this strange bird in the area. He had met him briefly one day and knew where he lived.

Fletcher was busy counting his berries when the white pigeon flew on his branch and knocked some of the berries to the ground.

"Now, who told you to fly in here so fast, look what you did. It took me a long time to gather these berries," Fletcher chirped out. "Now, Clay, was it so important?"

"A falcon is at the park, and she knocked herself silly trying to get me."

Fletcher looked at Clay in astonishment.

"There are no falcons here, and none since my great-great-grandfather's time."

Clay became his usual cynical self.

"Well, then there is a big winged bird with talons that almost had me for an appetizer."

Fletcher looked and him and said, "Well, pigeon legs, lead on."

\*　　\*　　\*

The cat was mad. His territory was gone. Caesar, the chosen one, was the felenex in the area and he didn't like it. On top of that, that ridiculous jay had spread the word on him. Pickings were sparse until now. The food had dried up on his usual paths these suns until he saw something that he never saw or heard of before.

A bird, larger than he had ever seen, lay on the ground helpless, ready for the killing. It was one of these exotic birds and probably good tasting too.

He would kill it in one attack. As he approached the bird with claws bared, another voice from his right side spoke out.

"Do not threaten that bird, mongrel."

"My name is Bear, and I am not a mongrel. Why should you care what bird I kill?" Bear spat out.

"Since I am sworn to protect this territory from mongrels like you and Caesar my felenex left me in charge to do so, I say leave the bird alone."

The voice was of a red cat in the shadows. Bear couldn't get a good look at him.

"I am not afraid of your felenex or of you. This bird is fair game."

With that Bear leaped toward the bird. The red cat leaped into the way hitting Bear with his shoulder, knocking him to the side.

"You will die today, red one," Bear spat toward his attacker.

As Bear said those words, he sprung with his claws extended. As fate would have it, a large rock lay nearby the red cat. The red cat moved quickly to his left and fell backward as Bear landed on the rock. Bear hit his head and fell to the ground.

The falcon, regaining her composure, flew up into the branches and looked down. It was a red cat who had protected her from the big gray one.

"Why have you done this?" asked the surprised falcon.

"My felenex, Caesar, has taught me never to harm birds." Arthur was getting up off the ground.

"I would like to meet this Caesar. He seems above his standing in wisdom. You have done me a service. Someday, I shall repay you."

Just then Fletcher and Clay arrived and alit on an opposite branch.

Fletcher spoke first, "Your majesty, what are you doing here? Are you lost?" he chirped sarcastically.

"Don't be insulting, blue, I was out for a fly," the falcon retorted.

"I saw what happened as we flew in. You almost got dead if it wasn't for Arthur our friend here, and leave my territory clutch alone. You scared Clay here senseless, which isn't hard to do."

"Yeah I saw my short miserable life pass before my eyes" Clay cracked.

The falcon looked at the two birds and was apologetic.

"It seems I made a mistake. How is it you are friends with a cat who saves a bird from another cat?"

"It's a long story, Your Princessship, come to my nest in my safe tree, and we will split some berries and don't bother any more of my clutch along the way."

The falcon nodded and followed the blue jay while Arthur tagged along toward home. Arthur wondered if Caesar would be proud of him today.

*   *   *

Gallo was curious. The Colombians were always selling and hawking their coke, but there was something else here.

The lowlife they captured on the beach was a higher than the usual operative. Mendes Ruiz was a captain in the cartel and he was never in St. Thomas, but he had to be here for an important reason.

When Gallo contacted Simpson, the DEA chief in New York, Simpson dismissed the fact that Mendes was in the Virgin Islands. Something didn't smell right. Gallo had heard through his snitches and from Sabrina, that there was a high-level cartel meeting last week in the Caribbean. This would explain Mendes being here.

Gallo was thinking out every scenario as he walked up the steps to his office with Caesar following behind him. Caesar never lost sight of Gallo and walked with him like a dog. The natives and the tenants would all laugh or comment on the black cat trailing the man.

It was Gallo's fault. He always liked dogs, and he was trying to turn Caesar into a trained dog. This he knew would never be possible. Cats just don't take orders, but Caesar seemed to react in some instances like a dog. Gallo was proud of him that day they saved Sabrina on the beach.

Gallo entered the office, and John was holding Sabrina's hand.

"So, Sabrina, you okay?" Gallo smiled as he sat down.

Caesar sat on the window stool and glared outside.

"Yes, yes, thank you. I wrote down everything that happened like you said."

Gallo reached out to the paper Sabrina was handing him and scanned the writing.

"This Trini you met at the airport, does he work for the Colombians?" Gallo asked as he lit a cigarette.

"No, no, he never knew those pigs. He was working for some other drug smuggler," Sabrina nervously said.

"Did he ever mention who or where?"

Sabrina grabbed a cop of coffee and sat down.

"No, he never did, but he mentioned a name he was deathly afraid of, a Mr. Frank or Franks. Every time he said his name, it was like he was afraid for his whole family."

Gallo took a drag from the Marlboro. Sabrina continued.

"He said he was going back to Trinidad to see this man and get out of this business."

"What was this Trini's name?" Gallo asked.

"Roby or Robby, or something like that."

Gallo thought of Furness. He knows Trinidad like the back of his hand.

Sabrina was talking.

"There is one more thing this Trini was always talking about heroin, not coke."

Gallo's head snapped. *Heroin, why the hell would this stuff be involved here? It is popular again, but usually the Mafia handled that from the East.*

Sabrina got up and walked over to Caesar.

"This cat that follows you, he is special, yes."

Gallo smiled, "Yes very special."

Caesar looked up and noted a nervous tension in the female. Caesar remembered her from the other day. The female stroked his head, and Caesar responded raising his body. Sabrina gave him a kiss.

"Does he understand English?" Sabrina asked nervously.

"I think sometimes he knows what I'm saying and thinking." Gallo laughed at the comment, but was worried. He must contact Furness but he can't through normal cell phone or email. He had to see him in person, and he knew Tony was there visiting.

"John, you stay and mind the store and take care of Sabrina. I'm going on a trip."

Gallo got up and was about to leave when Sabrina remembered something else.

"Mr. Gallo, one other thing, the Trini said Mr. Franks was only available on a boat. He has no real address."

Gallo nodded and left with Caesar for his hotel room.

"Guess Furness will be surprised to see me, huh Caesar?" Gallo smirked.

Caesar sat in his favorite spot in the back window and looked up at his master and thought where are we going now.

*   *   *

The Colombian family, Valli, established themselves as coffee growers first in the mid sixties. As the years went by, the coffee trade was too competitive; and when the drug cartels started to spring up and make billions from the banned bean, the patriarch, Carlo Gorda Valli, started growing the banned drug.

It was a dangerous business fighting off many of the cartels in Colombia, but because the Vallis had the network already established with the coffee trade, the Vallis became the top family. Carlos had three sons and one daughter, and the oldest son was the chip off the old block. He started to run parts of the cartel when he was twenty-one years old. By the time he was thirty, the father was ill so he basically assumed control from his father.

His father was reluctant to retire, but Eduardo pushed him out and the other two sons agreed. It was only the daughter, Malena, who cared for the father and hated the business. Malena was the youngest, and when her mother died she assumed the woman's role in the family.

Malena hated Colombia and its sick business. She wanted to get out and see the world and live on her own. Her brothers could have the ranch and the land and the lousy business; they were into killing people. It was of no use to her. Someday she would leave and escape this life, but she couldn't leave her father alone.

It was a hot day when Mr. Franks arrived, telling her father of the deal from the general and the Italians. Her father wanted no part of it, but he was ruled out as being backward or old fashioned by his sons. There was money to be tripled, and Eduardo wanted it. Sometimes she thought Eduardo would kill father; his temper was so violent.

Mr. Franks, as always, lusted after her, and bought her gifts and asked her to come with him to his yacht. Malena hated everything about him, even his voice. He was repulsive, and this made her even more determined to escape. If it weren't for her father, she would be gone. Malena was as usual by the oven cooking for her father when the tall man walked in. Dressed in mostly black, the tall man sat down next to her father and smirked at her.

She hated him, and it showed on her face.

"We'll, Malena, will you come with me this time? I'm traveling to Trinidad, and we can tour the island together. I discussed it with your brother."

"Senor, I am not interested in the family business or the people in it. My father is my main concern."

"So I see." The man in black smirked. "And if your father wasn't here, would you still stay?"

Malena turned and glanced at the man with hate. She turned back, cursing under her breath.

"Oh well, maybe soon, Malena." The tall man rose from the chair and gave his goodbye to the father and walked out the door.

Malena was frustrated. She must get her father and leave here soon. She left the eggs on the stove and ran to her room to look for her passport. It was still active, and she searched for her father's passport. Malena was only gone about ten minutes when she heard a noise. She ran toward the kitchen, and her father's body was on the floor but there was no blood. Her father had gotten up to get the eggs when he collapsed. There was no sign of foul play, but Malena knew he was killed. She screamed for the maid, but no one came. Her father was dead, and she was alone.

It was Eduardo's work, she knew, but how? On the table were her father's reading glasses, the local papers, and a coffee cup. She made the coffee herself. Malena lifted her father's body and hugged him tightly and started to cry.

She was alone now.

*       *       *

The international airport in Port of Spain has a fairly new terminal. Most of the airlines are either American or Caribbean, but the most popular is Caribbean Air.

Flight 410 was coming in late—at about 11:00 PM—when Furness and Tony were waiting at the Customs exit.

They couldn't wait for Gallo's arrival and that famous cat. He had wired them.

Gallo had a pretty pleasant trip from St. Thomas to Grenada, but the local Customs wouldn't permit Caesar in the airplane until some calls were made by the local authority to Washington, that's when the red carpet was opened for both of them. The Caribbean Air flight was held up thanks to the mixup, and Gallo was anxious to see his friends.

Furness had arranged for Customs to let them through fast since his cousins are in the regiment and the police.

To Gallo's surprise, Customs in Port of Spain went fast with all the people asking about Caesar and wanting to pet him. Word had spread of the famous cat.

One woman screamed out, "It's that cat. He's the one that killed all the rats and captured the drug dealers."

Just then, a whole group of tourists and Trinis came over, and even the Customs officials were mesmerized by the black cat. Finally, Caesar was free, and they walked through the exit door to Furness and Tony, who were all smiles.

They all hugged, and Furness gathered them into his SUV. Caesar was happy to see his savior Master Furness on this strange-smelling land. The scents here were much different than the other land he came from with Master Gallo. The ride here was pleasant enough with that same eerie feeling he got on the last trip. Master Gallo called it a jet and carried Caesar over to the window. All he could see was the sky, and he was flying like the birds. His stomach started to get sick, but he got over it quickly when a female brought him a pan of milk. Now he was with his friends in another land, but there was something not right about all this.

Caesar licked Furness's hand, and they all laughed. The cat was also surprised to see Master Tony here and without Mistress Libby. He wondered why.

Furness drove out of the airport on to the main road to Diego Martin.

"Gallo, you must see the sights while you are here. I'll take you to the north and the boat clubs, and we'll go out onto the bay. Tony here has seen it already, but I don't think he would mind."

Gallo smiled and just wanted to relax, but he had to bring up business.

"I'm here looking for someone, but let's go to your house so I can clean up and I'll fill you in."

Tony felt a foreboding in the way Gallo said it. Tony knew this trip wasn't going to be just a vacation after all.

\*   \*   \*

Brooklyn Heights was warm, and cars were trying to make their way down Montague Street. The area had become a mecca for business and the residents; and the areas beyond the Heights were selling quickly. All of Brooklyn was on a real estate boom from Greenpoint to Mill Basin—the land, houses, condos were selling for big numbers.

Libby Cassett walked into an old brownstone on Fourth Avenue in sight of the Verrazano Bridge. The brownstone was typical of the period. Large steps up to the second floor while five small steps below the stair took you to the first floor. Once inside, a large vestibule and stairs to the upper floors faced Libby. She sat down and waited for the so-called producer of small independent films.

Libby heard a noise and at the top of the stairs stood Bert Youngman.

He stared down at his prey. She was gorgeous as he had heard, and he felt maybe he could score. He was deceiving her this way, but fifty thousand is fifty thousand. She would be great in films. He thought back about his encounter with a tall man dressed in black a month ago while in the Caribbean.

Bert had traveled to the Bahamas islands to search out locales for bikini shots on the beaches for a film he was producing. The tall man had come over to him at the bar in the Paradise Island Hilton. They talked about fishing and women. Bert asked the stranger if he knew any unknowns looking for a film he was about to start.

The tall man smiled and noted a small New York City actress he was familiar with but had some problems.

"She's not too happy with me these days. We are former lovers, and we sort of broke up but I still love her." The stranger turned to suck on a lemon and smiled again. "And call me Frank," he said in a low tone.

"So what can I do for you, Frank?" asked Bert sheepishly.

"Well, we both can solve our problem. You need a beautiful actress to star in your film, and I want her back. I'll give you her address and maybe you offer her the starring role in your movie. I'll give you some money for your picture too."

Bert's eyes lit up. "Money, how much?"

Frank took out a cigarette and lit it and took a drag.

"Fifty thousand, and I don't care if you use her in your film or not."

Bert was astonished. *This guy is so much in love he's willing to give me fifty thousand to sucker his old girlfriend down here.* It was a home run.

"Sure, I'll offer her the job, and if she's any kind of desperate actress, she'll jump at it." Bert was jubilant.

The tall man got up, and they exchanged pleasantries, and they would work out the details later.

Bert heard the young girl stand to greet him, which caused his daydream to disappear. Now he would have to convince this woman to star in his film and come down to the Bahamas with him. As he descended the stairs, she looked up and smiled. She was perfect for anything he could film.

*Hmmm, maybe this won't be so horrible after all. I can use her in the film too. Lucky me.*

*     *     *

Sam was sitting on the steps at his house when he heard the noise from above.

"Hey, Firebreather, we have a new friend for you to meet."

Sam noticed a beautiful majestic bird float down onto one of Fletcher's branches.

She was gray and light brown with eyes that went through you.

"Her name is Ketval, and Arthur saved her a couple of suns ago. She's a—"

"I know what kind of bird she is, Fletch," Sam barked up to the tree.

"I've never seen one before around here."

"Hello, sir, the last two suns I've been a guest of the jay, and even though I don't like his living habits, it's been adequate."

Sam smirked. "Oh no, not another crazy bird."

"Nice to meet you too. My name is—"

"His name is Sam, the Firebreather, the head of this territory," Fletcher chirped out.

"Fletch, I can introduce myself."

"No, no. Ketval doesn't know about our clutch here, and I want her to meet everyone. Too bad Caesar isn't here."

Ketval turned and noted sadness in Fletcher's voice.

"Who is this Caesar you talk so much about?"

"He is destiny itself. No other animal has his bearing. He defeated many rats and humans too. He is of the line of Simmark."

Ketval, even in the lofty aeries of her family, had heard of Simmark and his exploits.

"If he is truly of the Simmark line, then I must meet him and take him to my clutch. My family must meet him." Ketval was excited.

"I am sorry, Your Princessness, he is far away on some adventure, and when he will be back I don't know," Fletcher sighed. "And I wish I was with him."

"I heard you common aves have clutch talk down the land coast that gossips about the goings and comings of anything of interest to human or animal. We, of course, the aeries of my family are not involved in such gossip."

Fletcher laughed, "Yeah, we got birds that talk like crows and clutches up the coasts from the gulls to the geese but not as far as Caesar is. He's in some faraway land. We have no clutch that far to the south. The birds there don't want to know us.

They're the south area birds. They think we're stupid so our network crackle stops at the great swamp in a land called Florida or what the geese and gulls call the flat lands."

Ketval noted Fletcher's frustration in the aviary network.

"Fletcher, you know, we the raptors, which include many of the turned-beak birds have our own crackle network only we don't gossip. We pass on useful information. Maybe I can investigate this for you. I know many ospreys who skirt the coast regularly."

Fletcher was surprised. He got the stuck-up bird to do something for someone else beside herself.

"You would do me great honor if you did this, Your Princessness." Fletcher bowed.

Sam almost choked. With that, Ketvel said her goodbyes, and with a great wave of her wings was up and gone.

Fletcher was beaming. "A majesty bird here and willing to help me."

Sam was laughing, "I thought you were going to kiss her talon."

"Very funny, Sam, but if it gets us some info on Caesar, it's worth it, and I hope it gives us some news."

Sam nodded and thought about his friend Caesar and wondered if he would see him ever again.

\*     \*     \*

Malena Valli woke up, and all she could see was the sun. She was lying on a bed of dry leaves and being eaten by various insects. She brushed away the pesky things and stood up. She hoped Eduardo's men hadn't spotted her in her flight. After her father was killed, she grabbed what she could and ran for the nearest tree cover. Her plan was to make it to the coast as fast as possible and grab the next plane to anywhere.

She had a passport, but she was afraid her brother would be out to kill her. He wouldn't stop at father. He wanted it all with no loose ends. It would be a long walk to the coast and to not be seen, especially by that Mr. Franks. He's the bastard that killed her father—she was sure of it. Eduardo must have told him to get rid of the old man. She started to run and run fast.

Just as Malena was running west, Mr. Franks was boarding his yacht. It was a glorious day. His plans were being fulfilled. Franks thought about what had happened so far, and he smiled. Eduardo trusted him so much he lured him to kill his father and paid him a large sum to do him in. He was in charge of the cartel in common with the general's stupid son, and the equally stupid Mafia.

If Cimbari really knew who he was, he'd be dead. They will all play into my hands. Then there is the fucking cat and Gallo. They're in Trinidad, according to his sources—*and just where I want them to be. I have a little job to do there to clean up that mess with Robie in St. Thomas.* And then there's Miss Cassett. He would handle her and get all of them at the same time.

"Neat . . ." he yelled out.

"Perfect," again he bellowed.

"Shit-head where are you," Franks cursed for his first mate.

"You sleeping again, you good for nothing Trini. You'll be happy to know we're off to your fucking little island to handle a quick job."

"Shit-head."

Just then, Woody, his first mate, came up from below.

"Yes, sir, we're going to Trini. I'm happy, haven't been there for last three weeks."

"Yeah, but first, take your imbecile friend and scout out the airport. I want to know where Malena Valli goes. She's not in my plans, but I'm going to make some room for the bitch. I need some fun too, ha ha."

Woody cringed. He didn't like when the captain laughed like that.

"Go, go, she'll probably get there in a day or so, and don't let her see you."

"Yes, sir," Woody replied and gladly walked away.

Mr. Franks sat on his captain's chair and laughed, "They're all going to get it. The fucks that tried to kill me. Heh heh heh."

*     *     *

Dr. Clifton Zine was a brilliant man. Son of a Chinese father and an English mother, he was born and raised in Hong Kong for the first fifteen years of his life. His father, after his English mother died, decided to travel to America to show his son the world.

It took his father years to raise the money, but he did it cleaning floors and selling electronics. Clifton was always interested in science and engineering. He excelled in physics, mathematics, and mechanical engineering.

His father got a job with a large electronics firm and saved all his money for his son's education. He wanted his son to go to college and be an American. Clifton was so brilliant he received a scholarship from UCLA, and majored in physics. Not stopping, he was first in his class and then attended graduate school at MIT for mechanical pneumatics and then on to a Ph.D. in physics and chemistry. His talent was so noted by the United States government that he landed a job at NASA. His father all along stayed in California, while he was in school.

At NASA, he developed new rocket fuel that was a breakthrough for the shuttle missions. He worked on a new hydrogen cell before anybody even thought to use it. His constant work started to get a reputation as a loner, a recluse, and an eccentric. It wasn't that he didn't like people; they bored him with their little stupid lives. They never thought about how to improve the quality of life.

He would think of a new invention or chemical formula almost every week and experiment on his ideas. So to experiment, he would stay away from the stupid parties and 'get togethers' as they called it. Something was rattling around in his head for the last three years. It was a fantastic idea for the government. They would love it. It would revolutionize transportation.

He thought of motion without any fuel. Oh yes, there would be a kind of fuel, but not by conventional standards. His theory would take sometime and a large space. So he took every free time he could to build his new theory. He gathered his sources and laid them out slowly as not to miss anything. He gathered blue algae, but not the common algae. It was hybrid blue green algae. It was a special growth from an area off South America. He had it flown in from Chile. Then Clifton got some stainless steel tubing about two inches in diameter. He built a little car and searched for special pale yellow quartz crystals. He found the quartz at a local gem store traders club. They were all happy to help him. He now had much of what he needed and locked himself in his landlord's basement. The landlord didn't care; Zine was paying him extra for the use of the area.

He started to build his laboratory for the blue green algae along with the steel tubing. He knew he had to get the algae at just the right temperature and humidity. He built a Plexiglas greenhouse and mixed different hybrids of blue algae until he got the chemical reaction he required. Wouldn't those idiots at the agency be surprised? *Let them laugh at me. I will change the face of transportation. They will stop laughing soon,* he thought.

Dr. Zine spent three months developing his theory until he had it almost perfected, and he got the interest of one of the top scientists in his division to gather up all the upper management to witness his invention presentation. They were always skeptical of anything new.

The day came for his presentation, and all the heads of staff gathered and were anxiously waiting for this breakthrough but scoffed at Dr. Recluse as they called him. Dr. Zine presented it, but it failed to produce his desired effects. The government heads laughed at him and his foolishness, and they ridiculed him. It was then he promised never to work for the government again. They were brainless amoebas and not worthy of his brilliance. He took all his money and bought a warehouse in Virginia outside Washington, and he experimented until he found the flaws.

Finally he had it; he had found the perfect answer, but will it work on the larger scale?

This was his next mission, and there were men who had heard of his experiment who were interested and wanted to finance him on a larger scale. These men were willingly to finance on a large scale the complete transportation rail system. He didn't care what their politics were.

Dr. Zine knew they were ex-government men not interested in government work but to increase their own bank account. He didn't care their motives just the outcome of his invention. He would improve the world. The end justified the means.

Dr. Zine went to work for them, but not in United States. They supplied him with a big new brilliant lab in the Bahamas where these men and other money backers owned land. Again he couldn't bother with who was backing him. Dr. Zine was happy and anxious to continue his work. Now he could work and prove to those jerks in the government, he was right. *They'll be sorry they laughed at me.*

*    *    *

Robie sat on his gallery overlooking his front yard. He had installed a steel gate with an electric opener, which kept the burglars and crooks out. His masonry walls were ten feet high and only blocked out his neighbors, but not his view of the mountains.

Robie grabbed a can of Coke and thought about St. Thomas. Sabrina, who worked at the airport with him, had disappeared and Robie wasn't going to stick around. He knew too much. He knew about the coalition between the Valli family and the Vietnamese heroin cartels. The American Mafia was also involved in some big operation under the sea from the Bahamas. He didn't know exactly where, but his guess was near Nassau. Sabrina and he used to talk about it constantly, and then the shipments came from the USA for large stainless steel tubing and large stainless steel sections—for what, he didn't know.

It was his job to hide all this from Customs, to be shipped to the Bahamas. Sabrina didn't know the whole story, but he didn't trust her completely either. Two American agents in the past months had disappeared who had gone out on dates with her. She, of course, denied any involvement with the agents, but Robie was not foolish enough to press the issue. She was dangerous, and he was sure a spy for the Colombian Valli family. That's why he quit and came home. She was going to meet that other American agent, and it was too much for him. Back to Trinidad, where it's safe and out of the way; and just in case something was to happen to him, he left a diary in a safe spot.

Robie got up to check his clock on the wall in the kitchen. It was eight thirty and he was getting hungry. Furness had said after lunch, and he said he had two friends from America with him. Robie knew Furness from his college days here on the island. His hunger pangs drove him to the refrigerator for a roti. He took one bite and placed it on the counter when he heard a noise by the front yard. He walked to his front door to see what was going on and he noticed his gate was open. Odd that it would be open without his direction. He opened his door to look around. Everything was quiet and the birds were singing on a nearby tree in his neighbor's yard. Beautiful black birds with yellow markings sang their daily song. Robie pressed the automatic button in the house by the front door and the gate closed. He shrugged his shoulders and reentered his house.

As he went into the kitchen to cut the roti, he noticed the birds had stopped singing. Robie arched his neck out the window by his neighbor's tree. Those beautiful blackbirds were gone, and there was an eerie silence. He walked with the roti in aluminum foil in his hand toward the front door and opened it. His gallery was quiet, and he sat down to eat.

At that moment he heard a noise under the house. The house was raised about three feet above the grade. He walked down the steps and to the side of the house where a black figure was seated under the house.

"Hello, Robie." The stranger smiled.

"Who are you . . . ?" were Robie's last words when a .22 caliber bullet entered his skull.

The roti fell out of his hand as he fell to the ground dead.

The black figure got up and screwed off his silencer from the gun. He grabbed the roti and took a bite.

"Not bad," he said as he dropped it by Robie's side.

The black figure left as quickly and quietly as he came.

\* \* \*

The black cat sat on the ledge overlooking the great front yard. There were brightly colored birds here that taunted the cat as they flew overhead. The cat didn't hear the cries of the strange-sounding birds. He was thinking of his friends far away and how much he missed them. He could hear the voices of the three men in the house, but he wasn't listening. He was only feeling this foreboding that had been bothering him since the human rat flew into the sea moons ago. His dreams were of the human rat that killed his mother and mistress. Every night he was haunted by the black figure with that voice that sent the fur on his back up.

Master Furness had locked up his dogs for the time Caesar was there. The dogs were friendly enough and didn't understand why their master penned them up, but humans assume too much between cats and dogs. Furness had rather not deal with it.

Caesar thought of the human rat again, and somehow he sensed the rat wasn't dead—yet he saw him go into the water. A bird broke his thoughts.

"Hey, cat, where you from?"

Caesar looked up to a blackbird with striped colors.

"From far away over the large sea."

Another blackbird joined the conversation.

"He's from a place called New York City. I heard the human talking. I heard of it. It's very big and has strange birds there," said another blackbird who alit on a nearby roof.

"What's your name, black one?"

Caesar turned and glared at them with his green eyes.

"Caesar, son of Vandal. The line of Simmark."

The birds stopped talking and looked in amazement. Could this be the cat that they had heard many tales of valor? The black one, they had heard from the sea terns, who had defeated the ships rats and saved humans.

"You are the great one we heard about, it is possible?"

Caesar smiled. "Not so great."

Word spread in the nearby forest and mountains, and dozens of birds appeared out of nowhere.

"We hear you befriended birds and blood swore to never kill a bird?" the blackbird with the long beak asked.

"That's true. My two best friends are Fletcher the blue jay and Sam the dog."

Caesar wished Fletcher was here. He could tell his tall tales. He missed the blue jay.

"It seems you make friends of enemies," the long-beaked one chirped.

"Yes, it's true, both saved my life. Did any of your clutch come upon any strangers in the area, say from the same area as me?" Caesar asked, hoping for information.

All the birds thought and shook their heads.

A small orange and red bird answered, "No, oh great one, but if we do we will tell you. Will you stay here?"

Caesar smiled and looked around at the beautiful mountains and smelled the fresh clear air.

"For sometime, I think. My master is on a search for some bad humans, and I protect him and my family."

The birds were in awe of him and stayed to discuss the land he came from. All were curious about Fletcher and the other animals.

Furness decided to take his guests to Robie's house but first they would go eat lunch in Port of Spain. When Furness came out to the gallery he would never be prepared for the sight. Hundreds of birds were gathered on rooftops, on trees, on power wires, or walls chirping away; and in the center of it all was Caesar. The cat was just sitting basking in the sun.

"Hey, guys, come out here, you've got to see this. It's a miracle."

Tony and Gallo joined him and their mouths were open.

Gallo laughed, "Caesar's holding court."

Furness said to be quiet, or the birds will fly away.

It was a sight for the books, so Tony took a couple of photos.

"No one would believe this."

Furness walked outside, and all the birds squawked at his presence and flew off to outlining branches in adjacent yards. He then gathered up Caesar, and Furness almost could hear the birds say goodbye while they flew off.

The three men got into Furness's SUV and drove out his gate to lunch and then to meet his friend, Robie.

A surprise would await them all, including the great one as the birds called him.

*   *   *

Franks was proud of himself. He had taken care of the Trini stoolie and the Colombian father in three days, and now it was off to the conference to meet fucking Cimbari's son. He was patting himself on the back. His revenge would come soon. His plan was easy. Gain the Colombians' trust and the Vietnamese son's trust, and fuck them both along with the Mafia. No one would suspect him and his motives.

At the same time he would settle the score with Gallo and that fucking cat who took his eye. As a bonus, he would get that bitch Cassett and her stupid boyfriend too. He laughed to himself. It was going as planned.

Next step would be one he didn't plan. It was Malena Valli. He wanted her for himself as a bonus for his genius. He lay back on the pillow in the cabin of his yacht. Woody, his first mate, was scouting the area in Caracas for him. Caracas was only about ten miles off the coast of Trinidad. His spies told him she flew to Caracas and was hiding out there from her brother, Eduardo.

The yacht sat in the Port of Spain harbor called the Gulf of Paria. It was a very hot day around ninety-eight degrees Fahrenheit when Franks went on deck. He had heard though his snitches that Gallo and the cat were visiting that stinking Trini who helped him in the past. After he dispatched Robie, he wanted to go after Malena but Gallo played into his hands. Franks laughed out loud. He thinks he's on a hot trail, the stupid fuck.

He checked his gun and magazine clip. He had bought another Browning Hi Power since he lost it on Long Island Sound with his eye. It was an exact match to his other gun.

"I will kill you, cat. Your days are ended."

Franks got into the powerboat on the side of the yacht. He called for his men to follow. Syps was his local Trini contact and hit man and Colin was half-Trini and half-East-Indian descent who had killed his abusive father and aunt at nineteen to get away from them. Both were wanted in different islands of the Caribbean. They joined Franks on the boat and headed for Port of Spain. Franks was ready for more death.

*     *     *

At the same time as Franks was heading for port, Sam and Arthur sat in front of the fireplace and thought about Caesar. He was gone again on some adventure, and they missed him. The Princess, the falcon Fletcher befriended, had put out the word in the raptor crackle line, and they had no clue of Caesar's whereabouts. The coastline birds had no word of him.

Sam was lonely. Mistress Libby was out most of the day, and Arthur would roam the neighborhood, watching and helping other cats as he had promised Caesar. So he was bored. Even Missy couldn't cheer him up. Fletcher tried, but Sam was depressed. He wanted to be out there helping Caesar, Master Tony, and Master Gallo. It seemed all his friends abandoned him.

Mistress Libby was excited for some reason he couldn't understand. She was on the talking hand box forever and not just to Master Tony, but to some man named Bert.

"Yes, yes, but I don't understand, you want to come here to my house to see me?" Libby asked surprised.

"Of course, to see you in your habitat within your environment. It helps me to make decisions on my films." Youngman was excited.

Libby paused and thought, *Well, if he tries anything Sam will stop him.*

"Okay, okay, when?"

"Today is Tuesday, say this week Friday at about seven," Bert answered confidently.

"A little late but okay, seven it is."

"Thanks. Goodbye, Miss Cassett." And the line went dead.

Libby sat down and wondered about this. He is a producer she had him checked out, and he has many films to his credit. It was just odd to meet here. Maybe he is strange like so many in the film industry. Heaven knows she's met many. She went over to Sam and Arthur and stroked both on their heads. Both animals responded raising their heads to meet her hand.

"Hey, Sam, I wonder how Tony and Caesar are doing. I miss them both," Libby stated to her two pets.

Sam looked up with sad eyes. "Yeah, and I miss them too," he barked.

*   *   *

Gallo started to fill in Tony and Furness as much as he could on the men he needed to see. They had gone to lunch at the West Mall when Furness dropped his fork and stared at Gallo.

"Did you say Robie?"

"Yes, do you know him?" Gallo asked anxiously.

"Yes, as a matter of fact that's who we are going to meet today. He said, 'Bring your friends too.' He's an old friend of mine from school. This is creepy. He's involved with smuggling?"

"Yes, I'm sorry Furness, but it seems so," Gallo said quietly.

Furness put his head in his hands.

"Oh no, Robie. I knew he was a bad boy but not like that. He's stole food from delivery trucks and ran some sort of numbers here but this." Furness was upset.

Caesar was sitting atop the barrier between the seats and noticed the human's voices raised and Master Furness looked sad. He hated to see anybody in distress, so he put his paws on Furness' shoulder.

Furness felt Caesar's paw and looked at the cat.

"Is it possible this cat understands us?"

Gallo looked at Tony and back to the Trini.

"With what we've been through, I think he understands more things than us."

Furness grabbed the black cat from the barrier ledge and hugged him.

"Thank you, black one."

Tony's eyes started to well up so to break the moment Tony blurted out, "So what's next guys?"

Gallo looked at Furness.

"Let's go visit your friend."

Furness hugged Caesar one more time and stated with a strong voice,

"Let's go."

Tony carried Caesar to the SUV and placed him on the back ledge, his favorite spot. Furness put the truck in gear and drove quicker than he normally did, to Belmont, a suburb of Port of Spain.

The SUV screeched its discomfort on the hot asphalt roads as Furness turned corners sharply and went through yellow lights. There was no conversation in the SUV, just anxiousness on the three men's part.

Furness steered the truck around the Savannah and into Belmont. It was three o'clock and the sun was beating down on the area. Gallo's forehead was constantly sweating, and he noted that everyone was wearing long pants except the children. He had on shorts and was still hot. How could they not be hot with everything covered up?

The SUV stopped in front of a black gate, and Furness got out to ring the bell. He rang it several times with no response. Furness tried to climb the gate to see inside but could see nothing.

He walked back to the car to call his cousin in the police, Dan Harvey.

Furness put the phone down.

"He'll be here in fifteen minutes."

Gallo looked at the visibly upset Trini.

"Listen, when he gets here don't tell him I'm working for anybody, not just yet. I'm not sure what the story is at this point and I don't trust anybody."

Furness nodded and sat on the hood of the car.

Caesar's nostrils noted a faint scent from the past. Caesar wouldn't believe he smelled something familiar. It couldn't be. He felt sick and wanted to wretch. As soon as he sensed it, it was gone. The wind had taken it. Something was wrong and that scent—the smell of death, he knew it well—was present and, something else was here too.

\* \* \*

New York City was cool, and the rain came down in a mist that fogged up car windows. Autumn had arrived early this year, and the trees were turning their red and orange colors quickly. The city as always buzzed with excitement as cars and tourists lined the sidewalks of Broadway and downtown.

Don Cimbari sat at Mama's in Little Italy on a quiet alcove table in the rear of the restaurant. He was expecting a very important government contact. He ordered his usual—mussels marinara with penne. His three bodyguards sat at the table across from him. The back alcove was not lit save for a small candle on Cimbari's table.

Dean Martin was singing "Volare" over the speakers in the ceiling, which was a personal favorite of the Don. The restaurant owner, Vince Lala, would always race to the stereo to put on the disk of Dino whenever the Don was dining. Mama's was the Don's favorite on Elizabeth Street, and he came at least once a week.

The three bodyguards were eating already, and Cimbari could hear them slurping their spaghetti, making approval noises.

Cimbari was annoyed with them.

"Hey, you're supposed to watch my front and back, you mamalukes."

Cimbari turned from them and sipped his espresso from the demitasse cup. He wasn't hungry. This was an important link he was about to make today. This man would guarantee the success of the coastal drug venture. No more would the Cimbari family worry about being caught with their pants down with drugs. It was fool proof but this G-man would give him all the last minute setups, payoffs, and intel on the eastern coast as directed.

Cimbari heard a door open in the distance with some low voices. Some seconds passed and a figure, a large man about six foot two inches, stood in the alcove.

Patsy, one of the bodyguards, frisked him for firearms and nodded to Cimbari.

"Sit, please. Sit. Would you like a caffé?" Cimbari offered.

"No, just scotch and water please."

Cimbari made a gesture to someone behind the tall figure, and the sound of feet scrambling toward the front could be heard.

The tall man sat down and the drink came instantly.

"So we are here, finally. Is my operation going to have problems with your people?" Cimbari asked abruptly.

"No, we have everything set. The Florida people are on board. The castles on the Georgia and South Carolina beaches up the coast are all approved by the local and state agencies. The liquor commission in each state has approved all the licenses. The Customs and DEA are under control. No one knows the whole story except a select few and those people are in the loop." The tall man finished his speech and took a drink of the scotch and water.

"Very good, and the money, what is your assessment?"

The tall man was waiting for this.

"The monthly fee is acceptable to all, except my end. I don't want to go back and forth on this but I need more, say another million."

Cimbari smiled. He knew this man was buried well beyond his means in credit and had large debts, especially gambling.

"So you want to dip your beak more or to say wet your head. We know of your vices, and since you have been a successful broker of ours, it is acceptable."

Cimbari took a sip of espresso when the tall man spoke again.

"There is one more thing. We have an agent in the Caribbean who is not on our gift list. He's a live cannon, and he's well known even to the FBI. It would be difficult to get him to accept anything from us and to kill him might draw attention."

Cimbari was ahead of the stranger.

"We know of that bastard with the fucking cat. They've hurt the family before, and I have a score to settle that doesn't include your operation. Don't worry about him. It will be taken care of. He has a price on his head."

The tall man nodded and got up and said his goodbyes and left.

Cimbari thought about Gallo and the cat. Right now, the Dino brothers are planning a hit on him. If they fail, there is another option.

It would be settled soon.

\*    \*    \*

Cat Island in the Bahamas is the definition of paradise. It is in the middle of the island group and is the favorite of fisherman throughout the world. Many Europeans holiday here and fish for trophy fish off the coast. The beaches are white, and the eastern side of the island is made up of resorts and coastlines. The weather is perfect with a cool breeze in the summers off the Atlantic Ocean.

It is here the cartel set up their main laboratory for Dr. Zine in a deserted ranch house. The ranch was off the beaten track within sight of no homes or hotels. The cartel dug out the side of the hilltop on the south side of the island. It was the brainstorm of the general who located the site, and it was Tom his son who engineered the laboratory since he was a structural engineer.

Cat Island was just the start of the story. Tom, along with the Cimbari wealth and political connections, obtained permits and licenses for all the Sand Castle Restaurants on the beaches from Nassau in the Bahamas to New Jersey. It was ingenious. The cartel had it all complete now; just some finishing touches and the route to Miami would be operational. The general's contact in the U.S. government found Dr. Zine, and it was like manna from heaven. It will be a perfect crime right under their noses.

Tom sat on the cliff outside the laboratory, watching the seagulls dive for fish. He was pleased. All was ready and his father, the general, was proud of him. Ha, that was unusual. His father was a pain in the ass, and he was tired of being constantly criticzed by his father. This was his time not the old man, and he would show everyone.

The Colombians at first didn't think it would come to pass, but they were on board now. Nothing would stop them now, and in about two weeks he would meet with the parties again and confirm it all and the operation would start. As Tom was sitting on the south of Cat Island, birds flew over the highest point in the Bahamas, Mount Alvernia. Atop the mountain peak was a monastery called the Hermitage, built by an architect/priest Monsignor Hawkes, in the nineteenth century. It was a refuge for him and a pilgrimage for many now.

Cat Island is a quiet island of 1,700 people who basically live in three areas. The capital Arthur's Town, the center of the island and the west side devoted to tourists. Under the ranch in the south cape, the cave under the house that the Cimbari family built for Dr. Zine was constructed by outside help from the United States. The Cimbari family employed the men. No one from the island was involved except a few laborers.

One such laborer came from Arthur's Town, up north. His name was Darby. Darby was a native Bahamian and traced his lineage back to the Loyalists of the American Revolution who moved here in 1783.

Fishing was Darby's life's trade, but his friend asked him to take him down the coast one day to work with him and get some easy money. His friend heard there was an American company that needed some help. The construction was fast paced and secretive. It was Americans who lived on site, and when Darby was cleared to work after some questions he would come to work regularly. Darby noticed all the Americans had New York accents—at least he thought from all the movies he had seen.

They kept among themselves, and Darby never worked on the underground portion past the large mansion. His friend, Smiley, always told him to mind his business and not look at their faces. After the house was built, he was paid handsomely and was told all the work was finished, but his natural curiosity got the better of him. Days later, he would travel with his fishing boat offshore of the ranch and crawl within 150 meters and watch the equipment going into a cave. The cave was built below the ranch on a cliff overlooking the beach. It was like nothing he had seen before, and he wondered about a ship offshore with dredging machines. They were laying something in the ocean, but he couldn't see. Many times he returned to the site, but he was afraid of getting caught so he stopped after a week.

No wonder the fish catch was poor these days. They were digging up the bottom of the ocean. No one from the Bahamian government was anywhere to be seen or ask the Americans questions. On the last day he visited the area, he returned to his pals in Arthur's town at the local bar and thought of the cave and wondered of its secrets. It bothered him all these weeks. The air was hot and the sweat poured off Darby onto the bar. He gulped down a draft of ale and returned to his fishing boat.

*Maybe I'll go around the horn with my boat one more time and see what's going on. They'll just think I'm lost.*

\*　　\*　　\*

The body lay at the west side of the house. It was Robie. Furness was visibly upset. His friend of many years was murdered. Furness called the police, and his cousin Dan came. The police started their usual investigation while Gallo knew this was the work of a professional hit man. It was not some local either. The use of the .22 caliber suggested American origin.

Caesar sat on the steps of the house, his nostrils aflame with a scent he thought dead. It wasn't possible. He followed it to the road, and it disappeared. Caesar then thought of that night in the winged machine. The human rat, Gallo, and himself had all fallen into the sea, but the human rat never came out. The rat had not died, and Caesar's revenge was not complete. The human pestilence must be found and destroyed because not just for past murders but also now for a new death. Simmark had told him his destiny was to rid the world of evil. This man was evil itself. Too many deaths are on his hands. He must be killed.

The humans were talking as Caesar sat still looking into his soul. He knew now what the dreams were about. It was either the human rat or him who was going to die. It was their destiny to meet again.

The police gathered the body and all the evidence, including the half-eaten roti, and Gallo picked up Caesar.

The cat had a faraway look and was not his usual self. Gallo had seen that look before, and trouble usually started after that. They entered their cars and drove to the police station where Furness would go over his relationship with Robie, and they would try to piece together who did this murder.

*   *   *

The money was pouring in from the Mafia and the Colombians. Their cost of the installation and equipment came to a large sum. The American Mafia had built the Miami Sand Castle project and was working on others up the eastern coast as fast food restaurants with scenic touches. The restaurant advertised a large greenhouse with exotic plants where customers could dine around its earth saving environment. It was nominated for an Architects Award as an environmentally green project. Lush palm trees and bushes, not found in the USA, were growing happily in each greenhouse. The food was also served with the same theme-seafood, or free-range chicken and organic grown vegetables. These restaurants were to be located in each large city from Miami to West Palm Beach to outside Jacksonville to Savannah to Charleston to Myrtle Beach to Norfolk to outside Washington DC and then on to Atlantic City, New Jersey. The first opened in Miami.

It was a massive undertaking and Tom was proud of it. His pain-in-the-ass father, the general, would call regularly on the progress of the coalition and the construction. They spoke Vietnamese over the phone but also in code in case of listening ears. The construction was almost ready. The special tubes to West Palm Beach were lain on the ocean floor. It was the last leg of the network to Cat Island from the Nassau-Miami connection that was held up. Dr. Zine would not accept a batch of pipe he didn't inspect first. The doctor was a difficult man, and Tom had to manage him along with the Mafia and the troublesome Colombians.

Their shipments would be the greatest in cocaine history, and with his father's heroin supply and the Mafias' connections all would profit handsomely. Cat Island was perfect. No one was here. The Cat Island natives were too involved in tourism and fishing to notice any work going on.

The laboratory was almost complete to Dr. Zine's satisfaction. Within two weeks time the coalition would meet one more time and final contracts settled and the deliveries would start. Tom was ecstatic as he lay on the beautiful beach on the eastern side of the island facing the Atlantic. The terns and seagulls fought over the food left by a tourist while the ocean rose and fell.

Tom stretched out on the blanket, awaiting the prostitute from town to come. He had used her before. She was not a native of Cat Island but a Bahamian nonetheless. They had made love on the beach during the day before. No one was nearby or would they care. He heard a car stop nearby and footsteps near him. It was her. She didn't waste any time but went right to work on him peeling away his trunks. Life was good, Tom thought, and it would get even better.

*　　*　　*

The blue jay perched on the tree branch in the morning sun. His cousin, Reginald or Reggie as he called him, was calling for a mate. As magpies go, Reggie was okay, but he had never had a mate—something nobody could figure out.

The persistent caw-caw call was driving Fletcher crazy coming from two trees away. No wonder no female was interested, he never shut up, from sun up to sun down.

*Caw, caw,* and *caw* in those constant three groups.

It was maddening.

Clay, the cynical pigeon, alit nearby Fletcher and wisecracked, "Is that bird going to stop sometime this moon?"

"Maybe I should talk to him about his noise he is producing from his ugly beak."

"Why don't you find that evil cat and lead him to the magpie, so I can sleep this week."

With that, Clay flew next to Fletcher.

Fletcher had known about Clay meeting with Ketvel the falcon two suns ago.

"How did your date go?"

"It wasn't a date, Fletch, it was a conference."

"She's okay in my book. The family of falcons welcomed me into their clutch. I was like a worm ready to be eaten, I met her father and mother and her brother, who I still think wanted me for an entree. They perched with me and discussed the territory."

Fletcher laughed. "What I wouldn't have given to see the sight. You a pigeon, with the royalty of the birds and there was four of them around you."

"What four? There were six. Their cousins and they want me to meet the red hawk that lives in the next territory."

"You've become the friend of the court. Maybe you're a court jester perhaps or a friend of the royalty."

"What are you crackling about, Fletch. What is a jester? Some television show you watched again at old man Lockwood's window."

"Yes, and it had beautiful birds on it too, but the birds had no billing in the credits at the end—shame."

"Fletcher, sometimes I think you have a tree bark stuck in your head," Clay said, shaking his head.

*Caw, caw, caw,* came the infinite call.

"Oh, by all that's alive, can I shut him up? Fletcher, please," Clay cooed.

"Yea, let's go talk to him. Can you fix him up with some bird you know?"

"Yeah," Clay laughed. "Yeah, she's got a great personality. You know her. She's the pigeon with the bad talon. She limps when she walks."

"I don't think Reggie would want a pigeon. He needs to meet another magpie."

"So let her disguise herself and say *caw, caw* all day," Clay snickered.

As they flew over to Reggie, Fletcher asked, "Clay, did Max and Ketvel tell you about the raptor crackle of birds that talk up the ocean coast?"

"Yeah, she said she hadn't heard anything yet, but would let us know. They talk to birds down to the Sunshine State she called it, whatever that is."

Fletcher smiled. He knew his extended family was growing, and he loved it.

*   *   *

The Trinidadian police lieutenant called them into his office. He was pleasant and knew Furness's was a cousin of Sergeant Harvey of the regiment. Robie was shot through the temple at close range with a .22 caliber pistol, not five hours ago.

The lieutenant asked Furness his relationship with the dead man and was satisfied. Gallo introduced himself as an American agent along with Tony and Caesar.

The lieutenant was an admirer of Caesar and the stories of the past year. Caesar jumped on the wood stool to stare out without a meow, as Gallo started to talk, "I think I know who did it. It was a typical Mafia hit, but down here would be unlikely. It's someone who either is a rogue of the syndicate or a former hit man."

Gallo didn't want to give the lieutenant too much information about his project. Furness' cousin arrived and sat and talked to him about Robie. Furness's cousin, Dan Harvey, was an officer in the Trinidad Regiment.

Dan informed the police lieutenant that they have a lookout for a man dressed in black, according to a local bystander who saw something.

Gallo had to ask, "A man in black in this heat?"

"Well, it is not unusual. Many Trinis wear black," Dan retorted back.

Gallo thought about Rattel. He always wore black and nothing else, but he's dead at the bottom of Long Island Sound.

"We're searching everywhere, and we will get him." Dan was confident.

Caesar sat and was in shock. That sick scent of the past moons. It was back. Something he thought he'd never smell again. It was horrifying.

He couldn't get it out of his nose so he would try to blow it out, but to no avail.

Enew, the cat god, had given him a sign. Destiny was not finished with him yet. Simmark, his ancestor, had said he would have many trials against the pestilence. It was coming to pass and soon he felt. What was in store he did not guess, but he would not stop until this disease was gone.

\*  \*  \*

The two figures stood at a truck across from the Port of Spain police station. At the rear of the truck was Syps, and he was selling coconuts and fruit, so it was easily camouflaged at the Savannah Park along with a dozen other trucks there.

The Savannah was a large interior park of Port of Spain with a main road circling its green expanse. All the government buildings were on the Main Street encircling the Savannah. Cars of all shapes and sizes sped up and down the road going to work or selling products.

So it wasn't unusual for two men to be selling fruit and sitting on their truck for hours at a time. No one would notice, including the police.

Syps and Colin were small-time local thieves in Trinidad, but their faces were not noticeable to the local authorities with all the kidnappings going on, and nobody cared about cell phones and credit card thieves.

The two men waited for three hours when they noticed their target leaving the police station along with other men.

Gallo was their mark and the others, if in the way, would die too. Syps recognized one of the other men. He was a local hero from this past year. He helped catch a big time drug dealer in New York City. He was a big Trini called Furness. Syps had to be sly and cool; the other man leaving with Furness was not known to him, but he was carrying the cat.

This was the animal Mr. Franks wanted dead but only by his hand. Mr. Franks impressed this on both of them

"Do not touch the cat. He's mine," Franks yelled as he looked at Syps and Colin with those cold dead eyes of his.

"I will be nearby when you hit Gallo. Leave the animal to me," Franks stated as he left them dockside.

"Call me on the handset I gave you." And with that he disappeared.

Syps noted the three men got into an SUV and started their way down the Savannah north. Ever so slowly, Syps and Colin jumped into the seats and put the truck in gear and started to follow.

The police and their do nothing positions exasperated Furness.

"So what if Robie had some criminal record before? He was still murdered."

Gallo sat in the back with Caesar. Both knew who had killed Robie, and Gallo sensed Caesar had the scent. Gallo was amazed the dead man returned. It was incredible.

"Listen, Furness, let's go to the Hilton so I can wash today away."

"Why don't I go to the hotel with Gallo and change too, and then we'll go to Chaguaramas where I heard of a great restaurant on the water. It will get our minds off today." Tony hoped to brighten up the night.

Furness said nothing but nodded his agreement.

"Good idea, see you in about an hour. I need to shower." Gallo smiled and Furness turned the SUV toward the Hilton.

*   *   *

Libby grabbed the phone and called Tony on his cell. Sometimes it would work depending on which area he was in. She's was super busy. The production company she was with was starting the off Broadway play next Friday, and she had to go over some dialogue with the lead actor. Bert Youngman had called and was ready for an interview with her soon. She still was uneasy having their meeting in her apartment, but sometimes you have to go to strange lengths to get a movie started.

Then there was the Hollander estate. The lawyer called her and said there was a meeting in his office with Hollander's cousin. It would be one of many such meetings and arguments. The cousin believed he was not in his right mind when he signed everything to his daughter or thought was his daughter, Elizabeth. Hollander went so far as to put in her nickname Libby in the will.

The cell phone was ringing, and a familiar friendly voice answered, "Hey, Libby. How are you beautiful?"

Libby smiled. "Busy, busy getting the play started and maybe getting into a movie soon."

"Hey, that's great. Listen it's been weird here today. One of Furness's buddies was murdered."

"Oh god, you okay? How's Furness?" Libby interrupted.

"Furness is fine—just upset—and I'm okay. Gallo's here too, and he and Caesar look good, but they both became quiet after the murder. Like they knew something." Tony's voice gave her the chills.

"What are you saying, Tony? Someone we know?"

"No, no probably just me being paranoid. So how are Sam and Arthur?"

"They're good," Libby answered with her mind somewhere else.

Tony continued, "What's this movie deal?"

"Oh, this producer—he is semifamous, Bert Youngman—wants me in a film to be made in the Caribbean. Some action film."

"Hey, we can meet. Where in the Caribbean?" Tony was excited.

"I think he said the north Carribean. Not sure. I'm going to meet him in about a week." Libby's mind was thinking out every possibility. "Tony, you don't think it's the Cimbaris trying to get us for messing their drug operation?"

"No, no, doesn't calculate—too far away, no connection. Seems the victim, Robie was his name, had a criminal record here in Trinidad and the police think it was drug related. Furness doesn't think so."

Libby was curious.

"What is Furness's take on this?"

"He has no answer. It's a mystery to him. Robie apparently just got back from his job at the airport at St.Thomas, maybe somebody followed him from there."

Tony didn't want Libby to worry.

"Listen, I love you, and as soon as were are back in New York we will set a date. Maybe in the spring."

"I love you too. Say hello to Gallo and Furness, and give Caesar a big kiss for me. Please be careful, Tony. I don't think I can go through another traumatic year like last year. I will lose my mind." Libby's voice was quivering.

"Listen, we are all fine here. Not to worry. Go give Sam and Arthur a hug, and stop your fretting. It's just a local thing, okay."

"Yes, okay. I love you," Libby whispered back.

"I miss you and will always love you, bye, bye," Tony said as he hung up.

Sam sat by his mistress as she talked on that strange box, and he knew it was his master's voice. Her limbs and back movements changed, and her voice was higher when she talked. There was something wrong. He sensed it. After she put down the strange box she went into the bedroom to lie down. Sam noted Caesar's name in the talk and he was okay along with Master Tony, but there was a shadow over the talk.

Arthur was sleeping by the bedroom door, no need to bother him about it. Sam would just watch and wait.

*       *       *

Chaquaramas, Trinidad, is a seaport on the northwest peninsula of the island. It was once a United States naval base up until the 1960s. The Trinidadian government at that time wanted the United States out. They didn't care about the amount of money that was pouring in from the base. Politically and socially, it was a mistake, and many a Trini knew it.

The admiral in charge of the naval base had hundreds of citrus fruit trees on the base that he was afraid would go to waste since the sailors would pick them each year and give the fruit to the locals.

The admiral offered the Trini government to come and pick the fruits for their people free since they would be wasted when the base closed. The Trini government told the admiral they didn't want his damn fruit, and to get out now. So the admiral, when they closed the base, left everything—housing, conference centers, and seaport—except the Admiral plowed the citrus trees to the ground. It was his way of saying "go to hell." Since then the buildings have not been updated but stand as monuments to the past.

Only the seaport has been used for yachts and fishermen to utilize. Some restaurants have sprung up on the shore and the area sports beautiful serene beaches.

Lately, the Trinidadian government declared it a national park and opened it for hiking and biking. It is a quiet desolate area with gray concrete paved roads poured by the United States Corps of Engineers.

It was this quiet waterfront that Furness was taking Tony and Gallo to eat and rest. It wasn't a long ride from Furness' Diego Martin home to the restaurant.

As Furness drove, Gallo noticed candy stores and grocery stores in broken-down buildings. Concrete walls were painted all different colors with makeshift signs spelling market with two *t*'s. Children ran into the streets and people on bicycles were on both sides of the narrow street. Cars inched by each other traveling at 30 mph or more. Gallo wondered how the accident rate was here.

It was dusk, and the sun was setting into the ocean in the west. There was calmness in Gallo now. He had a foreboding this afternoon, but it subsided. The thought that Rattel could be alive was chilling. *Rattel could have lived through that airplane crash last summer, but what the hell is he doing here?* It was gnawing at his brain, trying to think out all the possibilities. Gallo looked at Caesar. The cat was quiet and stared out the same window. Gallo would give good money to know his thoughts.

Caesar sat on the rear ledge looking out at the sea and the sun. His life had been thrown into torment by this human rat. Enew, the cat god, foretold him, "You will rid the world of pestilence of any kind." Caesar thought the human rat was dead, but his senses told him different. The pestilence still lived, and it was Caesar's vow to rid the world of it. He senses told him the meeting would come soon, and it would be here in this strange land. He prayed to Enew to give him the strength to deal with the human. It would not be easy this time. The human rat would be ready for him, awaiting his attack.

Caesar asked Simmark, his ancestor, for wisdom as he had vanquished the rats during the sickness many moons ago.

Caesar prayed that his Masters Gallo and Tony would be protected for this human rat was a killer of all species with no conscience.

He thought about Sam and Arthur at home and hoped he would see them again. Fletcher would have made him laugh by now probably squawking about his in-laws. He missed his home and Mistress Libby. Caesar looked out at the many faces on the path and awaited his destiny.

\*   \*   \*

Syps and Colin followed the SUV north to Chaguaramus. They hung back about four cars. It was easy to follow their prey, since the SUV was traveling slowly.

Once at the seaport area, the SUV pulled into the yacht club. Syps knew the restaurant well. It was on the water where patrons could dine outside on a veranda.

"Colin, this is a popular restaurant, it's not going to be easy."

Syps was thinking about how to do this when the cell phone rang. It was Franks.

"You two imbeciles there yet?" came the hard voice.

"Yes, we are. Where are you?" Syps answered sheepishly.

"Behind you."

Syps turned, and it was Franks in a small black car.

"Pull over," came the order.

They pulled over behind large dry docked yachts with no one in sight and got out of the cars.

Franks started to talk, "Listen, we have to make a disturbance to get the fucking cop away from his friends. I will fire a shot near the pier over there." Franks pointed toward a wooden pier with smaller boats docked. "Since he's a stinking cop he will come to investigate. If the friends follow Colin you stop them anyway you can. I just want the cop and the cat.

"Syps, you come with me. If you shoot don't shoot to kill. I want Gallo to know who killed him."

"And the cat?" Syps asked.

"I'm going to lure him to me and take him." Franks's face was red. "That cat will be sorry he ever took my eye."

Syps never saw Franks's face like this before. Nothing seemed to affect him, until now. It was an anxiety almost a glee to want to kill both the man and the cat.

"Put your silencer on the pistol, both of you. I don't want the local idiot cops coming here."

Franks took out his gun and stroked it and spoke to the gun.

"We're going to get even today." He turned and smiled and motioned Syps to follow him and Colin to get between the pier and the restaurant. Syps followed Franks with an uneasy feeling. This was a strange man, very strange.

*   *   *

Caesar sat at the human's table with the waitress petting him. She had an easy gentle stroke on his head. The humans were talking about him, but his mind was somewhere else. His senses told him this was a dangerous place, and he must warn Masters Gallo and Tony. They were too busy talking and laughing. The humans thought they were safe here. Why can't they sense things like I do? Toward water he sensed danger like a foreboding of things to come. Even the sky started to get dark and opened up into a rainstorm. Caesar noted these rainy periods would happen almost every day and last only a short time, but today, though, was an exception. The rain was coming down harder, and the wind pushed it toward the humans. Master Gallo got up and moved to a different seat under the covering.

After the new seats were taken, Caesar was brought out a bowl of tuna fish, which he loved. He started to eat when a noise he hadn't heard in a long time came from the water nearby. The noise was the same echo he heard many moons ago when his mother was killed. It sounded the same, and it made him sick to his stomach. He started to move toward the sound.

Gallo grabbed Caesar and told Tony and Furness it sounded like a gunshot.

"That was close. I'll go see. I'm sure it's nothing. I'll take Caesar with me. I think he recognized that same sound."

Furness looked at both the man and the cat. It was not coincidence that both jumped in reaction to the sound.

"If you don't come back in two minutes, we're coming."

Tony agreed.

"Okay, but don't start a riot."

Gallo put Caesar on the ground and the both walked toward the noise. Both knew it was he. This meeting was inevitable. The gunshot was his calling card to come, and we will decide who lives or dies.

Gallo followed the water's edge past the restaurant. There were many piers jotting out from the shore with all sizes of boats tied to the wood pylons.

The rain continued, and it wet Gallo's back, sending a chill into him even though it was hot. The wind whipped the boats against the docks, making a hollow clapping while the water churned onto the shore. There was no one nearby. It was like a ghost town of boats. Nothing could be seen. Gallo wondered if he was being paranoid about this Rattel thing, yet Caesar was on guard and looked ready for a fight. The hair on his back was full, extended and his eyes were intense.

*God help us both.*

The rain was hitting the metal roofs nearby harder, singing as it did. Rain spilled off the gutters onto the ground starting ponds in the dirt. The wind whipped at the shirt on Colin's back. He was waiting by a large boat near the restaurant with the back entry in sight. He saw the cop and the black cat pass him walking toward the gunshot. What was so important to kill the cat? Colin thought Franks was off or even mad, but he paid good money in American dollars, which was like gold here.

He was getting wet, and he was uncomfortable. This was stupid. He wondered if the cop had reached Syps yet.

Syps lay at the water's edge by a pier hidden from view. While Franks decided to sit in a large yacht docked almost twenty meters away. Franks wanted to get the cop and the cat in crossfire. Syps was to shoot the cop and Franks would take out the cat. Syps was consistently curious about the cat he heard so much about from Franks.

How could a cat be so smart? No way. A dog maybe but a cat can't be, yet Franks does have an eye missing. It was all very sick.

Syps heard a noise of a person walking. It was the cop. He didn't see the cat. He looked around, but the black cat was nowhere. The cop came forward with his gun hand in his belt, walking slowly looking all about him.

The cop walked past him and was almost to the middle between Syps and Franks when Syps noted a movement behind him on the pier. Syps never expected to be protecting his rear since he was so focused on what was in front.

Syps turned and saw only a black blur when the cat hit him on the back. A screech came from the cat alerting Gallo of an enemy. Gallo ducked behind a yacht when Syps fired at him and missed.

Syps turned to shoot the cat and he had vanished as fast as he came.

Gallo returned fire into the area where the shots came from and fired four times into a pier.

There was silence, and then a bullet grazed him on the left shoulder from behind. He fell in pain, grabbing his arm and shoulder. There were two of them one in front and one behind. Where was Caesar? He obviously alerted him of the first attacker. After Gallo fired those four shots there was no moment in that direction. Behind him the perp was somewhere near a yacht docked at a pier. Gallo checked his shoulder; the bullet had sliced some skin but no damage. He tore his shirt over to stop the bleeding and tied it tight. The rain ran his blood down his arm. He was in a cross fire and pinned down. He crawled to the rear of the yacht, which blocked him from both perps.

Gallo carefully approached the side of the yacht and scanned quickly the first perp's location. His head was down in the mud. One of Gallo's bullets found its mark, hitting the perp in the head. Now he had to find the second shooter. Just then another shot rang out, but this was in the direction of the restaurant.

Furness and Tony heard the first shots and ran toward it. As they approached the side of the restaurant looking for Gallo a man fired a bullet missing Furness by inches.

Both men fell to the ground behind adjacent garbage Dumpsters.

Furness reached into his pocket and pulled out a gun.

Tony looked at his friend in amazement,

"I thought you couldn't have these here?"

"Who cares? Use it. I heard you were good. I can't shoot a lick."

With that, he threw the gun toward Tony.

Tony smiled at his friend. "You're full of surprises. Go over to the right as far as you can go and make some noise like we're trying to run. Don't stick your head up."

"Don't worry, I won't."

Furness crawled to the next Dumpster and grabbed some gravel in his hand. The rain had made ponds everywhere and Furness was sitting in water.

Tony knew he would only have one shot at the guy and the gun was old and probably off its mark, if it shot at all. He readied himself and awaited Furness's distractions.

Furness threw the gravel at the bottom of the Dumpster and made some noises with his feet.

Colin thought they were running toward Gallo, so he stuck his head and shoulder out pointing the gun in that direction.

Tony had him and fired. The bullet tore through Colin's shoulder, breaking a bone. Colin went down in pain as Tony rushed him kicking Colin's gun away.

Suddenly from behind Gallo came running out of breath.

"Where did you get the pistol?"

"Furness. It's illegal, of course." Tony smiled.

Furness was walking toward the two men when Colin yelled in pain, "Get me a doctor."

"In due time, who's after us?" Gallo demanded.

"I'm dying. I need a doctor," Colin screamed at Gallo.

"Tell me now and I'll call one. Who is it?"—Gallo grabbed him and looked into his eyes—"who?"

"It's Franks. He wants you and that damn cat dead."

Gallo just remembered Caesar.

"Oh no." Gallo ran toward the last spot he saw Caesar.

As he ran, Furness yelled out in the distance he would call the police. Gallo vaguely heard him. His worry was about Caesar with this madman around. It's him. It has to be, and Caesar would go into hell to get him.

*    *    *

Caesar was on the scent. After he warned Master Gallo of the one man behind him he set out for the human rat. The stench from the human rat was causing him to wretch. He followed it along the water's edge. Nothing would deter him from his prey, and the gunshots in the distance didn't even get his attention. All that was important was the rat.

The scent led him to a big water house rocking back and forth in the water. This scent he could follow anywhere anytime. This was part of his nightmare following the smell of death of the killer of his mother. He reached the yacht and jumped onto its floor and noted that death was near and above him.

He leaped onto steps and toward the scent. A door was open to a small room and there was the smell of old fish all about the ship. In the room it was stronger, now coupled with that smell of what Master Gallo called gunpowder. He heard the human somewhere near him, and he decided to turn and retrace his steps to confuse the rat. He moved carefully and quietly and followed his nose throughout the many rooms. The rain made loud noises onto the ship and it echoed into the cabin masking the steps of a human with a purpose to kill. The ship rocked back and forth in the sea bouncing off the pier as it did. The ship made scratching sounds on the wood of the pier as the weather whipped the ocean.

The ship had many doors and cabins, and the man had moved through them all. The doors were open and they rocked with the ship. Caesar spotted an opening in the side of the wall with a small moving door close to the floor. He diverted his eyes for a second and peered down into the darkness through the small door. It was some sort of tunnel straight down to the lower area of the ship. He sensed a movement behind him, and he turned his head but it was too late to avoid the bullet. His head burned and all went black. The last thing he heard was a gunshot, and he was thrown into the tunnel, falling and falling into total blackness.

*    *    *

As Gallo ran toward the shot, he feared the worst. He hoped Caesar didn't attack the man himself. God he hoped not. Gallo easily approached the gunshot and heard a motor start and a boat starting to cut the water beyond a big yacht. He ran, but it was too late. He could hear the man laughing in the distance. The cat was nowhere to be seen.

Gallo yelled out for Caesar, but there was only the beating of the rain on the boat tarpaulins and on the water.

It was an eerie sound of silence to Gallo. He ran back and forth between ships docked among the various piers. He ran and ran, yelling as he did calling for the black cat, his friend but to no avail.

Tony came running and searched with him. When the police came Furness's cousin had to sort things out with law enforcement. Time was passing with no hint of the cat.

There was an empty feeling in Gallo's stomach. A feeling of dread he couldn't let go. There would be a vacuum now without his companion. That brave cat. Damn cat saved him again.

Gallo sat down at a pier as Tony Furness joined him.

"He's gone Tony. Rattel killed him. It was Rattel. I know that laugh." Gallo was wiping rain off his face as the three men sat looking out to sea.

"I hope God takes care of Caesar wherever he is." Tony's voice was cracking as he said it.

"Caesar will guard Him too," Gallo noted as he bowed his head.

Time passed and the rain stopped and the sun set in the western sky glittering on the ocean in front of the men.

A lone seagull could be heard squawking into the wind as the rain clouds disappeared into the northern sky.

\*　　\*　　\*

# LIFE AFTER DEATH, THE SECOND TIME

She stood in a hotel room in Barbados. It was a beautiful day on the island, and she was thankful to have gotten this far without being killed. She had evaded Eduardo's men in Caracas and flew to Port of Spain, Trinidad, and then to Barbados. She sat down on the bed and stared out the window. Where now? Her Colombian passport was a red flag for these hit men. She must change her name and get an American passport and disappear in America. It was easy to do this there.

Giving the local hotel clerk a smile and a promise of things never to come, she obtained a name of a forger in town. The cab took her on a crazy trip to a seedy part of the island.

The cab stopped in front of a broken down house with shutters in a dark green color. She knocked on the broken door, and an old man answered who looked her up and down.

"Who are you?"

"Jimmy, the gambler, told me to come to you," the woman said as the old man let her in.

"Oh, I see, you need a change of weather."

"That's correct."

He ushered her into a small studio with a laptop and pieces of paper everywhere. There was a smell of shit nearby that made her wretch.

"What's that smell?"

The old man smirked. "That's my dog. I can't keep up with him. He does it in the house, everywhere, so watch where you walk."

She decided to touch nothing except her feet to the floor.

"Listen, I need an American passport soon."

"No problem, you got the cash I work for you. You don't, sorry."

The old man sat behind his laptop smiling with brilliant teeth.

"See there." He pointed at his teeth.

"Yes."

"They were from a dentist from Venezuela who needed a passport. I took them as payment."

He smiled again.

"Yes, well, I have U.S. dollars."

"Very good, very good. My favorite. So what's the name?"

She thought Malena was a pretty name, and she hated to give it up but her life was at stake.

"Jenna Allison," Malena said questionably. She always liked the name Jenna since she heard the American president's daughter's name, and Allison was as American as she could think.

"How old?" The old man looked up.

"Make it twenty-four years old." This was a lie by one year.

"Birthplace?"

"Brooklyn, New York." Malena smiled, she had read and seen pictures of New York and loved it.

"Okay, we need a photo of you. Step this way."

The old man took a photo and processed her the passport in about three hours, while Malena waited at a nearly slimy café. Maybe now she would have peace and live her life as she wanted.

*   *   *

Word spread like the wind across Trinidad and then into the United States. Newspapers had pictures of the heroic cat and a man in black. Reporters hounded Gallo wherever he went asking dumb ass questions. Gallo spoke to Simpson the DEA Director, who he had been reporting to while in the Caribbean, and Simpson asked him to lay low and he would get back to Gallo. It was a lousy two days of it before Furness got the brilliant idea to get Gallo to a safe house in Belmont.

Gallo jumped the concrete wall in the rear of Furness' house and jumped into Furness' car. Tony was in the passenger seat. They drove for a while all around a poor section of Belmont to make sure they weren't followed.

The three men easily got out of the car and entered the broken down shack.

"My friend Walter owns this, no one knows of it but us. So it's safe."

The three men sat down in silence, and Gallo thought about Caesar. It was a loss he couldn't deal with. His heart was not with him these last two days but somewhere else. The police searched everywhere for Caesar, but to no avail. He must have drowned in the ocean; yet no body was found.

Furness got up and opened a bottle of rum and poured it out for the other two men.

"To Caesar, the greatest animal I've ever seen or heard of." Furness held the glass up.

All three stood and clicked their glasses.

Tony drank the rum and sat down.

"What now, Mark, what will you do?"

Gallo opened a new pack of Marlboro and lit the cigarette match then took a full drag.

"This Colin we captured has some important information. He'll talk but the Trini police have to let me do it."

Furness nodded. "I'll get my cousin to get you in. This shit head will lead us to Rattel. I know he will."

Gallo smiled at his friend.

"You guys have to let me follow the lead by myself. Too many feet spoil the chase. You have to stay here and keep in touch with me if I'm on a good lead."

"As much as I want to go get the son of a bitch, I agree. Right, Tony." Furness turned to the quiet one.

Tony's thoughts were of Libby and how she would take this news and there was something else, he wondered.

Tony got up and looked out the broken panes of the window.

"Gallo, you don't think he wants all of us dead. It appears he has been setting traps for us all."

Gallo looked at Tony and cursed himself for being so naïve.

"It's not only possible, but I think it's true. You have to be on the watch for his men."

"It's not me I worry about. It's Libby. She's as much in this as we are and more so, in some respects. I've got to warn her, even though she will be totally upset about Caesar she has to be told," Tony said with haste in his voice.

"Call her, but don't tell her about Rattel. Between losing Caesar and telling her about that madman it will frighten her too much. Tell her someone's after us, and be careful."

Tony then downed his drink.

"I'm going to tell her in person. I'm going back to New York."

The other two men couldn't argue with him, so they planned their schedules and Gallo stayed in Belmont while Furness and Tony were going to return to Diego Martin.

Gallo grabbed Tony by the arm before he left the shack.

"Don't trust anyone. Keep your eyes open and try to keep in touch with Furness or me. Remember, he will kill you in a second." Tony smiled at his friend.

"Don't worry about me, I'm pretty careful." Tony smiled at his friend again. "It's you I am worried about, you know . . . about being by yourself now."

"It's not me you should lose sleep over, it's the man who has made my life miserable and has come back from the grave to haunt us and kill a friend. Like Caesar, I will follow him into hell to kill him and anybody in my way. So don't fret about me, Tony. He will pay as sure as water is wet, he will pay.

*　　*　　*

Libby was all set for her trip with Bert Youngman to the Bahamas to film the movie. Bert was supposed to come today but was late, and the sun had set. Libby called his cell phone earlier and talked to him. He was pleasant and said he would pick her up at seven o'clock tonight to catch a nine o'clock plane to Nassau. Seven came and went and Libby started to worry. It's not like a producer to be late for a flight when he said he would pick her up by limousine.

Sam and Arthur sat on the rug sleeping next to each other. Libby's girlfriend, Bette, would take care of them while she was away.

A ring came from her doorbell. It was Youngman.

"Ms. Cassett, it's me," came the voice.

Libby pushed the button and was excited.

The door opened, and in came Youngman with three other men. It was frightening.

"These are my aides, Ms. Cassett. They wished to come along."

Libby had an eerie feeling about these men and Youngman wasn't himself. He kept looking around. It was a set up.

Libby started to walk for Tony's gun.

"Ms. Cassett, don't move," came a voice from behind Youngman. It was a swarthy-faced man dressed in a navy pea coat and he was holding a gun in his hand.

"You will take only a coat. This is all you will need."

The other two men went for Sam and Arthur.

Sam jumped and brought one man to the ground. Sam was furious. Sam continued to bite and bite on the man's arm. The man screamed as a dart entered Sam's torso. The dog whelped as the needle hit his body. Sam instantly felt sleepy and fell to the floor. Arhtur attacked the man with the dart gun, but was pushed to the side and shot with another dart. Arthur fell to the floor limp.

"So you see, Ms. Cassett, we have no intention of harming you or your animals. So please get your coat and let's go."

The other two men placed Arthur and Sam into two carriers and brought them out the door.

"You must be insane, everyone will be looking for us," Libby yelled at the swarthy man.

"No, they won't. You are on a trip with Mr. Bert Youngman, your producer. He's taking you to the Caribbean to film a movie. So you will be gone a long time.

Now, leave a note for your friend about the animals. Say you decided to take them too.

Libby sat down and wrote the message.

"Is this for money? I haven't gotten a dime yet from Hollander's estate."

The swarthy man laughed, "No, no Ms. Cassette, you will find out soon enough, let's go."

She sat at her desk and wrote the note and left it on the desk. He motioned with his gun and Libby and Youngman went down onto the street and into the limo.

Libby could hear her phone ringing, "Oh god, please let Tony find my message."

"Move Youngman," one of the kidnappers yelled as Youngman hesitated getting into the car.

The limousine pulled away as a blue jay noted some strange voices and activity that woke him. He had not seen the animal carriers that contained his friends, but he did see Mistress Libby leave and she didn't look happy.

It was night, and he couldn't fly at night. He was powerless to follow the car. He called out for Missy, Sam's mate, but with no luck.

He would have to wait for the sun to somehow find out an answer. Its possible maybe Mistress Libby didn't want to go to some boring human gathering. The same as the one Fletcher witnessed the other day on the street with loud noises that could wake up a dead magpie. Humans are always yelling at each other—anyway, probably just a meeting of some sort.

Fletcher turned on his branch and fell fast asleep.

\*     \*     \*

Tony had called Libby's cell number several times after leaving Furness and Gallo but with no answer. It was troubling. Libby always answered that phone. He tried the house phone and her work number but neither one was successful. He sat on the Caribbean Air flight to JFK Airport thinking of Rattel. How he got to Caesar and almost killed Gallo. Tony was anxious to get Libby and keep her safe away from this madman.

The jet landed on the runway with a hard bounce and then came to a steady roll. Customs at JFK took him a short time and he was jumping into a cab to head home.

New York was gray, it was November 1 and the air smelled of winter. All the trees when he left were green or almost turning their autumn colors.

It was about fifty degrees when the cab drove along the Brooklyn-Queens Expressway to Brooklyn Heights. It still looked the same to him.

He tried Libby again and again, but she still wasn't answering, then he started to feel a shudder in his stomach. He prayed she was okay.

The cab entered his street, and he noticed it was empty, like everyone was missing. The cab's brakes screeched and he paid the driver and got out. The house looked disserted as if no one had been there for a while. He quickly opened the front door with his key and entered the apartment, calling out as he did.

"Libby, its me."

A dead silence greeted him. No Sam to meet him; no Arthur at his feet rubbing his leg. He ran like a madman through the apartment but it was empty. There was no message or note anywhere. He sat on the sofa and racked his brain. Where would she go with the animals? *Oh god, please, he didn't have her, that sick fuck.*

A noise came from the front door; it was the sound of a key in the lock. His heart sprung. It was Libby. It had to be her. Disappointment was on his face when Sara, the cleaning woman, entered and saw Tony.

"Mr. Massaro what are you doing here?"

"Have you seen Miss Cassett?" Tony brushed off any explanation of his presence.

"No, no, just a note she left me yesterday."

"Can I see it," Tony said excitedly.

She reached into her pocket to retrieve a yellow paper.

> *Sara*
> *I'm going away to do a movie shoot and I'm taking Sam and Arthur with me. Clean the house as usual and my desk.*
>
> *L.*

Tony sat down on the sofa with the note trying to figure it out. Why take Sam and Arthur? She would need to set it up with the airline. His mind raced trying to think about the possibilities.

Could it be they wanted the three of them? All three had become famous because of the past year. He looked up.

"Oh, Sara, excuse me, I'm trying to sort this out."

"That's okay, Mr. Massaro, I'll just do my usual cleaning for today.

"Okay, okay."

Tony sat back and wanted to get the cops involved but thought better of it. *If he took her she would contact me some way, but she thinks I'm in Trinidad.*

He dialed Furness.

"Hey she's not here. She's gone and with Sam and Arthur. I wonder if we should call the FBI. I'll contact Gallo, maybe he'll know who to call. Have you heard from Gallo?" Tony asked

Furness's voice sounded distressed.

"No, he left here this morning for places unknown. He said he would call me."

Furness sounded tired.

"This monster may contact one of us if he has Libby. Keep your eyes and ears open."

"Will do, meanwhile my cousin is looking into the background of the man who was killed on the dock that day."

"Keep me informed. I'll get back to you, thanks."

"Watch yourself too," Furness warned and with that the phone went dead.

Tony searched the apartment for clues. It was too neat, not even a turned pillow. Then like a beam of light into his head he realized Sara was here yesterday.

She was dusting the bookshelves on the second floor when he found her.

"Sara, you got to help me. I want you to describe how you found the apartment yesterday."

Sara stared at him but went along tentatively.

"Well, when I came in, Miss Cassett had left the animals food in their dishes. So I cleaned it out and dumped the water dish. They wouldn't be here so I wasn't going to leave the food to cause germs."

"Go on, please."

"Miss Cassett had left her makeup all over her dressing table so I cleaned it and adjusted some knickknacks on her desk."

Tony then knew. Libby had mentioned her desk in the note.

"Come with me Sara to the desk."

They walked into the office, and Tony sat at the desk.

"Sara put the desk back the way it was."

"Mr. Massaro, I don't remember it all. It was a mess."

"Please Sara it could mean her life," Tony pleaded.

"Well, she had the calendar to the wrong month, so I turned it back and—"

"Which month?"

"I think it was on June."

Tony turned her calendar from Chase Bank back to June. The colored picture above the dates was of a Caribbean island.

"What else, Sara?"

"Well, she had some pencils here and some, and her pen set with the flag here."

Sara adjusted the desk as she knew it and Tony was trying to see any clues.

She was going to the Caribbean, but where, he thought.

"Oh, Mr. Massaro, she had a map of Long Island on the calendar so I put it away."

Sara retrieved the map and placed it down.

It was of Long Island, what the hell? Tony was confused.

"Was that it, Sara?" Tony asked frustrated.

"I think so, sir."

As Sara was walking out she turned to Tony.

"There was a strange thing, sir."

"Yes, Sara."

"The American flag in the pen set was upside down."

Tony's stomach got sick.

"Thank you, Sara. You helped greatly."

Tony sat down in front of the desk. The sign for distress—an upside-down flag. She was in his hands and there is still a clue here, if he could find it. He sat looking but he was tired and rested his head on the desk and fell fast asleep dreaming of Libby.

*   *   *

When Gallo left Trinidad, it was on the footsteps of the hit man who attacked him and Caesar. Gallo had a tip from Furness's cousin, Dan, to head to Sealots—an area near the airport at Port of Spain. It was on the ocean full of shacks and broken-down sheds where the ultrapoor lived.

Gallo, asking the locals, discovered his man was from there and that he had left with a man named Franks. Gallo had found the sister of the hit man. She lived in a slanted shed on the ocean, with roosters walking outside of her door. The shed was about to fall down. Her brother's name was Syps, and he was always in trouble—gunrunning, drugs, and he would hire himself out as a killer. He would have the police always on his back. Lately though, the local police left him alone so his sister said. She noted Gallo was an American and made it obvious sex was available to him.

The sister—Babe, as she called herself—had no use for her brother and wanted out of this sandbox now.

"So you go after him, huh?" She smiled at Gallo as she lowered her already lowered low-rider pants.

She was good looking and had a nice figure. *Used by different men*, he thought. Her crotch was about an inch away from the sunlight.

"I am looking for him to pay him some money I owe him. I borrowed a hundred dollars from him last week." Gallo hoped she wasn't going to strip.

"Give me the hundred, I will make sure he gets it." Babe then opened her mouth and inserted two fingers and sucked on them.

"No, no. I will give it to him. Where did he go?"

She was getting frustrated with this American.

"I'll tell you, but you must give me something."

Gallo started to get worried.

"What is it?"

"I want three hundred dollars U.S., and you can fuck me."

Gallo normally wouldn't care, but she had to be the area whore—but not for him.

"I'll give you the three hundred, but that's it. Tell me where he went?" Gallo peeled off three hundred dollar bills.

"Okay, okay, you don't want to lime with me. You'll miss a treat. I'm better than your American girls."

"It's okay, Babe, just tell me where," he said as he waved the money and stuck one of the bills into her crotch.

"He went with the tall one, Franks, on his yacht but didn't go too far. He mentioned a girl, a South American girl, Malena. They were chasing her. Franks had to go on a trip so my brother was to get the girl somewhere in Barbados, I think."

"He was heading that way?" She smiled as Gallo inserted another hundred into her sweaty shirt, which showed off her large breasts.

"Anything else?" Gallo asked.

"Yes, there is." She started to suck her fingers with that longing look again.

"He said that Franks was happy that one was down and the next would follow."

"You listen good." Gallo gave her the last hundred.

"I just don't listen, I use my mouth too." Moving her fingers back and forth into her mouth.

"Thanks, Babe, for the show and the info."

"You're welcome. Don't forget to come back. I'm always open."

*I bet*, Gallo thought as he walked away on the heels of Syps.

*       *       *

Barbados is a tourist dream. The farthest east of the Caribbean islands, it is a jet hop from Trinidad and Caracas. The people love the Americans and their dollars, and are very happy helping the tourists to their destinations. The weather is always perfect, and the beaches are white and pure. Multicolored fish dart by you in the ocean only to return to look you up and down. The Atlantic Ocean breaks on the beaches, and the wind from the ocean keeps it cool in the midday sun.

It was on one of these beaches Malena, a.k.a. Jenna, sat on a lounge chair hidden from view behind palm trees. She picked this hotel because it was not a tourist gathering, and she wanted to get lost into the masses.

The old man who made her fake passport smiled and handed her the American passport in her new name, Jenna Allison.

It was a good name to get lost with. She decided to rest today and travel to some obscure American town and disappear where her brother Eduardo would never find her. Malena would check around and behind her when she traveled and where she stayed. She prayed that God would let her live.

A man sat across the beach with sunglasses on, tanning himself on a blanket with the radio on to a local station playing old tunes of Sparrow. There was a cell phone in his hand.

"Yes, yes. I'm sure it's her. No, no not American, it's her. She went to a well-known forger here. It's her."

A voice with a Trinidadian accent spoke, "Okay good. Keep her in your sights. I'll be there soon," came the voice on the line.

"Where's my fucking money for my expenses?"

"You'll get your money, just stay on her." The line went dead.

The man closed the phone and sat back. Maybe he could fuck this bitch in the meantime while he waited for Syps and the guys.

*   *   *

Gallo was following Syp's sister Babe's belief that Syps went to Barbados, so he paid for a trip to the island and landed within forty minutes from Port of Spain airport.

The Barbados airport was busy, and he knew Syps wouldn't fly but use a boat—Gallo hoped. He guessed he had beat Syps here and decided to find out about all the main docks or yacht club moorings.

He checked into the Hilton under the name Grant and asked about yacht moorings and similar areas. The concierge was all too helpful to point out all the great docks on the island along with directions. He thanked the overenthusiastic clerk and hailed a cab.

In the hours following, he started to get weary, and the cab driver thought he was nuts until Gallo flashed some U.S. money his way and then butter could melt in the cabbie's mouth.

"Mr. Grant, what are you looking for?" came the ready to please response.

"Is there a dock where say, many boats dock that are not exactly on the legal side."

Gallo tried to be tactful.

"Jeb will take you. I know a place like this. Many boats come in from Trini and Venezuela there. You want some ganja?"

"No, Jeb, just take me there."

"Okay, Mr. Grant, now." Jeb stepped on the pedal, and the ancient Ford creaked and moved forward.

Gallo had only seen Syps briefly that day on the beach when Caesar was killed, but he would never forget that face.

After a ten-minute ride, Jeb pulled the cab into a vacant lot.

"This is it, Mr. Grant."

"Jeb"—Gallo thought Jeb might know some goings-on here—"have you ever seen a tall American usually dressed in black here or any other port on this island?"

Jeb turned and looked at the ocean.

"There is a story about such a man told by the cab drivers here. I thought it was a lie."

Jeb turned back to Gallo.

"My friend Morgan tells of a prostitute who was beaten so bad. She was in the hospital. Morgan took her to the hospital bleeding all over his cab. The man in black entered through this port."

"Do you know the name of the boat, Jeb?"

Gallo asked excitedly.

"Who doesn't? It's owned by the Valli cartel. That's why he wasn't arrested that night. It's called *La Vita*."

Gallo sat back and knew this had to be Frank Rattel. Who else would fit the description but working for the cartel out of Colombia? That was news.

"Jeb, thank you. Tell your friend that man will pay for his crimes soon."

Jeb turned to Gallo, "This is why you search. Jeb tell no one about you. Be careful, Mr. Grant. They are like snakes and will kill anyone. This is the dock the man in black was at that day."

"Thanks Jeb."

Gallo sat back and waited. Maybe he'll get a bonus and get Syps and Rattel in one day.

*   *   *

White clouds ran in front of his eyes. He blinked and blinked again, but the clouds stayed. He tried to walk, but he couldn't move yet; the landscape would change from clouds to a mist on a distant valley floor. The cloud in his eyes disappeared, and he could see a great valley. He walked into the valley where many cats gathered. They all smelled him and bowed before him. It was evident he was dead, and this was the land of Enew, the cat god.

A familiar voice came to him among the cats but above him. It was Simmark, the great cat, his ancestor.

"You have come to visit us, my son."

"Visit, am I not done with humans and their senseless killing?"

"No, you are the chosen one to help them, you more then I ever did. Your courage will save them again. It's through you Enew has decided to bring his help again to the humans, like he did before with me."

Simmark stood on a ledge with a white brilliance behind him. There was a warm feeling when he talked to Simmark. His anxieties and troubles were gone, all washed away.

"Great Simmark, I have saved them. What else can I do?" the cat asked.

"You will protect them again. You are the one. The one for one and for the many."

Quickly a fog entered the valley, and he was drifting into a human house filled with all of his loved ones. Each called out to him. It was Master Gallo and Mistress Libby asking for him to come back. He saw Sam and Arthur in trouble. His heart started to beat faster and he remembered Simmark's words, "You will protect them again."

As he ran toward his friends, he fell into a deep hole and blacked out. The last thing he remembered was voices, human voices.

\* \* \*

A young eleven-year-old girl walked throughout her father's yacht bored with her toys, and the men on board weren't going to pay any attention to her. She stopped on deck to look at the scenery. It was beautiful here, but she missed her mother. She was mad that God had taken her mother from her and left a big void in her life. These last six months were boring here while her father did work on the mainland. She had no friend or playmate and the computer games were not keeping her satisfied.

She strolled through the ship and went below to get her clean clothes. The maid would always stack up her clothes on the washer near the linen chute. As she approached the chute's door, a black figure lay at the bottom of the chute. She gasped at what she saw. It was a beautiful black cat. Her first urge was to call her father.

"Daddy, look it's a cat, a large black cat."

Her father couldn't hear her. He was too busy fishing on deck above.

Susan looked the cat over. There was a big gash on his head, where blood had oozed and formed a clot. He had a collar on, and Susan turned it over. Someone else owned him—her heart dropped. She had prayed for this, and now it would be taken away. Her father would search for the owner, but he didn't have to know, and besides, he was always busy.

This cat would be her playmate. She loved cats. But how did he wind up in the linen chute? She didn't care. Susan removed the collar and put it in her pocket. She picked up the large cat and walked up to the deck of the yacht to show her father. He was very heavy.

He was fishing with friends of his from America.

"Daddy, look what I found."

The father turned and was surprised.

"Holy smokes, where the hell did he come from, Susan?"

"He was in our linen chute, Daddy. Can I keep him? He has no collar." Susan smiled, hugging the cat.

"I guess so. Let me look at him."

Her father placed his boat rod on its holder and picked up the cat.

"He's a monster. Must weigh twenty pounds. He's got a large cut here, Sue. We better take him to the vet. Get him checked out."

Susan jumped up and down for joy.

"Thank you, Daddy. I love him."

The father smiled and hugged his daughter. Maybe it was God's way of giving the child someone to be with because he couldn't. Living in Trinidad as an international banker afforded him no time for his daughter. The cat would be a playmate and maybe fill the little one's heart with some joy since her mother died. He had help watching her, but he was always fearful.

Susan hugged the cat again.

"What are you going to call him? He has to have a name."

Susan knew immediately. "Blackie."

The men who were fishing laughed. "Original, isn't it?"

Susan didn't care, because Blackie was hers to keep. She ran down the steps. In the back of her mind she had lied, but no one would find out.

*     *     *

Malena had plans. She would take the American flight to Miami or Orlando then fly a small airline or a train into the heartland of the United States. Maybe Tennessee or Iowa. She didn't care. It was important to leave the Caribbean.

She checked out of the hotel and searched for a cab. Malena had dyed her hair light brown to cover her black tresses and left off all makeup. She looked about twenty years old. She dressed in a typical American miniskirt with blank colors so she would blend with the tourists. A red cab drove up in front of the hotel, and she told the driver the airport as she entered. He nodded and stepped on the accelerator.

The driver had a cell phone headset talking low as he drove.

"Yes, yes, I know where to go," he spoke into the wire.

Malena felt nervous and got a sick feeling.

"Excuse me, but do you know where I'm going?" she said in a good American accent as she spoke.

"Yes, yes. The airport," came the reply of the driver, without turning his head.

She sat back, still nervous. The airport was not far, and Malena did not recognize this route.

"Excuse me, but this is not the way, driver."

"Sit back, pretty one, you are in for a ride," came the chilling voice.

Malena panicked and came reaching for the door handles, but they were all broken on purpose and the windows were not operable either.

"You son of a bitch. Let me go."

"No, no, you and me, we're going to get acquainted, and then I will take you over to them. Ha ha."

The glass partition was locked between them. Malena was helpless.

*     *     *

Gallo sat in the cab for an hour and thought about his next move. Syps isn't going to expect him, but he's wasting time waiting here.

"Jeb, can you tell me where the cartel stays when in town?"

Jeb turned to Gallo. "I know where the man in black beat the prostitute. It's a small motel not far from here."

"Let's go." Gallo would try any lead now.

Jeb was right. The car ride was not good. It was a seedy part of the island where everyone looked guilty of something. The motel was a typical one-story cottage type with old roofs and older siding facing the sea. In New York City, this would be an expensive locale, but here it was left to rot.

Jeb pulled the Ford into an old parking lot across the way and turned off the engine. Gallo was starting to feel like it was a dead end when a red cab arrived. The driver got out and had what looked like a gun in his hand. A woman was his passenger and the man had keys in his hand.

Jeb saw the same thing.

"She doesn't look like the typical prostitute, Mr. Grant."

"I think I'm going to check this out. You stay here. If you hear shooting, call the police."

"Okay, watch yourself," Gallo heard Jeb say as he left the cab and ran across the street.

The motel had at one time a wooden fence, which had long since rotted away that Gallo jumped over. He retrieved his Colt pistol and walked slowly to the door marked no. 14, where the man and woman had entered.

He heard the woman yell, and a lamp fall. *This is no prostitute*, he thought. Gallo hit the door with his shoulder. The old door was in no shape to resist him.

Coming in from the sunlight, it was dark, but Gallo spotted the woman on the bed clutching her ripped blouse.

"Who the fuck are you?" barked the cabbie.

"Nobody," Gallo answered. "It's just I don't like rapists."

"Mind your own business. You don't know who you're talking to." With that, he raised his gun.

"Drop the weapon, rapist, unless you want a bullet."

"Fuck you, American," the rapist yelled and fired his pistol.

Gallo fired twice to the body. The man fell like a rock to the floor.

Gallo went over, and he wasn't dead yet.

"You'll be sorry, you fuck. I'll—"

His last breath was gone.

Gallo grabbed his wallet and other papers. The girl was crying, and Gallo told her to gather her things and leave with him. She fixed her blouse and left the room, grabbing her bag in the red cab.

"Who was that guy?" Gallo asked.

"Who are you?" she cried as she gathered her bag.

"Someone on your side. Who was he?"

"He was a sickie. I was getting a cab to the airport when he kidnapped me." She was still sobbing.

"Okay listen, I'm an American down here on vacation. I have a cab, and don't worry, I'll take you where you want to go."

"Thank you, Mr.—?"

"Grant, Mark Grant." Gallo almost said his real name.

She followed him to the cab, and Jeb's eyes were wild.

"I didn't call the police yet, Mr. Grant. Should I?"

"Yes, tell them you heard shots. Don't give your name."

"Okay."

Gallo looked at the woman up close now. She was strikingly beautiful, but he couldn't guess from what country. Her eyes were gray and her hair definitely was dyed. She was not American with that accent.

"Are you the police?"

'No, no, just a citizen that happens to be at the right place." Gallo hoped he was convincing.

"My name is Jenna Allison from Louisville, Kentucky. I was just on my way back from vacation when this happened. Why don't you want the police to know anything?" Malena wanted him to think she was a helpless American.

Gallo laughed to himself. She's definitely hiding something. No way was she an American from Louisville, and Jenna Allison?—give it a break.

"The police would just ask too many questions, and I know you don't want any publicity on this, do you?"

"No, of course not." Malena looked into his eyes. They were nice eyes, and maybe she could trust this American.

"Jeb, let's go. Drive to the other coast unless you have a plane to catch."

"No, no, I can take a later one." She smiled at Gallo. He liked her smile.

"Jeb will take us to a nice restaurant on the water."

Jeb laughed to himself as he turned the Ford. They were both liars.

*   *   *

The large yacht approached the small boat, and the men yelled out across the water to each other as the two vessels edged nearer. The sun was going down in the west behind the monoliths of skyscrapers. The Atlantic Ocean was calm outside of New York Bay, and it was a warm night.

In the smaller vessel of the two, the men started to pack their belongings and grabbed the girl and a man both with a sack over their heads. Two more sacks were grabbed and ready for transport. A growl came from one sack as the men gingerly held it. The yacht touched the boat and a ladder was dropped down. The sun was about to go into the horizon, and all would be dark soon.

A tall figure stood on the top deck of the yacht, smiling at all he saw. It was a pleasant trip here these last few days. One of his enemies he had killed and now would be the set up to get the rest of the scumbags. Revenge would be his at last.

The girl and the man stumbled on to the deck as the other seamen climbed the ladder with their sacks. The smaller vessel was sunk, leaving no evidence.

The black figure came down the ladder to the main deck and spoke, "Hope your trip wasn't too nasty, my dear."

The girl thought the voice familiar, but she was so frightened it didn't register.

"What do you want?" she asked.

"Yes, who are you? How dare you kidnap me?" The man in the sack over his head found his voice.

The figure in black pulled the two hoods off his prisoners.

A gasp came from the girl.

"It can't be you. You're dead."

"Not quite, beautiful, almost." He smiled. "But your cat is dead."

"What, Caesar?"

"Yes. I killed him myself."

She started to cry but tried to hide the tears.

He continued, "Your friend Gallo and your boy friend Tony are next. Soon to be brought to an island of my choice to be killed. All my murderers will be present and dead at one time. Sweet, isn't it? Ha, ha."

She reached out to punch him, but the seaman grabbed her arm.

"Very good spirit, but you are going to stay with me on our trip to the Caribbean, Miss Cassett."

The man yelled, "I was just doing you a favor. I didn't know about this."

"Ah yes, you were our agent in all this. Mead, Mead, come over here."

Mead, a swarthy man with a scar on his cheek, answered, "Yes sir."

"Did you grab the dog too?"

"Yes," Mead answered immediately.

"Very good."

"And a cat too." Mead smiled.

"A cat. What cat? That black demon is dead."

"No, sir, a red one."

"So, Miss Cassett, you have another cat. Well, we shall see this one."

"Wait," Libby yelled out, "he's not mine, he's just a stray I picked up."

"Too bad for him."

"You're a son-of-a-bitch, Rattel," Libby yelled.

"Yes, I know."

"Listen"—the man was getting nervous—"I'm Bert Youngman, people will miss me. What are your intentions?"

Rattel smiled at him.

"Our intentions are to let you go."

The man calmed down and said, "How? There's no boat."

"Like this." Rattel pulled out his pistol and emptied three bullets into Youngman's chest.

The body fell to the deck.

Libby screamed, "Goddammit, you're sick, you murderer."

Rattel barked some orders, and the body was thrown overboard.

"I let him go, didn't I? How easy was that?" He turned and smiled at Libby.

"Problem solved. Mead, let's see the cat."

Mead grabbed the sack and stuck his hand in and yelled, "The freaking cat bit me."

"Stupid fuck, dump its contents on the deck," Rattel ordered.

Mead turned the sack upside down, and Arthur fell out.

"What a beautiful cat you have, my dear."

With that, Rattel grabbed quick at the back of Arthur's neck.

"But the wrong cat Mead. I killed the other one. I have no use for this one."

With that, Rattel threw the cat overboard into the darkness.

Libby screamed and punched the seaman holding her and was about to dive into the ocean when Rattel tripped her and two of the seamen grabbed her.

"I'll kill you, Rattel, I swear to God. You're dead," Libby screamed.

"Get her below and throw the dog in with her."

"You bastard, I hope you fuckin' drop dead," Sam was barking through the sack.

"I hate cats, but dogs are another story," he laughed out loud. "But not for long."

Libby was crying as she was thrown into a locked room with Sam.

Sam was still in the sack, but he heard it all. He couldn't get out to help Arthur. His friend was thrown into the cold ocean, and he couldn't do a thing. Arthur wasn't like Caesar. Sam feared the worst. He bit his way out of the sack to reach his mistress, and he was in a dark room, and he saw his mistress crying. Sam approached her and snuggled her with his head.

Libby hugged Sam hard, crying as she did.

"My poor Arthur, oh god, oh god."

\*    \*    \*

He woke up in a daze. His eyes adjusted to the light, and a young female human was petting him. His head hurt, and he felt sore all over. His eyes had problems adjusting, and he was seeing all blurry as he blinked several times. Strange smells came from behind. The human young girl's and other human's voices could be heard. He started to move gingerly, his muscles responding slowly.

A dish of water lay by his feet, and he started to drink, and the young girl yelled to the other human in an excited way. He kept drinking until he finished the bowl of water. His strength was returning as he ate the bowl of dry food adjacent to the water. Never was he hungrier than now, but there was something wrong.

He didn't recognize this place, and he didn't know his name or where he came from. As he ate, he tried to remember where he had been before awakening. It was all a cloudy blur, with strange voices and strange faces of humans.

Who was he then? Where was he? He remembered being with Simmark, the great one, and of Enew's garden, but when he tried to think, his head hurt more.

The young girl was petting him now, laughing as she did. Was he dead and did he return to life by the great god, Enew?

It was frustrating not knowing. He looked around for clues of the past, but nothing here reminded him of his past. He was lost, and questions ran up and down his brain.

Susan Whittier lifted her Blackie up with her arms.

"He's healthy, Daddy."

"Yeah, the vet helped him. Even that gash on his head is healing."

Walt Whittier sat in his mountain home in Trinidad overlooking the north side of Trinidad. His mansion was the biggest on Trinidad due to his major investments here and in the Caribbean.

Walt was getting tired of the travel. He yearned for his home back in Westchester, New York. Since his wife died, his life had changed. Life wasn't worth the hassle anymore, and he longed for companionship. He missed his wife, and he was lonely.

With all the people he dealt with daily, he was still lonely for a partner, and Susan needed a woman's influence. He would settle all his accounts here and in Tobago and start getting ready to return to New York. It would be good for Susan. She's too isolated here, and the maid and her husband, though they were okay, were not a substitute for a mother.

This cat seemed to reenergize her, and he was glad the cat pulled through. It was risky at first. The vet first asked where we got him, and Susan was vague. She said she found him half dead by the street in front of the yacht club. The vet was surprised the cat was even alive, but due to the cat's strength and large frame, it was saved.

The vet gave Susan instruction, and he treated the nasty gash.

"You know if I didn't know better this looks like a bullet gash." The vet laughed as he said it, but there was something about this cat he found familiar. He couldn't place it, but he would in time.

Blackie would have to take some antibiotics for a week and then get him back for a second checkup.

Blackie "meowed" his approval to Susan's petting, and he snuggled into the young girl's chest. This must be his house and his mistress, he guessed, but something was nagging at him. It was something about a distant evil, and it bothered him down to his insides.

What was his life like before? How could he have forgotten? He would try to find out.

\*    \*    \*

The tall man stepped off the boat onto the beach where another man in shorts awaited him. Syps, Mr. Frank's hit man, waited on the white sand beach for a message from his boss. A cool breeze came down the beach from the south while large terns circled overhead looking for food on the sand.

The men exchanged handshakes and the tall man spoke.

"He's got the woman from New York. He said get Gallo and bring him to Cat Island. You know where on the island?"

"Yeah, I know about Gallo. Easier said than done."

Syps motioned to go into the shade. Both men walked under a palm tree.

"What's his plan once I get there?" Syps asked.

"Don't know. Mr. Franks was almost laughing when he radioed me."

"Okay"–Syps thought about Gallo–"did Franks hire you to help me get Gallo?"

"Yes, I've got two other men in the boat offshore who are wanted on every Caribbean island." The tall man motioned to the boat.

"Good, good." Syps nodded

"Gallo killed my man Grey in the motel where we were going to meet. Gallo has the girl Malena with him, but that's another matter. She has a price on her head by the Vallis. We could get a lot of money turning her into her brother." The tall man smirked.

"Mr. Franks wants them both alive on Cat Island. He has an urge for the girl," Syps noted, and the two men smiled.

"Okay, we know they are on Barbados and are planning to leave soon. We'll follow until the time is right. Okay with you?" Syps was asking, but telling him.

"No problem."

"Good. What do I call you?" Syps inquired.

The man smiled. "Advil like the pill. I get rid of headaches."

*     *     *

The Dino brothers had traced him to Trinidad and then to Barbados. They followed him on the streets of Bridgetown when he caught a cab, and they watched the cab stop and he entered a sleazy motel.

Big Al was eating some weird concoction he got at a local restaurant when Gallo came out. "Hey look he has a girl."

"Just great, we have to deal with the woman now too." Frankie shook his head.

"We'll follow him and pick the right spot and stop with the food you're going to get sick" Frankie grabbed the waxed-papered sandwich and threw it down to the seat.

"Okay, okay," Big Al mumbled with food in his mouth.

They followed Gallo to a hotel in Bridgetown and parked the car. This would be simple—kill him then retire finally. They had amassed a fortune in the New York Stock Exchange, and both were looking forward to retirement on an island somewhere faraway.

Frankie the Foot smiled and hit Big Al in the stomach.

"Look at him with the chick."

"Yeah, nice one too." Big Al laughed. "That's what he's been up to. Hah hah."

"This gets complicated. There's no contract on the broad," Frankie said as he shook his head.

"Then we take him out and leave the girl."

"Okay, let's wait until dark when they think everything is safe, or maybe they will go out to eat or something."

"We'll see." Frankie sat down in the car seat.

Big Al started to eat his second supper—a big roti with globs of sauce.

"Want some?" he said as he gestured to Frankie as sauce ran down Al's arm.

"You're going to make me sick too. You eat it."

*　　*　　*

Gallo and Malena entered the obscure hotel and took the elevator to Gallo's room. Gallo fell into a lounge chair and looked at Jenna, which he knew wasn't her name. She stared back at him.

"There's no way you're from Louisville, no way. Come on, what's the deal?" Gallo smiled at her.

Malena hesitated. The man just saved her from that cab driver. "But it is."

Gallo started to scan through the wallet of the rapist from the motel. He found a Trinidadian driver's license with the name Jason Grey. The other papers revealed nothing except for a piece of paper with a phone number. The phone was a cell number most likely. He recognized the exchange number; it was from Barbados or Trinidad.

Malena was worried. Should she trust this man? He seemed to want to help and she needed all the help she could get. She decided to trust him.

"Listen, you're right. I'm not from Kentucky. I'm Colombian. My name is Malena, Malena Valli. Some people would pay heavily to get me. What are you going to do?"

Gallo looked at her. She was beautiful and looked like she could use some help.

"I'm not your enemy. Valli, that wouldn't be the Valli, the Cartel Valli, would it?"

"Yes. I'm Eduardo's sister." Malena arched are back in defiance.

Gallo sat back. It is a small world after all, as Walt Disney had said.

"Didn't your father just die?" Gallo asked.

Malena stood up and banged the desk with her fist.

"He didn't die. He was killed. The murderous scum, I want to kill him."

Gallo asked her quietly, "Who killed him?"

"He did, my brother," she started to cry and sat on the bed.

Gallo stood up and looked out the window. *The son kills the father and now the sister is running away.*

"Who's after you? It's your brother, isn't it?"

"Yes, but he wouldn't soil his hands. He hired some men led by a pig who wants me." Malena was crying between the words. "He'll do anything to get me, even screw up my brother's big drug deal in the Bahamas."

Gallo started to get a familiar twinge in his spine.

Malena continued, "That's why he wants me dead. I know too much about his operation and this big deal with the Mafia."

Gallo sat back down. He had hit the mother load.

"Do you know what's going down?"

"Only what I overheard from the last three years. Eduardo and some Vietnamese guy got together years ago and hit it off. They were both into women and drugs. Not taking drugs, selling them. The Vietnamese guy hooks up with some doctor or something and invents a means to smuggle drugs."

Gallo was hanging on each word.

"What about the Mafia?"

"They founded the operation in America and they did the construction. I really don't know all of it but it is based in the Bahamas, on some island. I forgot the name." Malena wiped her tears away.

"Eduardo knows I know all this from father. My father had nobody but me, and we would talk consistently."

Gallo had to get to the bottom of this.

"Who's the guy who wants you for . . . well, for you."

"He works for Eduardo, even gave the pig a yacht. He takes it everywhere—that's how he gets around. He came out of nowhere. One day he took over as Eduardo's right-hand man. The pig's name is Franks," Malena spit it out.

Gallo was speechless. He got up and took two white wines from the complimentary bar, opened both and handed one to Malena.

"It's fate we meet then, Malena. Life does have its ironies. I'm after the same man—Franks, as you know him. His real name is Rattel, Frank Rattel."

Gallo took a hit from the small bottle.

"How could this be? How were you there at the motel?" Malena was surprised.

"I was following his men to try to find him. Franks killed a man in Trinidad and my cat. It's a long story." Gallo waved his arm and sat down.

"Your cat? Not a black cat?" Malena asked.

"Yes, black and smart," Gallo answered back in surprise.

"He would talk about a cat. I would hear him curse the cat. A black demon, he said he took his eye out. That he would kill the demon one day and the Americans who destroyed his life. Oh Jesus, help us."

Gallo knew now he must kill Rattel before he found the others. He thought of Tony and Libby. He must contact them even though it meant getting traced here. He could call his supervisor, Simpson of the DEA. Maybe Simpson could help and then he and Malena could leave the hotel. Gallo raised his bottle up to salute Caesar in death.

*　　*　　*

Every day his strength was returning, and the ache in his head was going away.

Young Susan was great at taking care of him and protecting him. After a few days, he ventured out into the front yard. The sights and scents bombarded his nose as if he never smelled before. It was a beautiful sun, and the birds overhead worried of his presence in the yard. He heard a dog barking nearby, perhaps in the next yard. Barking out his territory to all to hear. Mistress Susan came and started to bathe him with the hose. He didn't appreciate the water, but it was soothing to his body. She was very gentle.

She dried him off, and he lay near her in the sun as she read a book. Was this his life? It could not be. He had dreams, vicious dreams of men and a dog, and one particular man chasing him down streets into an alley and firing a gun at him. He always woke up shaking at that point. Mistress Susan would hug him when he had these dreams. The dreams always came every night haunting him. Why couldn't he remember his past? Was Blackie his name? It couldn't be. It was not familiar, yet the humans were good to him, and life was easy here. Maybe the nightmares will pass—he hoped.

Susan was drawing now on a sketchpad for her father, and the maid was serving her on an outside desk. Blackie sat at her feet as if he was always there while the maid went inside to do the house chores.

Insects larger than Blackie could ever imagine climbed over the grass in search of other insects. They passed his paw and he swiped at one making a game of stopping its progress forward. The insect chose another route and Blackie went to sleep.

The house had an electric gate, which opened from a button by the front door for security. Trinidad is the kidnap capital and Whittier worried when his daughter was alone even though the maid was there.

The maid, Fleur, was expecting her no-good husband. Cagney, her husband, named after the American actor, was always in trouble and usually was scrounging for money. Her husband had asked Mr. Whitter for a job, but it never worked out. Cagney would always screw it up.

The bell rang from the gate. It was Cagney. Fleur pushed the button, and Cagney drove his car into the driveway. No one noticed the gate was stuck open.

"Get your worthless ass out of here," Fleur yelled out to him.

"Fleur, my baby. All I wanted to do was ask you about our child," Cagney asked, getting out of the car.

"Bill is good. Don't you worry, my sister's watching him every day with her children. Looking for money, aren't you?"

"Well, I am a little low. Can you spare some? I got a job, but it's not paying until next weekend—"

"Save the excuses. Come in I'll get you some."

Cagney followed her in.

Susan was busy drawing on the lawn and never noticed the open gate. Many stray dogs roam the island looking for prey, scraps of food, or whatever they can eat. One such stray was on the Whitter's block and noticed an open gate. He looked inside. There was food and a young girl with a cat. He was not afraid of humans or their weak pets. He had attacked many and won. The girl was very small, and maybe this time, he would taste human blood.

He walked into the yard straight for the girl with his teeth bared when the black cat stood up. The cat was larger than any cat he had ever seen before. He had killed many a cat and was ready for this one. The black cat stood in front of the girl as Susan noticed the dog and screamed.

Fleur and Cagney ran to the door as Blackie attacked the stray dog. The cat's paws were like lightning and opened wounds on the stray dog's face. The dog tried in vain to grab the cat with its jaw, but to no avail. Even when he pushed the cat using his bigger size, it didn't work. The cat would jump to one side and open another gash on the dog.

"Go, get out of here, leave this territory," came the voice of the cat.

"You cannot stop me, cat. I want that young human."

"Then you will die," came the retort.

Blackie didn't hesitate when the dog barked. He went for the dog's weakest point, his nose. Twice he hit it with his paws, opening a wide cut from which blood poured out. The dog screamed and ran out the gate.

Cagney had grabbed a broom, but it was over in a minute. He went down to the gate and freed the gate so it closed.

Fleur ran and grabbed Susan.

"Did you see Blackie?" Susan yelled. "Did you see? He stopped that dog."

Susan grabbed Blackie and hugged him.

Fleur and Cagney looked at the cat and then to each other.

"Fleur, in all my days I have never heard or seen anything like that. That cat took on a dog twice its size and won."

"It's voodoo. That cat's a devil. Look at him. He knows what he did. It's as if he can understand us. He's looking at us with those green eyes."

"Oh, Fleur, stop. He's just a fighter. He was protecting Susan. Bet there is something about him. I don't know. I'll find out."

"Oh god. What is he?" Fleur questioned.

Susan hugged the black cat as the sun rose in the afternoon sky and birds squawked their tales in the trees.

*   *   *

It was the cold ocean water, and water in his lungs that made him panic. He reached for anything he could in the water, reaching out with his paws to keep his head above the water. The ocean had a strange taste and he tried to spit it out.

The cold was getting to his legs, and he was panicking. He was never this cold before. His stomach was sick, and he knew death was near. Then he heard Caesar's voice in his head about being frightened: *Don't let fear cripple you. Fight back. Keep your spirit. The Great Enew will help you when you persist.*

He remembered those words and continued to try to swim, but he was going nowhere. The ocean was mean and cold as if saying to him "there will be no surviving today." He swam—for how long, he didn't know. His spirit was low and his strength gone when he saw something ahead floating above the water.

It was a human not moving, and he sensed death. He grabbed for its side and with his nails lifted himself on to the body's chest. The human was cold, but the body protected him from the ocean waters.

His breathing was labored forcing air into his lungs. The human's body was above water, but for how long he didn't know. The man's head was underwater and looked as if it would stay above water. As he lay down to get his strength back, he sensed the body was being pulled with the ocean current.

The man Caesar thought was dead was alive, and he took Mistress Libby. There was nothing he could do. He could tell no one. He felt alone out in the cold ocean. His paws were frozen. What would Caesar do?

He could just hear him. "Arthur, get yourself together and think."

Maybe a human will see him.

The red cat sat on the man's chest in the dark for a long time. The ocean whipped its displeasure at the man's body. His stomach hurt and his body was weak from the swim. He could see lights in the distance but they were way off. He would wait for the sun. *Enew protect me, please.*

With that prayer, exhausted he fell asleep on the dead body as it floated with the ocean tide.

*     *     *

Advil and the two hit men trailed Gallo and the girl to the Bridgetown hotel. Advil had done this before many times. Kidnapping was his specialty, especially in Trinidad.

He had kidnapped many teenagers for ransom until the parents showed with the money. He always demanded American dollars, not Trinidadian dollars. This would be different. Gallo is an experienced policeman, and this is in a very busy hotel. He had to plan this correctly.

Syps had warned him about this policeman and his past, but the cop was at a disadvantage. He had the woman to protect.

He was on his way to the hotel when he received a call on his cell. It was the hotel desk clerk on the Valli payroll.

"They are checking out, hurry."

"Got it."

Advil slammed the gas pedal to the floor.

Gallo and Malena hurried out of the hotel lobby and to a cab. Gallo had placed a call to Director Simpson as to his situation.

Simpson wasn't too concerned, and Gallo read surprise in his voice that he was calling.

"How did you wind up in Barbados?" Simpson asked, astounded.

"It's a long story. I've got something to handle. Can't talk now."

"I understand." Simpson hung up.

Gallo felt uneasy with the call. It was strange the way Simpson reacted. Gallo dismissed it and concentrated on getting out of Barbados.

The cab drove them toward the airport but the cabbie was cursing at a car behind him.

"Son of a bitch is too close."

The dark green car behind them lurched forward and rammed the cab violently.

"Fuck, what the hell!" the cabbie yelled.

Gallo knew it was Syps.

The dark green car edged alongside the cab and pushed it toward the deep rain water canals on the side of the road. The cab hit a hole and a crack came from the front end. The cab's rear wheel hit another open hole and the cab slid along a concrete curb hitting a pole and coming to a stop.

Gallo jumped out of the car with Malena in tow and crouched behind the cab. The dark green car came to a screeching halt and two older men jumped out and started to shoot at Gallo.

The cabbie was hurt and unconscious. Gallo returned fire. Malena screamed that they were pinned down and tugged on Gallo's shirt.

"Listen, don't panic, we'll get out of this," Gallo said in a steady voice.

"Mr. Gallo, we just want you, not the girl, we promise not to hurt her," came a voice from beyond the car.

Gallo wondered who this was. *Didn't Syps want the girl too?*

Two more shots were fired into the cab when a black Lexus pulled up violently, shooting at the two older men.

"Who the hell is shooting at us?" Big Al yelled.

Frank Dino was surprised.

"Don't know, shoot back."

The Dinos and the black Lexus were in a gun battle when Gallo grabbed Malena and ran into the trees beyond.

Gallo wondered who was in the black Lexus. Malena and Gallo ran as fast as they could, but they didn't know where. The swampy forest floor was covering their tracks as they ran.

The Lexus had three men as far as Frank Dino could surmise, but when they opened fire with a submachine gun that's when Frank had enough.

"Al, let's scram."

"Okay, okay," Al obliged.

The Dinos' car was shot to hell by the return fire and they would have to run on foot. Nearby was a tall fence with bushes behind it and an opening in the fence. Both of the men ran into the yard and past the nearby house.

A large dog saw them and started to chase them down the side yards.

"C'mon, Al, you got to run," Frank yelled at his overweight brother.

"As fast as I can." Al was puffing as he talked.

"Jesus Christ, this is embarrassing, Al," Frank screamed at as he ran.

Al couldn't answer Frank; he was all out of breath. They ran until the dog gave up and the dog's territory was passed by the two men. They stopped when they were out of the strange shooter's range and sat on the street curb.

"You know, Al, we been doing this about forty years, right?" Frank was breathing heavy.

Al nodded, trying to catch some air.

"I think with our money in the stock market and our liquid assets, we do not need to be shot off a hit by who the hell I don't know, and then to be chased by a dog down these dirt streets, that's it. I quit."

Big Al Dino had just received some air and spoke, "I agree, this is ridiculous. Let's retire."

"You're right, Al."

"C'mon." He helped his brother up. "We'll go check out of that sleazy hotel and take a trip where no one will find us. Let Gallo go. Someone else wants him more than us. Good Luck."

"Let's live the good life." Big Al smiled.

The two men started to walk down the street, holstered their guns and knew life would be easier in their golden years.

*     *     *

She sat in the darkness, petting her dog. The dog huddled close to her and kept an eye out for strangers. The scents coming from beyond the door were strange to the do,g and at the same time he understood what had happened in the past sun. He had lost a good friend. An innocent soul was thrown into the sea for no reason at all. Humans never really have a reason to kill they just do it. It was his job now to protect his mistress. The ship listed to one side occasionally and an empty beer bottle rolled across the wood plank floor.

He heard voices coming closer to the door, and he recognized one voice pitch. It was the human rat that Caesar often talked about and thought he had killed.

The human rat entered the room and spoke in a harsh tone to his mistress.

"I kept you alive for one reason. To kill all of you who destroyed my life, all together in one place. Your fiancé, Tony, and Gallo will come to me. Gallo, as we speak, will be picked up by my men and brought to the island. Your boyfriend Tony will have some help to get there but he will show. So you see I will have my revenge on all of you finally.

"Your son of a bitch cat, the black devil, is dead. I killed him in Trinidad. He died too quickly. I wanted to give him more suffering.

"I let you keep your dog, because I like dogs and this mongrel didn't have a hand in my plans."

"Rattel, you have money, a yacht, and the world thinks your dead. Why all this?" Libby asked, trying to get more information.

"Why?" Rattel came closer and lifted the patch on his eye. Libby saw a white—yellowed eye with a scar through it.

"This is why, and because I wanted more and your two friends, helped to get me on the Mafia's shit list. The day of reckoning is coming for all three of you on the island."

"What island?" Libby asked quietly.

"It's a secret, but I can tell you. Cat Island in the Bahamas, it's going to be the moneymaker of all time. It will be a direct connection to the States for drugs and money or whatever. You will see it happen but not for long."

"Are you the one who started it?"

"No, no, some doctor got together with the Vietnamese gang. I'm just working for the Colombians but things are going to change, wait till they get there."

With that, Rattel laughed.

"Soon enough, honey, you will see. Ha ha ha." He was laughing in that sick sound as he slammed the door of the cabin and she heard it lock.

She knew of the island. If only she could get to her cell phone and call either Tony or Gallo, but her phone was most likely locked up somewhere above. She would bide her time and wait for her opportunity.

*     *     *

Tony had searched everywhere and was at his wit's end. Everywhere he turned was a dead end. Simpson of the DEA, Gallo's superior, couldn't help him. Tony tried Libby's cell and Gallo's and neither worked. Furness was on the case in Trinidad but there were no leads. All was silent with no calls.

It was maddening. He was sitting at his desk when he looked at the map Libby had left open.

It was a Long Island map, but there were no marks or clues as to what she wanted him to know or notice. He had reviewed the map several times, but nothing hit him.

He folded the map and slammed doors on the desk. He felt helpless. It was amazing no one saw anything. He walked outside and sat on the stoop. He thought of the good old days of Libby and Gallo and of Caesar. Never a cat shall ever be born such as him; then of Sam and Arthur, he thought of their friendship. He shook his head.

The sun was up, bleeding through the leaves and lighting the face of Tony. Tears welled up in his eyes for his friends.

Tony then heard a familiar sound. It was the perky blue jay, coming down from the top of the tree toward him. Tony felt as if the blue jay missed his friends too.

"I miss them too," he called out, and the bluejay answered with a *cay, cay.*

Both sat in the afternoon sun, thinking of the past.

*     *     *

Gallo and Malena ran through the deep rain forest. How far they ran, he couldn't tell. Both were out of breath when they finally stopped. They sat near a red flowering bush and listened. There was no sound except for birds calling out the two humans' presence.

"I think we lost them," Malena said, wishing it so.

"No, they're not going to quit. It's Syps. They want me bad. The other guys in the dark green car were definitely Italian hit men. I've seen enough of those types to know."

"I know about Syps and Rattel, but why is the Mafia after you?" Malena questioned.

"It's a long involved story, let's just say there was a guy in Italy who thinks I killed his son." Gallo waved it off. "We have to get off this island. They will have the airport covered. Your brother wants you back and Rattel wants me. Convenient, isn't it? Rattel's got something planned. I know it and your brother is in on it. This doctor, what is it he invented?"

"Some way to transport drugs to America. I don't know. It's all sick, sick. Goddamn drugs." Malena threw a hand fill of dirt to the ground.

"There was supposedly a big meeting between the three factions. The Colombians, Mafia, and the Vietnamese gang. This doctor has a scheme to ship out all their drugs. We got to find out and tell the DEA," Malena, said half crying.

Gallo was determined.

"Yeah, tell who?"

"That's right, how did these guys know you and where you were staying. That wasn't exactly the Hilton. How did the Mafia and Rattel know? Huh?" Malena stared into Gallo's eyes.

"That's the question I've been asking myself. Someone has a rat working for him or her. Only a select few knew I was in Barbados and I trust them all."

Gallo dropped it from his concern now.

"Listen, we got to get to a boat. The coast can't be too far away. We ran west so we have to double back to the coast. There are plenty of fishermen who will take us to another island for a price."

With that, he grabbed Malena's arm and started to walk east. The rain forest was dense and the birds loud in their disapproval of the human's presence. The rain forest swallowed them up and the sun grew hotter.

\*   \*   \*

The young girl sat in her classroom in Trinidad, listening to her teacher. The school day covered history of the Caribbean but was almost over, and she was to be picked up by Fleur, her nanny. The school was private and safely enclosed in a gated yard. The rash of kidnappings had grown in Trinidad in the last years, and the school was very nervous about the children's safety.

As always, the class stopped at 2:00 PM, and the children went to the front of the schoolyard, where their mothers or fathers came in their cars for the students.

Susan waited for Fleur by the gate near the street as she always did, and as always Fleur was late. Susan was daydreaming of Blackie. She couldn't wait to see him. She loved that cat.

As she was daydreaming, a stranger came up to her.

"Susan, your father needs you to come with me."

Susan always shied away from strangers.

"No, sir, my nanny is arriving soon to pick me up."

"No, she won't."

The stranger grabbed the girl, and a blue sedan came up quickly, and she was thrown in the car seat. She tried to scream, but the stranger's hand was over her mouth.

"Your father will pay plenty for you." The stranger scowled through missing front teeth.

One of the teachers in the yard talking to one of her students saw the kidnapping through the gate and started screaming for the police, but no police were nearby. The teacher ran to the office phone and called the police.

When Fleur arrived five minutes later, she didn't see Susan at the gate, but noticed her teacher outside looking frantic.

"Oh god, little Susan, she's been taken," yelled the teacher.

Fleur's heart dropped. *Oh Jesus no*, she thought, *not the sweet one*. Kidnappings have been going on for years in Trinidad, but she never thought it would hit her charge. She started to cry and called her husband, Cagney, on her cell. She was taken into the school office and sat down.

"What should I do? Whittier will be beyond himself," she asked her husband.

"I'll tell him," her husband said quietly. "Are the police there yet?"

"No, not yet. Oh god, not Susan," Fleur cried.

The sun was high in the afternoon sky as cars rolled past the school gate, speeding to their various appointments.

\*     \*     \*

Dr. Zine was ready for his demonstration to his benefactors. His creation was in perfect working order, and he had already tested his small car in the tunnel. He called it a car, but it was almost six feet long and only two feet wide but it would carry a ton, maybe more.

The design the United States government didn't want was now going to work out and travel into the USA and up the eastern coast.

Tom, the general's son, was ecstatic with joy. His father will be pleased with the start of the venture even though he could care less what his father thought, and soon the money would roll in, and he could be free of his father.

Tom walked down to Dr. Z, and they exchanged their checklist for next Tuesday's meeting.

"A week and a half and this operation will be in full working order, shipping drugs into the biggest market of them all, the USA."

He awaited the arrivals of the son of Cimbari, Alfredo, and Franks and Eduardo of the Valli Cartel.

Like General Motors, it will be an assembly line—from his father would come pure heroin, from the south the Vallis will bring cocaine and marijuana, and the American Mafia will distribute it along the coast. No one would be wiser. It was foolproof in every way.

There was a rumor Eduardo's sister was on the run, and could be a loose cannon and a threat to this operation. Eduardo had sent Franks to get her, but Tom had heard nothing of the quest. Then there was something else that bothered Tom. The Vallis were chasing a well-known agent of the USA. That agent Gallo and that black cat were famous for breaking the largest and best smuggling route this year. Tom was unnerved by this news, but the Vallis assured him not to worry. His stomach was not eased at Eduardo's promise. He hoped this Gallo thing disappeared soon.

Tom climbed to the top of the mountain on old stone steps that had Stations of the Cross engraved on them, and then out onto the cliff's edge on the south side of the island. A monastery was built here years ago, and it was now abandoned. A bell tower was erected at the highest point, and the bell had survived the years. Some tourists would visit occasionally. Tom leaned against the tower and looked over the ocean to the east. It was a two-hundred-foot drop from here to the jungle and then to the ocean. Terns flew over the ocean, grabbing at fish as they dived and Tom could see fishermen's boats off the coast.

He breathed in and then out. Life would be fulfilling soon for him, and money would be flowing like water. He would achieve all he deserved within the next weeks. A storm cloud passed over, and rain started to fall washing the island down. Tom stayed on the cliff in the rainstorm smiling up at the clouds as rain fell and washed his face.

\*     \*     \*

The black of night turned into a hazy gray morning off the Long Island shore. The sun rose over Montauk Point, and the ocean calmed in its approval of the morning light.

The ocean had been a black and bumpy ride for the cat. He was wet and tired from lack of food and sleep. He had gotten some sleep, but his rests were fretful. The body of the man was bloated now, and it was becoming more difficult to stay on the chest of the man. He had to constantly grab with his claws to hang on with the ocean's movements. This in turn wouldn't permit him to sleep. His muscles were aching, and his stomach growled in dissatisfaction.

He would call out as loud as possible, but there was no one in sight. The cat forgot how many suns he was on the man, but when he had fallen asleep at last, a prayer to Enew was answered. He was awakened by a noise.

A metal cage sat on the water. Tall and noisy with a clang he didn't understand. Off in the distance he could see land of some sort but didn't recognize it. The man's body was now almost underwater, and his footing was too loose to hang on.

He had one chance. Oh Enew, if he could only make it. The cat jumped onto the ledge of the metal cage using all his remaining strength. His rear two claws slipped, but he held on. He lifted himself on to the metal cage, as the body of the dead human disappeared into the dark water. He meowed as loud as he could, but only the clang of the metal cage could be heard. He lay in an exhausted heap.

Wet and tired he fell fast asleep, dreaming of Caesar.

"Tell me what to do?" he asked Caesar.

"Have faith. You're not lost. You have friends, Arthur. Have faith in Enew." With that Caesar faded into a dreamy haze.

The bell clanged its song for all to hear, but the ships and boats passing didn't see the red cat on the red buoy. The sun rose into the morning, and the seagulls sang their calls to each other of the many fish available in the ocean.

\*　　\*　　\*

The young couple was not noticed in the restaurant in Barbados. They had walked from the highway by the airport though the dense rain forest.

The man called from a pay phone to the cabbie that had helped him in the past. Jeb was all too pleased to come and help them out.

The man sat down on the veranda and sipped his scotch sour.

"What else do you know? How does your brother get the drugs to the States? How?" he asked the woman.

"He's an expert. Plane, boat, mules, you name it. Now it will be easy. He will bring it to an island and then it will be taken care of." Malena took a sip of white wine.

"Do you know anything about the particulars of the boats he uses?"

"No, never, besides he changes them constantly to not be caught by the U.S. Coast Guard."

"Damn. If we knew how we could follow the yacht's path to this island." Gallo slammed down the glass.

Malena wanted to help Gallo. She felt a trust and respect of the man. "I know how the Vietnamese group get their drugs here. I mean, it's something. Eduardo would laugh at because it was so simple it was never thought of by the Americans."

"And?" Gallo asked anxiously.

"They own an airline called Pacific Rim Airlines. The drugs are in the plane's wing with the gas."

"Wait a minute. It would be an expensive project to remove the gas from the heroin and—" Gallo was interrupted.

"I didn't say in the gas. I said in the wing with the gas. A compartment built into the wings separated from the gas. It was never detected because they make many stops from Vietnam to the Caribbean. So they just gas up at each location. No one is wiser to it."

Gallo was amazed.

Malena continued, "When they get to a destination they have the local crew on the payroll to off load the drugs as they fill the gas."

Gallo sat back and marveled at the simplicity of it all.

"These airports they serve, do you know one nearby?" Gallo asked, hoping.

"I think St. Lucia or a stop on Grenada."

"No wonder your brother wants you out."

Malena's eyes started to well up with tears.

"My father told me this to protect me in case . . ."

Gallo moved over and hugged her. She had been through too much, but it wasn't over yet.

Jeb the cabbie arrived and was all smiles. He knew these two would be grabbing at each other soon.

"Were you involved in that shoot-out near the airport?"

"*Shhh*, quiet don't be so loud. Sit down, Jeb."

Gallo explained the situation, and Jeb was ready to help. He knew of a fisherman with a large boat who traveled to the other islands and had a woman in all ports. Gallo and Malena stepped into the cab and Jeb drove off to the piers.

Gallo thought they had a good chance to find this island and maybe he'll find Rattel. He's part of this whole mess. First chance he got, he would call Furness and fill him in.

Barbados was hot and humid and a quick afternoon rain started to fall on the cab as it whined its way through the narrow curved streets.

*        *        *

Furness sat at his cousin's desk in the police station. He had searched for a week to find anything on Robie and his travels this past year.

It was a mystery. Even Dan, his cousin, couldn't find out why he was shot that way. Furness had not heard from Gallo, and that worried him. Gallo went after Rattel—or so Furness thought—and now he was frustrated and started throwing paper clips into the garbage can.

"Hey, those are government property you are throwing away." His cousin smiled at him as he walked into his office.

"Sorry, Dan, this shit's getting to me. There's something we're missing."

"Yeah, well, that's the story of police work," Dan said as he walked over to the coffee.

"Have you heard from Tony in New York City?" Dan asked.

"Yes. He's desperate. He can't find Libby, and he's going to go to Gallo's DEA boss. Libby's gone, Gallo's missing, and Caesar's dead. It's sad." Furness threw the last paper clip down.

Dan wanted to get his cousin out of this funk.

"Hey, there's been another kidnapping by that gang at the Savannah in front of the Barnes School. It's a very prestigious school. Only the rich can send their children there. The girl kidnapped was an investment banker's girl name of Susan Whittier. Shame. She was waiting for her nanny to pick her up and she was gone."

Furness seemed mildly interested.

Dan continued, "Seems the father wants to look for her with us. Says he has a cat that knows her scent. Wants to lead us with the bloody cat."

Furness's eyes looked at Dan.

"I know what you're thinking, Cousin, but isn't your cat dead?"

"Yeah, boy he is." Furness slumped in the chair.

"The father says the cat was her constant companion and stopped a rabid mongrel dog from attacking the girl."

Furness looked at Dan.

"Do you have a report on that fight the cat had?"

"No, no, but the local paper probably does. What's up?" Dan asked curious.

"What papers, where's your computer?" Furness got up quick and ran to Dan's computer.

Furness searched the *Trinidad Guardian* and found the article from last week.

"Cat stops dog from attacking child" was the headline news story Furness read on.

"A black cat saved investment banker Whittier's daughter Susan from an attack from a rabid dog yesterday." There was no photo of the cat.

Furness turned to Dan.

"There's only one cat that I know of that could do this on this island. He must be alive."

Dan shook his head.

"I thought you said he was shot by this Rattel?"

"Caesar was dead before and came back. It's him. Call the father let me see him." Furness was excited.

"Okay, okay. I'll contact him. Dan grabbed the phone and called Whittier to come to the police station. Whittier happily agreed and said Blackie would accompany him.

Thirty minutes passed and Mr. Whittier walked into the station with the cat under his arm. He sat the black cat down on Dan's desk.

Furness heart rejoiced. It was Caesar alive. It was God's miracle.

Furness went to pet the cat, but something was wrong. He didn't act like Caesar.

"Caesar. It's me your old friend," Furness said excitedly.

The black cat didn't acknowledge him but turned away toward Whittier.

"Wait. This is strange. Where did you find him, Mr. Whittier?" Furness asked.

"I didn't. My daughter did." Why do you call him Caesar? It's discouraging. Harvey, where are the police searching for my daughter? I told you Blackie knows her scent well and could help." Whittier was agitated.

"Yes, Mr. Whittier I understand, but these cowards are not hanging out on a corner for this cat to smell them. They're in either a cellar or an out of the way safe house. We are doing our best."

"It's not good enough for me." Whittier was very upset.

Furness stood in front of Caesar. The cat didn't look at him but he saw a mark on his head. Something a bullet might cause.

"Mr. Whittier, you say your daughter found him, but where?"

"I don't know. I think she said on the pier or the yacht." Whittier sat down exhausted.

"Was your yacht docked at Chaguaramas about two weeks ago?"

"Ah, yes. It was a Friday night. I was having some meetings there, and Susan was with me. Oh, and we brought the cat to a vet. He checked out but had a large gash on his head like he fell or something."

Caesar's big green eyes looked at Furness now, sizing him up. The cat stared at the man and Furness looked deeply into Caesar's eyes. It seemed like minutes, but it was only seconds they were transfixed.

Furness turned.

"Mr. Whittier, this is the cat that saved that ship in the North Atlantic and busted one of the biggest corporations dealing drugs in North America. You must have read about him. His name is Caesar, and the men who we are after shot him—only, he seems to not know me. Could it be he has amnesia?"

"Oh god, I read about him. The DEA gave him special agent status. Yes, yes. I remember this year months ago but amnesia for a cat!" Whittier was astounded.

"It has to be, but, Mr. Whittier, let's take care of one thing first—your child. I'll help you find her and then we'll get to the bottom of this. It's a miracle." Furness petted Caesar's head.

"Thank you. Now, Lieutenant Harvey, can we search now for Susan?" Mr. Whittier said anxiously.

"Right, let's go. I know an area they are known to hang out. We'll start there." Harvey holstered his pistol.

Whittier went to lift Caesar, but Furness motioned he would.

Furness lifted the black cat. Caesar meowed his disapproval, but let this man carry him.

Something was familiar about this man. He wished he could remember.

*   *   *

"He has to be killed if we are to control this tunnel. I don't want to pay any goddamn Vietnamese general money for this. We have to kill him and his son now," the man with a heavy Spanish accent yelled.

Don Cimbari held up his hand to quiet him down.

"We are in process to relieve ourselves of that burden soon. The son will be taken care of too. Your cartel and our family will control the tunnel.

"If all goes well, what I put into motion soon we will control the entire heroin distribution from Southeast Asia too. So calm yourself, Mr. Valli, calm yourself"

"Okay, okay. We are in agreement. Once this jerk is out of the way, we will split all of it." Eduardo lowered his voice.

"Yes, yes. We have an alliance. There is one thing. My son Alfredo says your man Franks was a former employee of ours. I want him dead. That is the only term for this bargain."

Eduardo Valli laughed.

"You can have him once he kills the Asian. I'll have him taken care of."

"Good. Bene. Now about your sister and the pig, Gallo. What's the update? Cimbari lit a nonfiltered cigarette and blew the smoke upward toward the red and gold ceiling.

"My men are on their trail. He's as good as dead. My sister, on the other hand, may be a casualty too."

"Ah, blood. It's a dangerous game killing the father and now the sister." Cimbari smiled at the Colombian.

"Like you did, Don, to get all this," Eduardo raised his hands upward.

Cimbari laughed.

"Touche', amigo. Let's have a toast to our friendship and our trillion-dollar enterprise."

Both men had a dry pale champagne poured into large glasses and raised and touched the flutes. Cimbari looked at the stupid asshole and wondered if he would ever catch on.

"Soon, amigo, we will be in control of 70 percent of the drugs in the world."

*     *     *

Brooklyn Heights was beautiful in late autumn. The streets are lined with tall trees that have variations of orange and red leaves. The trees started turning their colors and a quiet sereneness engulfed the area. The multicolored season was Tony's favorite, but not this autumn. He was still stalemated in finding Libby's whereabouts. She just basically disappeared. The FBI director whom he had met months ago couldn't find her and the director called him regularly.

Gallo was also missing. Furness had called him two days ago, and they couldn't get in touch with Gallo. He had gone off after Rattel somewhere in Barbados.

Tony felt helpless and sat by his television, watching his favorite team, the Yankees, in a rerun and they were losing by one run and had the bases loaded; yet, even that couldn't lift his spirits. *What to do, what to do?* he kept asking himself. He walked over to his desk and sat down opening a drawer; he removed the questionable map Libby had left behind.

It was a Long Island map, but nothing was marked up or pinpointed. In disgust, he threw the map down and it opened to a page on the floor.

Tony glanced at it and then cursed himself for being so stupid. Nassau County was in large letters. Nassau. That's in the Bahamas. That's what Libby was trying to say. It was the island of Nassau. Tony rushed to the telephone. He called Gallo's chief, Simpson.

"Hello," came a dry voice.

"Is Mr. Simpson in?" Tony asked excited.

"No, not here, shall I take a message?"

"No, thanks."

Tony hung up the phone.

He'll drive to Simpson's house and get him to assign an agent to find Libby.

Tony tried the FBI Director too but just left a message.

He ran out the door and into his car and sped away to the Long Island Expressway.

"God, oh Libby," he said out loud. "I hope I'm not too late."

*     *     *

These past moons had been lonely for the blue jay. There was no one to chirp or talk to. All his friends were gone off to some adventure, and he sat here, unable to help.

Abigail, his mate, was teaching the chicks, but they were already almost full grown and should have been on their own already. Everybody stayed with him because Fletcher was such a good provider and was fun to be with, but not these past suns. The loss of his friends made him quiet and alone.

Fletcher was reviewing the last time he saw Caesar when Max the seagull came by for a visit.

"Hey, Fletch, let's go invade the Red Hook barges."

"Nah, I'm okay. Thanks for asking." Fletcher moved over to give the bigger bird room on the branch.

Max looked down the men's path and saw Clay the pigeon.

"Hey, come on up here," Max chirped in that gull high voice.

Clay flew up to a nearby branch.

"What's new, birds?" Clay cleared his beak of popcorn.

"Just crackling here. Fletch any word on anybody?" Max cawed.

"I just saw Master Tony go out in a rush. I know something is wrong. I wish I could help," Fletcher moaned.

Max wanted to give Fletcher some hope.

"Hey, the bird crackle from the warm coast says there's a lot of chirping about a big wind coming soon."

"They're called hurricanes, Max," Clay cracked. "Get rid of that bird talk. This is the twenty-first century already."

"Yeah, hurricanes, a lot coming." Max nodded.

Fletcher looked at Max and wondered,

"Max, does your coast gossip tell you anything about strange going on along the coast?"

"Yes, all the time. I heard talk of a finding of a human the other day in an area called the Great South Bay. A man was found dead on the beach washed ashore. He was dead some three days."

Fletcher started to perk up.

"And?"

"Well, crackle says he was dropped off a boat at night. The gulls there say he was murdered. The loons noted his name." Max stopped to grab a leaf and chew.

"Go on, his name," Clay chirped loudly. "What are you always in an eating mode?"

"Oh, his name according to the loons was Bert or Hert or something like that."

"Bert, Bert," Fletcher repeated the name over and over.

"Seems I've heard that somewhere before, but where?" Fletcher racked his brain.

"Maybe on old man Lockwood's television?" Clay asked.

"That's it on the television. His some big shot and I saw him here one night before Mistress Libby left." Fletcher started to get a chill up his spine.

"Oh no, that was the last day I saw Sam or Arthur too."

Fletcher turned to Max.

"Can we talk on the crackle coast line?"

Max was astonished.

"But it's many birds up and down the coast who bring this crackle to us. We would have to visit the area of the dead human."

Fletcher looked at Max and Clay.

"So?"

"But Fletch you can't fly as fast as me and neither can Clay," Max said saddened.

"I know, but we can do it in short flies."

"You've got to be loony," Clay exclaimed.

At that moment, crows nearby were sounding their warnings.

It was Ketvel; the princess came to visit too. The falcon swooped down onto a higher branch above them.

"Nice to see you birds together again," came the smooth voice of the falcon.

Clay chirped back, "Yeah, nice to still be alive."

Fletcher looked at Max.

"You arranged this, didn't you? You bone picker."

Max smiled.

"I had to somehow cheer you up, but I never thought you would want to fly to the Great South Bay."

"Great South Bay? What for? the Princess asked.

"Princess, come with us, we need you to guide us. We're on an adventure."

"On an adventure are you daffy," Clay muttered to himself.

"I'm on to something. You know I am." Fletcher turned to Clay and he took aloft and the four birds started southeast.

Princess could do it easily but she held back for her friends. Max led the way with Fletcher not too far behind and Clay dragging on the end.

"Hey, Clay, get the drag out of your wings," Fletcher cracked.

Clay muttered to himself,

"Why does everything have to be a pain in the wings with this odd crew? They're as nutty as the squirrel."

\*     \*     \*

The general sat on his porch and had just hung up from a call from his son, Tom. Everything was on schedule for the drug tunnel, and all was going well. Soon his empire would be enormous. From Vietnam to the States—without question the biggest drug distribution in the world.

His Pacific Rim Airlines was turning a profit, and with this initial money spent he would be a trillionaire.

His home was ten miles west of Thanh Pho Ho Chi Minh, the capital, which was once Saigon, and he would visit the city to buy women for sex on a regular basis. He would also visit his cousins weekly who managed his airline from there. The general would drive an American Jeep regularly and loved American items so he collected everything American as a hobby. The Americans managed to leave items behind thirty years ago that had some collectible value to a few in the country. The general also saved vintage cars and some American weapons.

Knowing he collected everything American made the local people search out remnants of the war. They would flock to him to sell artifacts. American uniforms, canteens, belts, ammunition, or even an American truck—he would buy everything. His collection was housed in one large quonset metal building on his property. Every chance he had he would use the items to his glee, but new American items excited him. Calls would come in from all over the country.

One such a call came in this morning.

"Sir, we have a special American item. It's a beautiful collectible. It's in great condition. It's an American car. Some American general left it behind and it's been sitting in a mountain cave near Da Lat. It runs too."

The general, savoring the car, agreed instantly. The general would meet the seller near Da Lat at a house the car was brought to.

"Tell me what is the brand?" the general asked excited.

"It's a 1973 Cadillac," came the voice.

"I'll be there in two hours."

"Okay." The phone went dead.

The general jumped in his Chinese car and started his drive.

"A Cadillac and from the seventies. I can't wait."

He turned his car north as he smiled.

\*   \*   \*

The people visited the Granada airport and walked the tunnel along the secured area. Now with all the terrorists' threats, the airport wasn't as loose on security. The couple moved outside the secure area and walked along a chain link fence to spot the jets. This was definitely not the area for Pacific Rim Airlines.

The young woman sat down disgusted.

"It has to be here. I heard them talk."

"Look, let's walk down to the other side of the airport, maybe we'll spot something." The man smiled at her.

She listened and got up. He was a good man, and he did save her life. She wasn't ready for this feeling at this time, but it hit her like a lightning bolt. She started to care for him and in a strange way wanting never to lose him. It was something she never felt before. She tried making it pass.

Gallo led Malena down a sidewalk to a hangar they could spot through the fence. There were many planes jockeying for position, and at first nothing was even close to the name they were searching for.

A four-prop plane moved out to take off from the hanger when they noticed a blue logo in the background. It was Pacific Rim Airlines. It was an older two-prop plane taxiing into the hanger. It moved slow and then disappeared into the large building.

"That's it, Mark." Malena was excited.

"Yeah, now let's go into the terminal and ask about destinations. Maybe that will tip us off on where this special island is located."

They walked back to the terminal and asked a friendly airline representative for the schedule of Pacific Rim Airlines. She handed them a schedule, and they walked over to the bar. Gallo ordered a scotch sour and Malena a rum drink.

It was a large schedule serving many countries and islands, but their fleet were all old propeller planes, no jets. Their popularity was that they flew to locations that no other airlines visited.

It was astonishing. The airline traveled from Thanh Pho Ho Chi Minh in Vietnam to Manila on to Indonesian cities, which were many, and then onto the Pacific Islands. Each Pacific Island group was stopped at, including Hawaii. From Hawaii to some Mexican island named Revilla Gigado, then on to Marco, Guatamala, then Panama, Colombia, Aruba, Trinidad, St. Lucia, islands in the Caribbean, and on to the Bahamas, and the last stop in Nassau. It was amazing, but there were no stops in the USA.

Malena looked at Gallo, slamming the schedule down.

"It's hopeless. It could be anywhere."

"Wait, stands to reason it's not in the Lesser Antilles of Aruba and Tortuga. It had to be on the end of the trip or near it."

"It's just a guess, and let's take it. We have nothing to lose." He smiled at her and there was a feeling between them. Something Gallo hadn't felt since his first wife.

"Okay, Mark, lets go book a flight to Nassau." She smiled at him.

"First time I got you to smile. It's a beautiful smile." He grabbed for her hand, and they headed for the Pacific Rim Airline counter, never suspecting their moves were being watched.

\*   \*   \*

Cagney sat by the broken window and thought about the last twenty-four hours. He had done it. This was the big money kidnapping this time. The young Whittier girl was in his old shack he used to live in as a kid. The neighborhood was old and broken down. The three men he hired for the kidnapping were hoodlums in Trinidad and would do anything for a buck, especially U.S. dollars.

Susan Whittier didn't see him approach after the three men brought her to the shack. She was blindfolded. It was perfect. Whittier pays the ransom and I can get away from Trinidad and my wife. She was a pain in the ass.

One of the men, his name was Lou, entered the shack.

"How's the young bitch, any crying going on?"

"No, haven't heard a noise from upstairs. It's quiet, and I should be hearing from Whittier soon. I know the cops know, but it doesn't matter. He'll pay for his little girl. I'll call in a couple of days. Makes them pay quicker when they sweat."

The other man laughed and sat down turning on the television.

Cagney smiled; his wife Fleur would never guess this about him. She thinks he's off at work at some oil industry job. He gave that up months ago. It's been very profitable kidnapping kids and getting the money, but this time he was hitting closer to home. He was tired of the small businessmen's son or the landowner's daughter. He wanted bigger money and to get away from this island.

Whittier was perfect. When Fleur landed the nanny job, he knew it was made for him. Whittier was too trusting of him and his wife, so he planned it down to the hour and place.

This old house no one knew about. His father had died here six years ago, and he just let it rot until he used it for the first time for a kidnap location. No one would guess and especially in this neighborhood. This area no one ventured in just to visit. Cagney would keep the victim in a secluded room on the second floor, and the men would take turns watching her. The floorboards were rotted in some spots and you had to be careful not to step in the wrong location or you would land on the floor below. If the kidnapped person ventured out of the seat they put them in then they would fall through the floor and die. Cagney didn't care if they did. He just wanted the money.

He had purchased a pit bull terrier as a watchdog and called him Rogue. He was a killer. The dog had ripped open a man's arm once and the owner didn't want him anymore.

Just then Rogue came over to Cagney.

"Good boy, watching out for us."

The dog nuzzled his hand and growled.

"Hey, if that fucking dog comes near me, I'll kill it. He attacked John yesterday, almost ripped his arm off." Lou yelled from the dirty kitchen, such as it was.

"You leave the dog to me. He listens only to me and he hates stupid people, and John is a fucking retard."

"Yeah, yeah, just keep him away." Lou went back to watching *Gilligan's Island* on the television.

Cagney rubbed Rogue under the ears,

"Don't you pay any mind to idiots, we're going to be rich."

\* \* \*

It was raining hard in Trinidad. The month of November was hit with a lot of rain and this was no exception. A black SUV ran up the avenue looking for a little girl in all the bad areas but with the rain, and with no word from the kidnappers, morale was low.

Even the cat couldn't sense anything, and Furness knew it. Three days had passed since the kidnapping and still not a sign. The kidnappers had called two days ago and said they would arrange the meet. They called from a pay phone in Port of Spain, which was in the West Mall shopping area. Thousands of people shopped there. It was impossible to spot anybody suspicious so they returned again to the police station.

When they walked in, Fleur, Susan's nanny, was there frantic about her husband, Cagney.

"Mr. Whittier, he's missing. I called his job Mr. Whittier, he's hasn't been there in months. What's he doing? Oh lord."

Whittier grabbed her and sat her down on the bench. Dan suggested going into his office and they all followed.

"Mr. Whitter I don't understand, if he didn't want to come home he should have told me," Fleur cried again.

"Fleur when did you hear from him last? Whittier asked.

Furness grabbed a soda and sat down and lit a cigar.

"It was a day after Miss Susie was taken. He said he would be gone a day working overtime." Her voice cracked as she spoke.

Dan wondered, "Did he ever do this before?"

"Yes, yes, last six or seven months he's disappeared for three, four days at a time. I just thought he was just liming with his friends."

Dan motioned to Furness to come out of the room.

The black cat was on the window ledge, watching the birds singing.

Dan grabbed Furness by the arm.

"You don't think he's the one? There's been a rash of new kidnappings on the island of late, especially the last six months or so. With this Whittier girl taken, it's too coincidental."

Furness agreed, "I think it's worth digging deeper."

The two men returned to the office. Fleur was calmer now smoking a cigarette and drank some water.

"Fleur," Dan asked, "when Cagney came back, did he ever say where he was?"

"No, no just out liming and with his folks."

"Folks?" Furness asked.

"Oh, his relatives, he says they live in a small town near the airport called Cumuto. They hang out and drink and get foolish drunk and lime and forget what day it is."

"Can you show us where in the town he may be at?" Dan asked.

"Why?" Fleur asked. "You think he's up to no good, right. Oh lord. What? Not with Miss Susie, no he couldn't."

"We are searching everywhere, and he is a suspect since he is your husband and he's missing." Dan sat on the table and grabbed a Coke.

"Okay. I saw once his father's house, rundown as it was. He didn't know I knew about it. It's in a valley. He father died there," Fleur said wiping tears away. "I'll kill him myself."

"Let's go."

Furness picked up the black cat and they entered Dan's police car. The black cat sat on the rear window ledge and wondered where could this lead now. He listened to all the human conversation he knew Mistress Susan was taken, and they were on their way to get her. He hoped so. He missed her.

Lately even in the day he had visions of different humans and this one in the car with him he sensed was somehow part of it. He hoped the light would shine in his mind soon. Things were too jumbled now but he must find Mistress Susan.

*   *   *

The four unlikely companions pressed east until the pigeon stopped.

"Can we take a break already? C'mon, my wings aren't as large as yours, and I'm getting dizzy"

"Yeah, let's branch it."

"Okay," came the gull's voice from ahead. The gull sat on a nearby house looking for food morsels.

"Hey look a half-eaten chocolate bar on the walk below. You want some?"

"Knock yourself out, gull," Clay answered dryly.

Fletcher was tired but was trying to get his bearings. They had flown into the night, stopped and slept and continued on the first sun. He figured they were more than halfway there.

The falcon came down and rested on a higher branch.

"I can see the Great South Bay from here. It's another quarter sun trip," Princess cawed.

"Oh great, just great. Another quarter sun she's talking in riddles again. My wings feel like I got rocks on them. C'mon Fletcher, you must be tired too," Clay squawked.

"I am, but I keep my beak shut about it. Try to glide like the gull. It's a trick I learned about twelve moons ago."

Max, the gull chirping and chewing on chocolate said, "Yes, come with me and I will show you."

"Stop talking with your beak full. I can't catch my breath up there with you. It's lost, I can't make it. It's no use." Clay perched on a larger branch.

"Yes, you can. You heard Princess; she can see the Great South Bay nearby. It's close. You don't want to be pigeonholed as a quitter?" Fletcher said sarcastically.

"She can see into forever with her eyes and where do you get this stuff? Pigeonholed. It's got to be the television you watch. You know some studies I've heard shows it rots the brain," Clay quipped.

"In your case, it's a physical impossibility," Fletcher answered quickly.

"Very good, very nice. I'm dying here and you're joking."

"Trying to get your mind off your defeatism."

"Okay, okay I'm in. Where now to, which way as if I didn't know." Clay gave up.

"Yes, toward the sun and toward the water. Princess lead on," Fletcher crackled.

With that, Ketvel, the falcon, opened her large wingspan and took off in the direction of the bay.

"Let's go, bird team," Fletcher squawked out on purpose to get Clay's blood boiling.

"Let's go, bird team. Let's go bird team," Clay imitated Fletcher's call. "Let's go on to oblivion. Will somebody please shoot me?"

Clay lifted up as high as he could and followed the other three birds cawing to himself as he did.

*     *     *

The waters around Cat Island were still and calm except for a local fisherman's line penetrating the smooth surface. The weather was perfect for November in the Bahamas. White sand spread out everywhere on the island from north to south. The southern edge mountain rose two hundred feet above sea level.

The white yacht was entering the harbor outside of Arthur's Town when the first mate, Mead, dropped anchor. He was tired and had gotten little sleep on this trip with Mr. Franks. Franks was a hard captain, and the men didn't like him. Mead had another problem. The men were interested in the woman, and this took their mind off their work. She was pretty and helpless, and Franks laid down the law not to touch her in any way; but the men grew restless and talked in inner circles among themselves. Something was brewing about, but with Cat Island in sight it took their mind off the woman to their seamen duties.

The yacht was circling the east side of the island and dock at the most southern tip near the base. Mead spotted some fishermen offshore, but otherwise the waters were empty.

Mead was busy getting the ship ready for docking when he noticed two seamen missing on deck. They were the two men he trusted least and didn't want to hire them, but Franks insisted.

Mead went to their posts but they were not there, so he walked to their bunks. Both were empty. Then he got a sick feeling about the woman. Mead ran to the locked cabin below as fast as he could. Outside he could hear voices and the dog scratching nearby. He opened a closet, and the dog pounced on him. The leather muzzle protected him from being bit, but the dog was large and ran toward the women's cabin door.

The dog's weight hit the door, and it wasn't latched completely so it flew open. On the floor tied up was the woman with the two men stripping off her clothes. The dog instantly hit one of the men with his body pushing him to the ground. The other man reached for his knife to fight Mead. Mead was about to draw his knife when the woman hit the man with her head into his jaw. He fell screaming of pain in his jaw. While both men were down, Mead ran to the woman and freed her and ripped off her gag.

Sam was fighting off the first man when his muzzle loosened and he was able to bark and use his teeth. Sam grabbed the man's ankle and bit down. Something snapped and the man screamed in agony. When the second man came back to his senses, Mead subdued him with a knife.

Libby called Sam off the rapist. Sam ran over to his mistress, and she hugged him and started to cry.

"They were going to rape me. Thank God you came with Sam."

"I was afraid of this, and I'm surprised it didn't happen sooner. Get yourself dressed. I'll talk to Franks."

"No need, Mead." It was Franks and he had his gun in his hand. Libby got a chill up her spine when she saw him. It took all her strength to hold Sam back from attacking Rattel.

The seaman in pain from Sam's bite spoke,

"Mr. Franks, she invited us in, she wanted it."

"You know, you pig, that normally I wouldn't care about a woman, and I would have let you do your deed, but this one is special. She's bait, and I said from the start I want no one fucking touching her. We are near port. You couldn't wait to get to shore to use one of the whores there? I can't fucking have trouble in any part of my plan."

Franks pulled the trigger on the gun, and the first seaman slumped down. He pointed the pistol toward the other seaman.

"Your turn." The man was about to say something when the pistol spit out again and the man fell backward.

"Mead."

"Yes, sir," Mead answered meekly.

"Good job, take the girl to any upper cabin and put the dog on a leash. Get her some food and water. We want her to be presentable at the base." Franks walked out as easily as he came in.

Libby was shook up and followed Mead upstairs to an upper deck room. Sam was close to his mistress on a chain leash.

When Libby got to Franks's cabin, she could see land and for the first time in days, the sun. She drank some water and gave some to Sam who licked at it viciously. She had to escape and get word to Tony, but how? On a desk to her right were pieces of paper and a pen. If only Mead would leave.

"Mead, I want to thank you for your kindness, but I have a terrible headache, can you get me some aspirin?"

Mead liked her and was all too willing to oblige but was afraid to leave her alone.

"Sorry, I can't leave you alone."

"What can I do? I'm tied to a chair and Sam is too. Please." She used her best pleading voice.

"Okay, okay. I'll be right back."

He left, locking the cabin door behind him.

Libby stretched her head to the desk and grabbed a piece of loose paper on the desk and arched her head to her hands. She grabbed the paper and folded it as small as possible. Inching the chair closer, with her mouth she reached for a pen with her tongue hitting the top of the desk. She tasted a foul liquid in her mouth, but it wouldn't deter her. Libby finally grabbed the pen with her teeth and had nowhere to place it but her open blouse, ripped as it was. She dropped it into her cleavage, hoping it would not be seen.

Mead returned with two aspirin and Libby asked to use the bathroom. He consented and she hoped the pen wouldn't fall out when she stood up. It was about four steps to the bathroom and she knew Mead's eyes were on her ass. The two rapists had ripped her skirt up to her hips, and her whole leg shown now. She would use it to her advantage on the way to the bathroom.

In the bathroom, she started to write a note to anyone but she wondered how she would get the note to civilization. Only one way and it would be a hard one but she had to chance it. Libby placed the note in the side of her panties since it was so easy to get to now and returned to Mead.

Franks entered the room and smiled pointing out the porthole.

"Look, Ms. Cassette, Cat Island, the gold mine of the future and you are going to help me get rid of my demons here."

"You are sick, Rattel."

"Maybe but I'll be fucking rich too and no one can stop it. It's all set up. Your boyfriend is going to walk into a trap. Gallo is going to be captured soon and brought here and I will have my final revenge on you and your friends.

"And to top it off, I will have my vengeance on the Mafia Don too."

"How's this all going to happen?" Libby asked sarcastically.

"You will see, you pretty little thing. Too bad, too bad you won't see the ending. We could have had a beautiful relationship but I need you as bait." Rattel smiled.

"Yeah, maybe as one of my nightmares," Libby retorted.

Rattel laughed.

"Let me take you on deck and get some air, you look ashen. We want to keep you beautiful, huh Mead."

"Yes sir, beautiful." Mead looked at Libby.

"Ha ha, you even have Mead smitten. Let's go." Rattel grabbed Libby by the arm, and Mead grabbed Sam's leash.

On deck, Libby could see the coastline, maybe a mile swim or less. She couldn't do it but maybe . . .

Rattel started talking about Cat Island and barked some orders to the crew and took Libby to the side of the ship.

"Beautiful, isn't it?" Rattel beamed.

"Yes, er, Mead, could I pet Sam? I think he's scared."

"Sure, Miss Cassett." Mead looked at her longingly.

Rattel was busy pointing out the island and its coast as Libby reached into her panties to get the note to slip it into Sam's collar.

Rattel reached down to Libby.

"What the fuck you doing?"

"I just wanted to reassure my dog he's okay," Libby said calmly.

"Fucking dog's okay. Why I let you keep him is a mystery. Now your cats, I hate them. Bad luck forever, especially that black devil. Did I tell you I killed the little fuck? Yes, I did and right in the head too, ha, ha, ha. Go ahead, pet your dog and Mead watch her. I have to yell at your fucking stupid crew." He walked away and Libby kneeled down to Sam and hugged him.

She turned to whisper to the dog.

"Sam, you must jump and swim to shore. Go find Tony, find Tony. Go to Tony."

Tears welled up in her eyes; she knew there was a chance he couldn't make it.

"You must, Sam. Find Tony."

The dog knew what mistress Libby was asking, and he didn't think for a second about his life, but what his mistress had charged him with.

Mead had a loose grip on Sam's leash, and Libby was going to make it looser.

"Mead, thank you so much for your help." Libby touched his hand and showed some breasts doing so by bending over Sam.

Mead's eyes lit up, and his mind was not on the leash. Libby grabbed the leash from Mead's hand.

"Go, Sam," Libby yelled out as the dog jumped the rail and dove into the water.

"Swim Sam, swim to shore," Libby yelled out as Rattel ran to the rail with his gun. He fired two shots but missed both times, cursing as he did. The dog was a good swimmer.

"Very sneaky, Miss Cassett. but it will do you no fucking good. Even if the dog makes it to shore, who will find him to help. A fat fucking chance he will make it. You may have killed him anyway. It's a mile to shore." With that he grabbed her and tossed her at Mead.

"Stop thinking about her tits and take her below."

"Yes, sir." Mead grabbed Libby to descend the stairs.

"Please help Sam. Oh god, please," Libby whispered as she cried.

*   *   *

Syps sat in Port of Spain awaiting word from Advil and his two men. His cell phone rang and he flipped it open.

"Yeah, it's me," came the voice of Advil. "They're on the flight going to Nassau. What do you want me to do?"

"Good, let them think they're clear. Get a ticket and take the flight. I can't meet you in Nassau. He knows me by sight, but not you. When you get there take him and the girl to my safe house. I'll give you the address when you get them. When you are set, I'll give you the place to go to drop them off. You will be paid by Mr. Franks."

"Okay."

The phone went dead.

Syps knew Gallo was dangerous but not with the girl in tow. He would be worried about her too much.

The couple sat on the jet together talking about many things. She explained her life to him, and he was telling her about his marriage. Both didn't notice the tall man getting on and walking down the aisle. The tall man noticed them and sat two rows back with two other friends.

The plane took off and the first stop was to be St. Vincent, then on to St. Lucia, San Juan and then Nassau.

It was a usual quiet trip with stopovers that lasted two hours. When the plane set down in St. Vincent, the couple remained on board. The three men also stayed but when the plane touched down in St. Lucia, the couple decided to visit the airport.

Gallo was hungry, and they sat at a bar and ordered drinks. Gallo got a local hamburger while Malena ordered a salad. They sat and talked mainly about what they would do when they got to Nassau.

Gallo couldn't call anybody in the government. Someone had to have told of his whereabouts and since Malena is a target he'd wait till he was sure. His cell phone wasn't working anyway.

Three men joined them in the bar but at a table nearby. Gallo noticed them out of the corner of his eye. They were Caribbean but he didn't know what country but they were on their flight.

Gallo thought he caught the men looking at them, but it could just be natural curiosity.

Gallo and Malena finished their lunch and boarded the plane. He wanted to look these three over again. When they entered, one was very tall and looked like a boxer with a broken nose and an ear misshaped. The other two actually looked alike—maybe cousins—but he noticed one of them staring at Malena. This bothered him since she was a target by her brother. He would be on his guard now with these men.

San Juan, Puerto Rico, came and the aircrew announced a small delay due to a rainstorm in the Bahamas. Malena decided to go to the restroom, and Gallo followed her just in case.

"Are you going in with me?" she asked shyly, but flirting as she did.

"Er, no, just watching your back."

She smiled at him and entered the small bathroom.

As he stood by the bathroom, the three men moved uneasily and gave off signals he had seen from the past. They were up to no good and he or Malena were their mark, probably when we get off the plane in Nassau.

Malena came out and smelled great, and they returned to their seats. Some of the passengers got off the plane during the delay but Malena just wanted to sit.

Her hands he noticed were smooth and when she brushed against him she was soft.

He was starting to get that old feeling again as he did with his wife, Gina, years ago. He looked at her mouth and then her hair. She was very beautiful and even with all that had happened to her, she was optimistic they would succeed.

She noticed his glimpses at her.

"What's up, Gallo?"

"Just thinking about Caesar," He lied.

"You miss that cat very much," She said touching his arm.

"Yes, it's going to be tough going back to New York without him."

"Do you have a nice apartment there in New York?" She looked into his eyes.

"Yes, it's great, but it will be empty without the cat."

"Maybe you'll get another cat," Malena said, coming closer to him.

"Yeah, but not as great as—"

They kissed and the kiss lasted a long minute, both holding each other tightly. He held her for a time and they kissed again. She wanted to hold on to him forever and she buried her head in his shoulder. They talked all the way to Nassau on the plane. Gallo was perhaps in love again, but there was danger ahead on the island—for both of them.

\*　　\*　　\*

The black car came to a halt in the town of Conuto in central Trinidad. The roads were barely roads outside of town and the house Fleur directed them to was located on a half paved road.

Dan parked the car two blocks from the house and signaled his police car behind him to do the same. Furness and Whittier got out and Caesar jumped out and instantly smelled something familiar. It was Mistress Susan.

The cat started to walk briskly toward the smell and the men followed. Dan told Fleur to stay with a policeman in the car.

The three men and two police officers neared the house in question. It was a two-story house made of concrete block that had seen better days. Pieces of the block were missing in the walls and some windows were knocked out. It was big though and Dan told his men to split up.

Furness and Dan went on following the cat while Whittier was told to remain back. Caesar sensed a danger in the house beyond the human scents. It was a dog.

John, almost half asleep, noticed movement outside the window and fired a bullet in that direction.

Cagney yelled down, "What the fuck are you doing. Trying to get us noticed?"

"Someone's here, I saw them out there." John pointed out the window.

"You fucking asshole, let me see." Cagney was nervous.

He saw Dan and Furness running under bushes and opened fire in their direction. Amatt and Lou on the second floor did also, firing at movement in the bush.

The two police officers returned fire, killing Lou on the second floor through a window.

Cagney yelled out to the police, "I'll kill the girl, back off."

Whittier heard the shots, and Cagney's threat and ran toward the house, stopping at Furness's location.

"My daughter, he's going to kill her."

"No, sir. He won't. It's his only edge," Dan yelled.

Furness looked around for Caesar but he lost him in the firefight.

Caesar knew Mistress Susan was on the top floor of the building, and he also noticed a large tree nearby that he could climb. He mounted the tree with ease and an open window was within a jump. He leaped into the window and tried to scent out the area.

The floor was dark with pieces of wood everywhere. Two scents hit him hard but both were intermingled; one was his mistress and the other a strange dog smell. He never smelled this scent before.

As he walked toward the scent, he noticed holes in the floor. He could hear men yelling outside but he paid no mind to the noises, he was on a trail.

Whittier had broken free of Dan and Furness and didn't care about his life but just his child's. He ran off to the left of the house and spotted a doorway. Whittier ran into the door and up a broken stairway, falling twice as he did. Amatt was too busy looking out the window and worrying about the cops to see Whittier's noisy approach. Reaching the second floor, he called out his daughter's name and he heard noises in a nearby room off the stair. He broke into the door and found his daughter tied up and gagged. He reached to her frantically ripping off the gag and ropes. She was crying and hugged him and wouldn't let him go.

Whittier squeezed his daughter, but heard a noise behind him. It was Rogue, the pit bull terrier, growling at both of them.

Whittier knew of this breed and its viciousness and their deadly jaws. He grabbed a loose piece of wood to try to fend off the dog when another sound to the right of the dog stopped him.

Susan yelled excited, "It's Blackie, he's come to save us."

The cat had run through an opening in the wall placing himself between the humans and the dog.

Rogue smiled at the black cat.

"Get away while you can, cat, you can't save them from me."

"Maybe not, but I'll stop you long enough for the humans outside to come here and they will stop you." Caesar spit at the dog.

"The humans, ha, ha, they are just as afraid. No one can beat me as you will see."

As he spoke, he ran for the cat with his mouth ready for snapping bones.

The cat was quicker than him, and ran to one side burying his claws, and digging welts into the dog's side. The dog didn't react to the cat's wounding him but turned on the cat trying to grab at his neck or even a body part.

The black cat swiped once again, this time with accuracy and speed hitting the dog's face and opening a gash near his nose as blood poured out. The dog staggered for a minute getting his bearings.

"Nice move, cat, but do you think your little claws can stop me? You have to do better than that." With that, Rogue quickly moved toward Caesar opening his jaws as he did.

Caesar knew he could scratch this dog all day and it would do no good. He needed a better plan and it dawned on him. He turned tail and ran out of the room and down the hall and into a larger room. The dog followed in a blind rage barking that he had the cat.

Whittier grabbed at his daughter and she cried as he did, "Blackie saved us."

"Let's get out of here, sweetie" Whittier snatched up his daughter and ran for the stairs. Cagney never noticed Amatt was not watching the girl as he was firing into the cop's area.

In the room Caesar ran to, there was an opening in the floor, large enough for a dog. Caesar leaped the opening and turned toward his pursuer. Caesar counted on the dog's rage to not notice the opening. Rogue barked, as he ran not looking anywhere but at his kill. Blood raged in his brain. At the last moment, he saw the hole and tried to leap over it. Rogue managed to leap the hole landing near to Caesar but he was on the edge with one paw dangling. The cat's paw struck again on Rogue's face and blood gushed onto the broken floor. Rogue was scratching for a foothold now on the broken wood floor.

"You're dead, cat." With that, Rogue bit toward his enemy.

The cat once again avoided the jaws of death and moved to his side opening a new gash on the dog's leg.

Caesar leaped onto the side of the dog biting and scratching at a furious pace. The dog couldn't turn but kept trying to turn his neck to get the cat's leg.

The weight of both animals was too much for the old floor and it cracked under the strain. Both animals fell biting and scratching as they did.

Luck was on the cat's side. Caesar hit the next floor but landed on a rotted table hitting his head. The dog was not as fortunate. He hit the floor going through the wood planks and into a crawl space below; some workers years ago had left nails in boxes in the crawl space and nails found Rogue's heart. The dog was dead instantly. Caesar lay still on the table.

All was lost for Cagney. He heard the Whittier's girl voice outside and he cursed under his breath. He must get away and leave the two idiots to fight the cops. John would never notice him leaving since the cops had him pinned down in the front room. As he ran for the rear door to the dank swampland behind the house, he caught the fight and fall of the two animals. He recognized the cat. It was the one Susan had found and Whittier bought to the vet. He had heard of this cat. After the cat chased the dog in the Whittier's rear yard he made inquires. Cagney had hung out in a local bar and heard word of a drug smuggler, one called Syps, who had told people of this famous cat killed by his boss. The cat was described as a demon from hell, who killed rats and attacked his boss, the one-eyed man. This was that cat after all. It had to be the one spoken about by the smuggler. It had to be but they claimed he was dead. Shot by that one-eyed man a month ago now.

This had to be the cat and what a reward he would get bringing this prized cat to the one-eyed man. Cagney could find this Syps, the right-hand man. He knew where to look, especially if he hears the cat's still alive.

Cagney looked out the front window. The cops were still fighting off his men. Good. He ran to the black cat. He was still alive but he saw his dog below the floor. Rogue was dead.

"You got Rogue, you devil cat. The rumors of you are true"

Cagney picked up Caesar and grabbed a sack; placing Caesar into the sack, he lit a match and threw it toward the garbage on the floor.

"This place will go up and all the evidence with it."

He pushed the wood and paper toward some of the other garbage.

"This should cover me."

Cagney ran out of the back door with his precious bundle over his shoulder.

*     *     *

Tony sat on the plane, anxious and nervous. The plane had been late to take off and it made Tony think more of Libby. His mind could picture horrible things being done to her. He was on edge even when the attendant asked for his drink order. He never really drank but now he needed it to calm down.

Simpson on the other hand was as cold as yesterday's cucumber. Good morning here, hello there. It was bothering Tony, the head of the regional DEA office came with only one agent.

It didn't take Tony any time to convince Simpson to go especially when he heard all the facts and with Gallo missing too.

The attendant came back with his drink. She was a full-breasted woman with long black hair. Something all the men on the plane took notice of. Larkin the other agent was as talkative as a sponge. He just sat there reading some magazine. Simpson didn't say much to Tony on the flight except to tell him of their next connection.

"We're going to fly into Nassau and take an island hopper to Eleuthera. We have a base there. It will be easier to operate our search from there. Nassau has too many tourists."

With that, he fell fast asleep dreaming perhaps of little drug plans in his head. Tony downed the Captain Morgan and Coke and asked for another.

The flight landed in Nassau International Airport, and the three men hopped on a two-prop plane with seats children would find small. Tony hit his head several times boarding and sitting.

They landed on the island of Eleuthera and a man met them with an old Japanese car. They drove to a town called Governor's Harbor and went into a white stucco building with no flag outside.

Tony was given coffee and he sat by the office window. There were two agents here receiving some information on computers. Larkin sat down and didn't say a word.

The man who picked them up spoke, "Nice flight?"

"Yeah, yeah," Simpson spit back, annoyed.

"Where's my message I requested from my contact?"

"Sorry, sir. It did come for you today actually." The man looked nervous.

"Good, good. Find anything on the girl?"

"No, sir, not even a whisper from the emails or cells."

"I see. Did you hire up a boat for me?"

"Yes, sir. It's just out in the harbor. It's called Sidney for Sidney Portier. He was born in the Bahamas."

"Yes, I know. We'll Larkin guess we can go now. Bring Messaro."

Tony noticed a strange look in Simpson's eye.

Larkin pulled out his service pistol and fired twice into the agents. Both men's blood splattered on the monitors and the keyboards.

Tony jumped and looked at Simpson.

"Surprised, Messaro? You should be. You think I'd come all the way down here to find your stinking girlfriend. It's you I want. There's a certain person who needs you and he's going to be on the next island within a day.

"Boy you must have a ton of questions running around in your head. Let's just say I sold out to the highest bidder."

"Your men?" Tony looked at the dead agents.

"Que sera, sera, let's go now." Simpson gestured to Larkin and the other man and he pushed Tony out the door to the car.

"And your girlfriend is with my, your old friend. You will see her soon, and don't worry about Gallo either—he will join us all. It's going to be a team meeting, you might say. Ha Ha."

Tony got in the car, and Larkin stepped on the accelerator and steered the old car toward the harbor.

\* \* \*

The ocean at Cat Island was warm and sparkling blue. The breezes from the Atlantic Ocean flowed from the east, washing the coast for the many fishermen. The sun beat down, warming the sands of the white beaches, keeping the terns happy with washed-up food.

In the bay, there was movement far off all the normal fisherman's waters. It was movement in the water by a strange figure paddling toward shore. Exhaustion was in his limbs, and his body asked him to stop, yet his heart told him to continue. He would not quit as long as he was breathing.

The tide, by now, was tormenting him, forcing him side to side and back toward the ocean. Water was in his lungs, and he labored at each breath. He barked, calling for help, but only the sea answered with a moan. He could hear voices. His mistress telling him "Go on Sam, go on," and Caesar, his friend, meowing his encouragement.

He refused to go under. The waves pushed at him, pulled at his legs, and hit him in the face. Then he saw Boeko, the great god of dogs, in front of him, sitting on the shore in the distance.

"Come, my son, you can come to me."

"I am trying, Great One," he barked.

When at last his breath was gone, his legs stood still, and his mind went dark. He thought he heard a strange voice somewhere on the water.

An old fisherman spotted a strange wave to his stern. He turned the wood boat around to investigate. It couldn't be a school of fish—not that kind of movement. As he heard the wave, he thought it a dolphin. It was as big as a dolphin, and sometimes they die of old age and float to the top.

No. It was a brown color with a tail. Couldn't be. It was a dog. He grabbed his big net, and as he approached the animal tried to pick him up with the net. He was too big for the net. The fisherman stripped off his shirt and dove into the water.

The dog wasn't moving, and he grabbed it under its shoulders and lifted him onto his boat. The fisherman couldn't believe it. It was a husky or German shepherd of some kind, out here with no boats or ships around. He couldn't believe it.

The animal was alive but had swallowed much water, so he gave it some CPR he knew for people. The water poured out of the dog's mouth, and he barked a weak bark.

The big brown eyes of the dog opened, and the fisherman was glad.

"Well, dog, I'll take you in to a vet. You swallowed half the ocean, but you're alive. Luck was on your side, dog."

The fisherman turned the boat toward shore as Sam lay still, breathing quickly.

\*   \*   \*

"Can we stop flying? I can't feel my wings anymore." With that, Clay alit on a nearby branch.

"Come on, lazy, we're almost to shoreline," Fletcher yelled back. "You can glide there."

"Glide, glide on what? You have got to be mad. All three of you," Clay answered back.

Max was ahead of Fletcher and Clay while the Princess was way overhead, looking down. Max let out a scream and moved his wings to soar downward.

Fletcher glided over the last row of trees and saw the shore. It was beautiful. The sun glistened over the vast sea before him. The water rushed to the sand, breaking in waves onto the beach. It was peaceful, with no humans to be seen or heard.

Fletcher branched it on a tree and followed with his eyes Max soaring into a pack of gulls. They squawked some gull language, which he didn't understand, and the gulls landed onto the sand. As they talked, Clay arrived, branching it next to him.

"Oh, there's a sight. There is more of him. There is no hope after all."

"Cool it, Clay, we need them to find out about Mistress Libby and Sam and Arthur. Try not to be too insulting."

"Yeah, yeah, I know, but it's a meeting of the mindless over there."

"Calm yourself," Fletcher scolded him.

"Okay, I'm going to fly down and look for some food, I do eat you know."

Max came back with another gull—probably a spokesbird for the group.

"This is Coby Tern Gull. He's the leader of the Great South Bay gulls."

"Glad to meet you, Coby. We were wondering if you had heard about a downed human washing ashore here lately?" Fletcher asked anxiously.

"Yes, yes. The humans found him dead just down this shore. Crackle has it, he was tossed overboard by other humans." Coby indicated with his beak toward the east.

"Can we go there now to see? We think we know this man."

"Yes, but—"

Just as Coby was speaking, Princess alit nearby on a pine tree.

"Fly away, it's a raptor." Coby started to wing it when Fletcher stopped him.

"Don't worry, she's with me."

"She's with you? Can't be. They're killers. They kill everything. Look there's an unsuspecting pigeon eating on the beach. You're dead," Coby cawed out to warn Clay.

Clay heard the noise and flew to the group.

"Who are you?" asked Coby.

"I'm Eleanor Roosevelt," Clay stated calmly.

"Don't pay attention to my bird friend. He likes to joke," Fletcher laughed.

"You four are unlikely friends. It must be very important what you seek," Coby noted.

"What gave you your first clue, Einstein?" Clay chirped.

"Who's Einstein?" Coby asked. "My name is Coby."

"He saved all the birds from extinction," Fletcher quipped. "Let's fly east. Show me the spot."

They all took off towards the east. After flying about halfway up the beach, Coby landed at a spot near a rock jetty that extended into the sea some length.

"His body was found here, by the rocks."

"And we heard his name was Bert. Is this true?" Fletcher asked.

"Seems so, my clutch says so. They heard the humans speaking. He was some big shot with the humans." Coby went on, "My mate, Lulu, overheard it." Coby squawked into the wind, and a female floated in from the west.

"Hello, my name is Lulu."

"And that you are," came the remark from Clay.

"Lulu, this is Fletcher the blue jay, Max our cousin the gull, and this is Eleanor Roosevelt."

Lulu looked at Clay with a strange face but dismissed it.

On any other day, Fletcher would have extended the joke, but he had no time now.

"Lulu, please tell our friends about the day we saw the dead human."

"Oh yes, it was frightful. He was blue in the face, and his body was all broken. The humans gathered him up during the morning sun."

"What did they call him?" Fletcher asked.

"Oh, Bert. Bert Youngmen. I remember, and he was a producer director, whatever that is."

"Anything else they said?" asked Fletcher.

"Something about a woman being missing who was with him? They said she was going with him south to work on something."

"Did they mention her name?" Fletcher was excited.

"Oh, oh I think. It was so hectic here that day. I couldn't get any closer to eat until midsun."

"Missed your clam breakfast, did you?" Clay inserted.

Fletcher gave Clay a stern look.

"Come on, you can remember. Was it a name like Libby?" Fletcher hoped.

"That does sound familiar. It was something like that or Bibby, Sibby. I don't remember."

"There you have it," Coby noted. "Then it was your friend?"

"Yes, it was and she was with him, but where she is now I don't know." Fletcher was sad.

Max asked Lulu, "Was there a mention of a dog and cat?"

"This Bibby had them with her, but that was it," Lulu noted.

"So Sam and Arthur are with Mistress Libby, not to worry. The red cat will take care of himself," Clay quipped.

"Red cat, red cat," Lulu was chirping now, excited.

"Red cat—yes, a red cat," Fletcher said.

Even Coby was bothered. "What's wrong?"

"I never connected it," Lulu chirped. "There has been a report by the deep sea terns that there is a red cat stranded on a human perch in the water. Maybe he's your friend?"

"What, where?" Fletcher asked quickly.

"Let me get the crackle together, and we will find out." Lulu and Coby flew off.

"How long has it been, Fletcher? How many suns since they disappeared?" Clay asked.

"Hard to say, maybe a half moon, don't know. Oh, Great Aves. He must be near death."

"He's dead. You know it," Clay cawed.

Princess flew and alit on a rock.

"Fletcher, can I do something for the red one?"

Fletcher cleared his mind of depression and sadness.

"Yes, you can. Only you and Max can go out that far. Soar to your highest point and find Arthur for me, please. He's on a metal cage of some sort out in the ocean." Fletcher was hopeful.

"If he is there. I will see him. Max. come with me. but don't continue if you can't breathe," Princess said quickly, and Max nodded.

With that, the two birds went aloft with the south sky soaring higher and higher until Fletcher couldn't see them. Fletcher prayed to all the gods.

"Please let him have breath in him yet."

*　　*　　*

The Pacific Rim Airlines jet plane touched down on the landing strip and taxied into the gate. The people exited calmly, but briskly. Some were on vacation and some here for business. Three men followed a couple closely.

After Customs, the couple headed for the nearest coffee shop and sat down. The three men loitered within the airport, awaiting their prey.

Gallo knew they were from Syps. It had to be him since Barbados. It's Rattel that wants him dead.

Gallo told Malena he would grab a map of the Bahamas, and maybe it might shake her memory of the name of the Island. Gallo got up and saw maps of the Bahamas on the counter. He paid for it and walked back to Malena.

"Look. Here's the island group. I'll read the names.

"Abacos? Andros? Bimini? Eleuthera? Harbour Island? Cat Island? Long Island? Eh—"

"Wait, that's it. Cat. Cat Island. That's where they are." Malena's face lit up.

"How ironic. Cat Island."

He read about the island on the map.

"It's known as a hideaway. It's great for fishing and resorts and the highest peak in the Bahamas. Arthur's Town is its capital, and look, Sidney Portier was born there."

"We have to get a plane there, but we have to shake our tail."

"Listen, we're going to go to a taxi stand and take a taxi, but only *I* get into the cab. You will jump out the other side and go back into the airport to get tickets to Cat Island."

Malena was going to object, but Gallo stopped her.

"I will lose them, don't worry."

She kissed him hard on the lips.

"Seems, Mr. Gallo, you have my heart in your hands," she said breathlessly.

"It seems so. How did this happen with all this going on, Malena?"

"It doesn't matter. I am in love with you. So don't get killed like everybody else I love."

"Don't worry, I will get back to you."

They kissed again and left the shop.

They noticed three shadows, and the couple walked outside the airport to a cabstand. It was eighty degrees out and the wind was from the east, whipping Malena's hair and clothes.

"You are beautiful in the sun you know," Gallo noted.

"Come back, Mark."

He hailed a cab, and they both got in. There were four or five cabs in a line, and Malena slipped out of the side door and crouched down to the back of the cab line.

The three men, in their intent to catch a taxi, never noted the pretty legs of Malena passing them on the side of the cabs. Gallo's cab took off, and the three men jumped into a cab to follow.

Marlena was free and, as she saw the two cabs pull away, stood up at the end of the last cab. She walked toward the front doors of the airport to enter when a sharp object was pressed into her spine.

"Miss Valli, please don't make any sudden movements. I have a knife at your back, and I will use it. Please walk to the right toward the hangar at the end of the street. Give me your left hand to my left hand. I will keep the knife into your back as we walk. And we will walk like lovers, yes. Just like you and Gallo were just now."

"Who are you? I saw the three go into the cab," Malena said, shaken.

"Yes, and they did, but Syps didn't just have those three imbeciles follow you. He hired me as insurance. Smart huh. Gallo only noticed the three hit men, but not a businessman traveling between islands. Let's walk now."

The two people walked, and to any onlooker they appeared as a couple in love.

"What do you intend to do?"

"Well, Syps wants you, but Mr. Franks wants you more for himself. Seems he's stuck on you."

"And your name?" Malena asked, trying to get information.

"It's not important, just call me Honey. Ha ha ha."

Gallo knew he could lose these jokers by getting out of the cab into a hotel. They would follow into the hotel, and he would lose them and catch another cab to the airport.

Gallo instructed the cabbie to the nearest large hotel. When the taxi reached the hotel he got out and disappeared into a housekeeping closet on the first floor.

The three men exited the cab when one of the men Advil got a cell phone call.

"Yes, good. We will see you soon." He returned to the other men and they entered the hotel.

They approached the desk and left a note with the concierge and then disappeared into the hotel.

Gallo watched from a slit in the housekeeping closet while they searched for him. When they were out of sight and he was sure he would not be seen, he left the closet and walked briskly into the lobby.

"Mr. Gallo, eh, Mr. Gallo a message for you," came the voice of the concierge.

How did the man know his name? He retrieved it and it read,

We have Malena Valli. If you don't want her dead, join us outside. She couldn't slip away at the rear of cabs.

He felt foolish. No wonder this was easy. She was caught and not by these three. Another one he didn't spot. He walked out the double doors into their hands. He felt stupid.

"Well, Mr. Gallo, did you have enough sightseeing for one day? Come with us. We have an appointment with a one-eyed man who craves your company."

\*     \*     \*

Syps was in Trinidad on the west coast, cleaning up Mr. Franks's affairs. Franks told him he would get away from the Vallis and go away, so he wanted all his money from the local banks. He also told Syps to make sure the Trini police weren't on to anything he had done. Franks wanted to be sure he wasn't being brought up for either the killing of Robie or the gunfight with Gallo at the yacht club.

Syps had spies in the police force, and found out there was no danger on the island. They couldn't find their dick. So Syps had gathered up all Franks's money, which he would get 10 percent, and was ready to shove off when a call came on his cell. It was a strange number from Trinidad.

"Hello, Mr. Syps," came an excited voice.

"Yes, who is this?"

"You don't know me, but I met your men once in Chaguramas, and I know about the one-eyed man." The voice got more excitable. "I have a package for you. I think the one-eyed man would really want."

Syps was curious.

"What package?"

"It goes meow when it talks. Where can I meet you?" The voice was now rushed.

"That animal was killed and—"

"No, no he wasn't. My ex-boss's daughter saved him. Can we not talk on this line? I must see you."

"Okay, okay. Do you know Pietro's Tavern on the road to Chaguramas?"

"Yes, I will meet you there in thirty minutes." The line went dead.

It couldn't be, but they never saw the cat's body or heard of the police finding any evidence of a body.

Syps jumped in his rental car and drove south to the tavern. This he had to see and if it was true, Mr. Franks would want the cat brought to him.

\*     \*     \*

The day of his life-changing project was approaching, and Tom was excited. Dr. Zine had all the necessary tests, and the tubes and the car worked fine. Dr. Z was a genius.

All the investors would arrive soon at their ranch house, which was built up just for this occasion. The Cimbaris would have Alfredo Cimbari with his men. The Vallis would have Eduardo along with his posse including that son-of-a-bitch Franks.

Tom never trusted that lowlife and would keep a close watch on him. Strange as it may seem, his father hadn't called in these past two days—and that was a good thing. He knew his father was interested in the project since it was partly his idea, but he wanted to not hear from him.

Tom made inquiries with his men in Vietnam, and they had said he was on his way to look at yet another Cadillac for his collection. That was days ago, but they got an e-mail from him, saying he was searching out another Cadillac

Just as he sat down to grab a drink, his cell rang. It was Franks.

"Hey, I'm in the harbor and will join you in about two hours. I got a prize with me too." Franks sounded happy.

"What prize?" Tom hated him.

"Oh, something from my past I have to settle. There will be other surprises tomorrow too. Don't worry, it won't interfere with our schedule. All our plans are up to speed."

"Good, keep it that way. Is Eduardo on his way?"

"Yes. He's due to fly into Arthur's Town this afternoon."

"Good. Come on in, we will talk about your surprises."

"Sure, sure." Franks hung up.

As Franks put his cell away, Mead was dragging Libby on deck.

"Hungry, my dear? Here the local entrée is fruit, have some."

"No, I'm not. I think I'm sick." Libby was tired, and after not sleeping very well for days, her eyes were bloodshot and her clothes were dirty and ripped from the attempted rape.

"Hmm, Miss Cassett, you need some new clothes.

"Mead, go out to the nearest village and grab some appropriate garments for our lucky guest. I'd say size 4. Yes, 4. Go, Mead, now."

Mead got into the side boat and sped to shore.

"You see, I want you to be presentable when you die with your boyfriend, Tony, and that bastard, Gallo."

Libby breathed hard at the mention of Tony's name.

"Your eyes show your concern. He's okay for now but in good hands, on his way here, and Gallo too. Ha ha.

"Gallo and his traveling companion, Eduardo's sister, have been caught finally and will be here soon. So you see, we're going to be one happy family. I can't wait for the reunion and my revenge."

His smile turned into a harsh stern glare at her, and his eye stared into her soul.

"You see what your fucking cat did to me? Well, look at it again." With that he removed his patch. The eye was white completely with a scar in the center.

It made her wretch.

"Not so pretty, right? Well, your hero cat is dead. I put a bullet in his fucking head, but your turn for my bullet will come. You will be last. I need to enjoy you first."

Libby choked and spit at him.

Franks slapped her hard, and she fell to the deck.

"Enough foreplay for now, sweetie. Let's get ready for our reunion."

Two men helped her up and handcuffed her to a side rail of the ship.

"There, just sunbathe until Mead gets back. I want to see you in something sexy. Ha ha ha."

\* \* \*

The old fisherman visited the local vet with the dog. The dog was exhausted, but in excellent shape. He left the vet's office and returned to his shack on the water's edge. His friend Darby was coming in from a day of fishing when he saw the dog.

"What you got a pet?" Darby yelled out.

"No, found him in the ocean like a fish. He was almost dead. Vet says he's okay, but just tired. He gave him a shot of something and said go home and let him rest."

"Let me see him." Darby walked from his boat to the shack.

The dog was lying down with his eyes looking very tired.

Darby petted the dog.

"It's been a long time since I had a dog. My Bessie died two years ago, and it's been lonely ever since."

"Why don't you take him? I know nothing about dogs and you love them."

The old fisherman smiled at his friend.

"You're sure. Yeah, he will help me on the boat. Okay. Thanks."

"Oh, here's his medicine. Put it in his food."

Darby picked up the dog and walked to his small house up the coast. He laid the dog on a bed and searched around for food for the dog. He found some meat he had in the refrigerator, which would be nourishing. The dog loved it and wolfed the meat down.

As the dog ate, Darby noticed a collar.

"Do you have an owner?"

Darby removed the soiled leather collar. There was no tag—just a collar. The ring that held the nametag was gone. The collar had an opening and a piece of wet paper fell to the floor. After carefully opening it, it read:

> This is my dog, Sam. Please get him to Tony Massaro, NY.
> I am being held on a ship at Cat Island. Contact police.

There was more but the ocean water had washed some of it. Darby retrieved his magnifying glass to read the rest. Scribbling, but as he scanned the paper a word sent a chill up his spine. On the note read:

> Frank Rattel.

And that's all he could read. That was the sick nut who worked with that group in the south who built that labyrinth. He didn't know what to do. This Tony Massaro, who was the dog's owner, what was his connection? Darby sat and looked at the dog.

"Sam, your master is trapped on a ship with a madman. What am I to do?"

Sam looked up at the fisherman with sad eyes and fell fast asleep.

*     *     *

The pigeon was restless.

"If he's been on the sea all this time, he's got to be dead."

"Shut it, Clay," Fletcher cawed and walked onto another rock. He watched as the gulls flew over the eternal sea.

Fletcher could hear human cars in the distance going the speed of hawks. Humans always were going somewhere, but did they ever find what they were looking for? He couldn't care now. All his friends were in danger, and if Clay was right, maybe Arthur was dead. He couldn't think that way. He would do anything to save the cat and Caesar would want him to.

Fletcher thought about the happy times outside Sam's house and everybody laughing at the clumsy cat Arthur. Caesar had found him as a kitten wandering the human debris looking for food, and adopted him on the spot.

Arthur adored Caesar and would do anything for him. It was this love for Caesar, Fletcher hoped, that would keep the cat alive.

The sea rushed to the shore and slammed into the ground calling out to the world as each wave came and went.

Fletcher fell into a daze staring at the sea as it came and went. He never heard Max's call.

"*Caw, caw, caw.* Fletch, we found him, Fletch."

Clay was speaking,

"Hey, come out of your dream, blue, it's the gull."

Max alit onto the rocks by the shore. Lulu and Coby flew to the group.

"We saw him. Princess spotted him. You were right, Lulu, he's on a noisy perch, and he's lying still. We called out his name, but he didn't answer."

"He's dead," Clay chirped.

"Keep your beak motionless, Clay," Fletcher said in a loud chirp.

"Where's Princess?"

"Oh, she's out there gliding over him. Look can you see her?"

"No, no too far for these eyes, but how do we get him? We can't pick him up and bring him here. We need human help."

"No, no, no. They kill everything," Clay chirped again.

"Not always. We can't get him here nor help him if he's sick. We got to somehow get them to help him."

Max looked at Fletcher.

"That's going to be tough. They won't go out of their way for a cat and how do birds bring humans here to get him?"

Fletcher thought about all the angles.

Clay started his cynical thought pattern.

"Yeah, maybe those fisherman will think he's a tuna and take him in their net after we show them."

Fletcher loved Clay,

"You see, with your little pigeon brain you came up with the solution."

"I did?" Clay looked at Fletcher questioning his brilliance.

Fletcher motioned Max with his wing.

"Why not guide fishermen boats to that perch? If they see him they just might save him."

"And how do you propose we do this?" Clay cawed.

"You will do it, with me," Fletcher answered.

"Now I know you've been picking on those red berries again by old man Lockwood's house," Clay chirped. "I can't fly that far without perching," Clay squawked.

"Yes, you can. Your great ancestors did it across great areas to bring messages. I was told this by my sire," Fletcher noted.

"Yeah, and your father was berry witted too."

"You have that in you, Clay. It's in your wings to do it," Fletcher quipped.

"Yeah, where is it?" Clay looked around himself.

"Wait, I have a plan. Lulu, how many boats are out here in the morning?"

Lulu thought a moment, "The sea is full of them like the fish. Are you and Eleanor Roosevelt going to fly out on the sea?"

Fletcher looked at Clay with a wry glance.

"Good. We are going fishing for fishermen. All of us, in the morning."

Fletcher sat on the rocks.

"Max, go get Princess. The sun is almost down. We can't do anything now. We'll fly out in the morning."

"Fly, fly where? Yeah, we'll fly, but into the sea, and the fish will eat us. You're crazy," Clay said as he sat on a pointed rock. "Ouch. Even the rocks are annoying. How did I get my wings into this one!"

*   *   *

Pietro Restaurant was a hangout for drug dealers, smugglers, and pimps. It was within a block of the sea, and fishermen would come for lunch or dinner after a good day's catch. A disheveled man entered the restaurant with a burlap bundle and scanned the tables. He looked anxious and uneasy with his package.

There were outside tables, and the man entered the porch. He spotted his quest and sat down besides the man.

"Here's the package I told you about." He opened the burlap covering, and in it was a cat in a cage. The cat was asleep. There was no doubt as to the cat's identity.

"How much?" the other man asked.

"Ten thousand U.S., I have to disappear."

"You realize I don't have that with me."

"Yes, yes, but where and how?" The disheveled man was nervous.

"Let's go. Follow me to my car."

They both got up and walked to a graveled lot alongside the restaurant.

"I have money in my car. Put the cat down by my car and I will get the cash."

The man walked to his car on the edge of the lot by the trees. The other man placed the cat on the edge of the grass and awaited his money.

"What's your name so I can tell the one-eyed man who to thank?"

"Oh, the name's Cagney."

"Okay." The man pulled out a gun and it spat twice.

Cagney's face was full of surprise and then dread. He fell to the ground like a stone.

The man unscrewed his silencer and retrieved the cat. He turned to see if all was quiet and if anyone had seen or heard anything. He placed the package in his car and drove off to the docks. *Won't Mr. Franks be surprised when I get to Cat Island?*

\* \* \*

The yacht docked at the nearby pier as Tom overlooked the beach from the ranch. Two people were led off the yacht with their hands bound with plastic handcuffs. Behind them was a huge man. This was the man Syps told him about. His hands were bigger than his head. Two other mercenaries followed each holding their captive by the arm. The man Tom knew was Honey. He was a hired killer.

Tom motioned them his way and the big man arrived first.

"Here's the two Mr. Franks wanted." His voice matched his size.

"Bring them into the house. Mr. Franks hasn't arrived yet. He's due within the day."

"Once these two are in the house my job is done, and I expect to get my money now." The big man held onto the girl captive's arm as he motioned the other man to bring the man captive into the house.

"Well, your contract is not with me, it's with Mr. Franks. Have a drink and something to eat and he will be here soon." Tom hoped he was convincing.

"Fucking shit. I don't want to hang around waiting for someone, fuck." The big man grabbed the girl's arm and led her into the house.

Tom followed behind and offered them rum and cokes. They sat down and said nothing but drank the glasses dry.

The captive man spoke, "Can we have a drink too? It's been a long trip."

"Are you Gallo?" Tom asked as he got the two drinks.

"Yes, in the flesh."

"And this must be Eduardo's sister, Malena." Tom handed her a glass.

"Yes, I am. How is my murderous brother?"

"He's well. He will be here soon too. He traveled to New York to settle some affairs with our other partner."

"Hey, how about the handcuffs? Where could I run to?" Gallo asked as calmly as he could.

The big man answered, "No fucking way. Not until my package is delivered."

Gallo looked at Tom, who was the only civilized man in the room and wanted some answers.

"So tell me, eh, what's your name?"

"Tom, just Tom for you."

"Tom, what the hell are you doing here? That sick Rattel is in league with you? Smuggling drugs perhaps?"

"I'd shut up if I was you." One of the mercenaries slapped Gallo hard across the face.

Tom stood up.

"That's no way to treat our guest. Since he will not live much longer, I will indulge him."

"You ever hear of a coalition or limited liability company?" Tom smiled at the joke.

"Yeah so what?" Gallo looked at Malena. Maybe this will buy some time or information.

"We formed one here and in two days all parties will be here to witness our ribbon cutting of our new venture. A venture no one could believe exists. Never again to be harassed by the Coast Guard or the DEA. A genius invented it, and we built it and, gentleman and lady, it is perfect. No detection, no by-products, no evidence-just water. Ha ha ha."

The big man was getting annoyed.

"Hey, this is fucking enough, give me the money now."

Tom was about to answer when a familiar voice came walking into the house. The room smelled of death and death greeted everyone who met him.

"You found my friend, Gallo. It's been a long time policeman since we met." He turned toward Malena, "And, Malena, my love, did you miss me?" He smiled that sick smile Gallo had remembered from months ago.

Mead, the first mate, entered with another captive, it was Libby. He threw her down onto the couch.

"Here she is Mr. Franks, all dolled up."

Mead, in his sick taste, had brought Libby a short skirt and small tank top. They barely fit her.

"You look great, my dear. Oh, let me introduce my other guests. You know Gallo, but you don't know Malena, my other love. Sorry, my dear, but Malena and I are going to be engaged soon."

Malena looked at him in disgust.

"Never in your dreams."

"Your brother, Eduardo, wants you dead. You're a danger to him. I would expect some gratitude from you since I am your protector."

Gallo annoyed with Rattel, spoke up, "What the hell is all this, and why are we still alive?"

"Very good, Gallo, I want you to witness my complete revenge on you and your friends. That fucking black cat is dead and your friend from Brooklyn in on his way. Soon Gallo all your questions will be answered."

The big man was tired of all this shit.

"Give me my money so I can leave this fucking place."

"Oh yes, Syps hired you to capture Gallo and Malena, and you did a good job too. I have your payment in my bag. Let me get them."

Rattel moved over to a large brown leather case he brought in. The big man and his men were salivating at the thought of the money. They moved closer to Rattel, and Gallo grabbed Malena's arm and motioned her to move away. Libby noticed Gallo's movement and braced herself.

Rattel came out of the case with his Browning pistol and fired four shots, one into each man. The two in the rear fell dead but the big man was still alive and reached for Rattel's neck. Rattel moved quickly to his left and fired two more shots into the big man. He fell cursing Rattel. Honey looked at Rattel surprisingly as he fell to the floor.

"Well, now that payments have been made, Mead, get those pieces of shit out of here.

So, Tom, when are our benefactors coming?"

Tom was a little shocked by the killings, but gained his composure.

"Tomorrow. I got Dr. Z prepped for a walk through with them."

"Good, good. Meantime, Gallo, you and your two girls can be our guests for the night. Mead, take them to that secure cellar room and take off their handcuffs. I want them to be comfortable before their impending death.

"Malena, you will not die if you will come with me."

Malena turned as she was being led out.

"I choose death."

"Fucking suit yourself," Rattel yelled out.

Tom turned to Rattel, "Why this bullshit? We got bigger fish to fry. Doesn't Eduardo want to cut out the Cimbaris from this? He's spent a ton of money to get this away from them."

"Don't worry. He is icing on the cake. Eduardo thinks he's coming to kill the Mafia and me, but I have an ace up my sleeve. He thinks by telling the Mafia about me, he will get it all. Neither Alfredo Cimbari or Eduardo know what's going to happen tomorrow.

"The Italians think they are making a deal with Eduardo, and Eduardo thinks he can kill me and you and grab it all. I see his deal. He's playing both sides, against you and the Italians. Greedy fuck."

"Should be an interesting day."

*　*　*

The ocean whipped its waves against the rock and outcroppings of the island. The wind called out day's past as fishing boats came in with their catch. It was almost four o'clock when the boat with four men approached the dock at Arthur's Town.

None of the fishing boats noticed the men and their captive. The captive was led to a nearby bar and drinks were ordered. The captive sat staring at one of the men.

"Well, Tony, what did you expect? I can't live any kind of life on a DEA salary. Where did you think I got the money for that house?"

Tony glared at the man.

"I heard your wife was wealthy."

"Yes, she was but I have expensive taste, and her money wasn't enough."

"So you were the one who led Gallo into getting caught. You knew his every move."

Simpson smiled.

"What are friends for anyway."

"And now?" Tony asked, looking around.

"Ah well, we are on our way to join our friends and partners tomorrow. Your friends are going to be history, and me, I will have one of the pieces of the pie."

Tony looked around, scooping out every detail. No one in the bar looked even interested in their conversation.

Simpson turned to one of the men. He was dressed in dark clothing and had a Southern United States accent.

"Go look for a good fishing boat. The one we have is fucking no good. We barely made it here."

The man got up and left the bar.

Tony turned to Simpson.

"If you made a deal with Rattel, forget it. He's the lowest of the low."

Simpson laughed.

"I didn't make any deal with that fuck. He thinks I'm on his side. The Cimbaris want him dead, and thanks to you and your friends hurting their little drug deal months ago, he's a big liability to them. He knows too much. In fact, Rattel is going to get a big surprise. Ha ha ha. You're just part of the whole setup."

Tony looked at Simpson with disgust.

\*   \*   \*

Syps reached Antigua and docked at St. Johns—its capital. The yacht needed fuel, and he needed to take a break with food and drink. He walked from the pier to the main street, and in an open mall was a restaurant where he could rest for a couple of hours. The trip to Cat Island would be about another day and a half, and he wanted to make it for the big meeting with the Vallis and the Italians.

The cat carrier he bought from a stop in Grenada was half broken but it would hold the cat. The cat made no sounds during the trip, and Syps assumed he was still out from his fall. The cat had taken on a pit bull and lived according to that asshole Cagney. It was amazing to him, but Syps couldn't wait till Mr. Franks saw the cat. *He'll go crazy, and he'll give me a bonus.*

The cat was still dreaming, and he walked in a fog. Clouds were everywhere, and a sense of well-being and joy surrounded him. He sensed a divine presence.

It was Enew, the cat god, sitting on a white rug. His fur coat was white and everything surrounding him was white. A tall man in robes approached and caressed Enew's head. Enew responded to the man's hand. He could feel great love here, a love he never felt before. It put him at ease. A brilliant light beamed from the man's eyes and looked into the cat's eyes and all his fears and misgivings were gone. He felt at peace for the first time in a long time. The man left as quickly as he arrived. He wished the man had stayed. This was heaven, and he was dead.

Just then, a familiar voice came from behind. It was Simmark, his ancestor. The Great Simmark he had spoken to before.

"You are not dead."

Enew then spoke. It was a voice as quiet and calm as he could imagine.

"Your life is not at end. Oh, great ratter. You are to continue to help others. You have saved many lives up to now but your greatest challenge is to save human life like your predecessor Simmark. You must make a choice. Your life or the life of someone you love. It is your choice, only you can decide."

He stood in shock. He was to have the fate of someone in his decision.

"You have great courage, and I think you will choose correctly." Enew then disappeared and Simmark smiled at him.

"Don't be questioning the will of Enew, he will protect you always."

"And the man who came in and vanished? I never felt that before. He looked into my soul," Caesar asked.

"He is who is. He is love." Simmark's eyes shined as he spoke. Simmark started to fade out and his mind started to drift and his eyes became foggy. Clouds came and went pushing him into different territories. He saw many cats lying by water's edge.

He recognized none but they saw him and called out his name. He tried to move, but couldn't. Clouds came again and he was starting to feel his paws. He awoke from his dreams.

At first, he smelled fish and was instantly hungry, but his head hurt badly. Then he remembered the fight with the dog. He was lucky he wasn't killed too, but the dog must have fallen farther than him through the man's floor.

He tried to move out of the box he was in but it held firm. A gate where he could see through allowed him a perspective of the surroundings. He was on a man's boat on the sea. Strange aromas assaulted his nose but there was a familiar smell nearby he couldn't place.

He tried to strain his body against the box, but it wouldn't give. He lay down and tried to soothe his head and thought about his life, his life he couldn't remember.

He wondered how Mistress Susan was and if she was safe. His head throbbed so he let it down softly onto his paws. He would think harder to remember his life.

Enew told him to be courageous and take care of someone he loved. How can he save someone if he doesn't even know who it is?

\* \* \*

Dr. Zine was beside himself. He realized now, after all these months, what these men were going to use his invention for. Not for humanitarian purposes or a new means of travel but for drug trafficking.

At first, he wanted revenge on the U.S. for their pushing him aside and not giving his ideas a chance. Ten years ago when he was on the commission to investigate alternate energy sources he was at the top of his form, but now revenge was his driving force.

*Revenge. Ha. The U.S. doesn't even know about me, just these gangsters. I've been a fool, an ass.*

He was deliberating his options when fate played into his hands.

"Dr. Z," Tom called him, "here's some guests for your entertainment."

Tom and two big men with guns led in a man and two women.

"This is Mr. Gallo and Malena Valli and Libby Cassett. They will be our guests for the night and witness the maiden voyage of our enterprise.

Tom motioned to the two men to bring them into the back lab room behind the main laboratory. Gallo and the women were locked into the room, and Tom smiled. It was a steel door, and the only opening was a slit in the door.

"Dr. Z, you can keep them company until tomorrow." With that, Tom and the two men left.

Gallo called out to the doctor.

"What's this enterprise he's talking about?"

"I'm afraid it's serious. I've invented a means to travel great distances on basically water and some additives."

The doctor sat down on a stool and spoke toward the door.

"I was mad at the commission established by the president years ago to investigate clean forms of travel. The top executives refused my invention saying it was too expensive and it would never work; yet, they were wrong."

"Doctor, is it possible you can get the key to get us out?" Gallo yelled through the door.

"Yes, yes maybe. They have several keys around here, maybe I can."

"Doctor, don't do it now, wait until the night when they will be off guard."

"Yes, yes, I will. I'm sorry, very sorry for any stupid revenge. Are you with the U.S. government?"

"Yes, Doctor, I am with the DEA, and the one women here is the sister of Eduardo Valli and the other is a friend of mine. They mean to kill us, Doctor, after their big meeting here." Gallo looked at Libby, she was exhausted and frightened.

"I will help you."

"Doctor"—Gallo was curious—"what is the invention?"

"It's all through nature. I developed super blue green algae, one that emits hydrogen in a stabilized environment. I harness the hydrogen along with methane byproduct and developed a canister in simple terms to insert into my traveling railroad car. The car is not very big now, but it could be made bigger. Yes bigger, to house many people."

Gallo was intrigued.

"But, Doctor, don't you need a spark or a match to light it?"

"Ha ha. A match—that is very good young man. Now are you wearing a watch?"

Gallo was about to laugh.

"Yeah, so?"

"Is it a quartz watch?" The doctor was amused; he finally could share his idea.

"Yes, it is. So what?" Gallo said, questioning.

"Quartz, my son, is the most abundant mineral on the planet. It's the sand on the beach. It's in all our rocks and mountains. It's even on your girlfriend's finger or neck, but there's one thing about quartz that's important. When a certain amount of pressure is applied to a quartz gem, it generates an electrical charge. This is my idea. In crude terms, I developed a match as you said in my hydrogen canister using quartz. It pulses continuously giving the spark for the fuel to ignite and push my car."

"Doctor, that's amazing. You have to get this to the right people to develop it further." Gallo tried to encourage him.

"I was with the right people, but they thought the canister was too small to make it last for long trips like from New York to Washington or Florida."

"Were they right, Doctor?" Gallo asked.

"To a degree. I surmounted this problem with the help of your captors."

"How?"

"I developed a rail system that fed the hydrogen mixture to the canister as it traveled on the rail. It is fed continuously through its connection in the rail. The problem was solved. Have a rail system like this and you can have this rail from California to New York. Think of it."

"And the Mafia finished all this along with the Vallis?" Gallo asked.

"Yes, and don't forget the Vietnamese connection too. They built an underground rail system for delivery that was the size of a small car. It spans now from here to Miami, and they are building it farther, maybe all the way to New York City."

Gallo was astounded by the genius of it all, yet the enormity.

"How is all this algae not noticed?"

"That's the genius of the American Mafia. They are building restaurants on the East Coast and called them Sandcastles and as a sales gimmick built immense greenhouses adjacent to each restaurant so the people who eat there can marvel that the Sandcastles, even though fast food, can return something to the environment. Once more are established up the coast, the rail car can visit each one underground and get fed with my hydrogen mixture."

"Let me guess, you are growing in each location, the blue green algae as per your special specifications." Gallo smiled. It was sweet. Right under everybody's nose.

"Yes, that's it. I'm sorry I ever thought of this idea."

"No, Doctor, it's not you. It's everybody's else's stupidity and greed that got you here."

Gallo sat down on the table while Malena and Libby sat on chairs, both amazed at the story they just heard.

Trillions of dollars could be made here using the doctor's car for transporting drugs into each major city at their fast food locations right where everyone eats and basks in the sea. Suddenly, Gallo wanted to sleep a long time. He put his head in his hands and called out.

"Doctor, let me know when you are trying to get the key."

"I will, I will," came the disappointed voice.

\*      \*      \*

The old man lifted his coffeepot and lit his antique stove with a match. He took out some coffee and loaded it into the pot, looking out his window as he did.

He could see his boat and thought of days past with his wife. She was a good woman who settled here with him. Not expecting too much, she lived an easy life with him. Children never came, but they did have each other. She was gone now, and he had no one to talk to. Oh, he had his friends, the other fisherman, but it wasn't the same as a wife of thirty years. The dog moved in his bed.

"Hey, dog or Sam, are you okay? You must have slept over a day."

The dog looked up at the human. A sun he had slept. Was Mistress Libby okay? he wondered.

The human gave him some food. It wasn't his usual, but it tasted better than ever.

"I got to go down to the boat to check some things. You stay here." The old man left with his coffee and walked to his dock.

Sam investigated his surroundings. It was a big room he was in, and there were two rooms off it. A stair went up to the second level—perhaps where the man slept. Sam peered out the door that the man left ajar. The sea was not that far away. A river from the higher mountainous area off the left dropped off sharply into the ocean, and Sam noticed some birds, mostly gulls of some type, floating about the water's edge.

He thought of Fletcher and Max. They must think him dead. So much has happened since he last saw Caesar. He wondered where that cat was.

A man approached the old fisherman and he had an American Southern accent.

"How much to rent the boat?" He lit a cigarette as he talked.

"Not for hire, thanks for asking though."

"Any other boats around here now?" the American asked.

"No there all out fishing today. I took a day off."

"Okay, okay, thanks." The American walked away but only down the empty pier, and dialed a cell phone.

After a conversation, he returned to the old man.

"What's your name?

"It's Darby."

"Well, Darby, it's your lucky day, you will make three thousand American dollars today. I want to buy the boat."

"I told you. It's not for hire or sale. It's my life. I couldn't live without it."

"Out of your mouth comes the answer." The American pulled out a gun and pointed it toward the old man. He motioned the old man toward the house.

"Are you crazy? You can't do this," Darby yelled out.

"Shut up. Go toward that river. I want it to be an accident. It will look like you fell and hit your head and drowned."

The American really never saw it coming. When his back was toward the house, the dog hit him hard. The dog's teeth grabbed for the man's neck. They both fell tumbling as they did into the river's inlet. The water swallowed both of them, and the tide of the river pushed them out to the sea.

Darby could only see the dog biting at the man's neck, and then they both disappeared into the open ocean.

Three men approached as Darby was blessing the dog.

"Where's Lou, old man?"

"He's dead."

Simpson hit Darby with the pistol across his face.

"You fuck. How could you have taken him?"

"It wasn't me. It was the bravest thing I've ever seen. It was a dog."

"A dog? You're lying." Simpson grabbed Darby and motioned to Larkin to grab Tony.

"Let's get on the boat now."

Darby and Tony were locked into the cabin while Simpson steered the boat south.

Darby introduced himself.

"I'm Darby Orderay. I'm a fisherman here."

"I'm Tony Messaro, and they mean to kill us all."

"Does this have to do with the south of here, with the tunnel?"

"Don't know, but it's a man called Frank Rattel, kidnapped my fiancé and animals, a cat and a dog."

Darby remembered the dog,

"Did you say dog? A big husky type or German shepherd?"

"Yes, why?"

"That's it, Tony's your name."

"Your dog was with me these past days. I fed him, and he just saved my life from that big man."

"Where is he?"

"I hope alive. They both went under out in the ocean. I'm sorry."

Tony was about to weep. His dog, he was so close to seeing him.

"Oh god." Tony put his head in his hands.

"Oh god, Sam"

Darby put his hand on Tony's back.

"He was very brave. He saved me."

Tony looked at the old fisherman.

"I know. I just wish he was here with me."

*    *    *

Furness and his cousin, Dan Harvey, were disgusted. All their leads were gone. Cagney had disappeared along with Caesar. The Whittier girl was safe with her father, but it was a dead end. Susan Whittier was upset at the loss of her cat. Her father tried to explain, but the young girl was despondent.

Furness and Dan sat in the police station, discussing their options when one of the police officers came rushing in.

"We found Cagney. He's dead."

"Where?" Dan asked.

"At a local bar on the road to Chaguaramas."

"Let's go."

The men jumped in a police car and sped to the scene.

The police had the body in the coroner's truck when they arrived. His body had two bullets in it, direct shots to the heart. The local barflys were very curious in the parking lot at Pietro Restaurant, so they walked away from the scene and talked at the truck.

Cagney's body was there at least three days. The smell was horrific.

"Did he have anything on him?" Furness asked.

"Yes, these papers." The police handed them to Dan.

There was a cell phone number and a name Syps.

Dan called out to his sergeant.

"Check this name and number now." The sergeant nodded and entered his car.

"What the hell was Cagney doing here?"

He had opportunity to leave the country. He could have hopped a boat and disappeared. Something kept him here and to this place. Makes no sense. Dan shook his head.

Furness thought about the name Syps. He thought he heard it before.

The sergeant approached.

"Lieutenant, we have an address on Syps."

The body of Cagney went on to the medical examiner while they continued onto Syps apartment in Port of Spain.

Syps's apartment was a mess. There were papers everywhere and stacks of maps, but only sea line maps of the Caribbean along with the Bahamas.

Furness searched for something to give him a clue. He was nervous for his friends. He had not heard from Gallo or Tony or Libby in at least two weeks. He was praying for an answer when one stared at him.

"Why does he have maps of the Bahamas?"

"He has a yacht according to this, Furness," Dan answered.

Dan held up registration papers that were Colombian registration papers for a yacht.

"Maybe two yachts."

"Yachts, why, and what about Cagney?"

"Maybe Cagney was hitching a ride and it went bad," Dan mused.

"No, no. It's more than that. Look at the Bahamas map. There's an island with pen marks on it."

There were several pen marks on the map of Cat Island.

"And it's on the south of the island."

Furness's back started to chill.

"Dan look at the name scratched on the side of the map."

"Mr. Franks."

Furness got that old feeling.

"We got to go there. That has all the answers."

"I have no jurisdiction there," Dan yelled. "We can't just go there like that."

"I'm telling you Cagney was killed for a reason, and the answer to my friend's fate is there along with the cat. I know it."

Dan looked at his cousin and knew this was serious.

"Okay, but I got to get the local police involved."

"Let's go."

*     *     *

He dragged himself onshore. His legs felt weak, and he fell down from exhaustion. Swimming against the tide and on to the beach was painful. The man he jumped on was dead, hitting his head in their fight on a rock. They were both washed out to sea. He clung to the body until the tide hit them. It was a laborious swim, and he was still tired from his last ocean swim, but this was a much shorter distance.

He had just hit the sand when he heard voices—very faint human voices. It sounded like his master. His ears stood up and strained to listen. It was his master with other voices.

He willed his body up off the wet sand and in the direction of the humans. He reached the area too late; the humans were gone at sea and out of swimming range. He paced up and down and decided to follow the direction of the boat toward the afternoon sun.

Sam knew he would somehow find his master and mistress. He sensed it.

*     *     *

Syps tried calling Rattel on his cell, but it had no service at sea. He was approaching Cat Island when a storm came up. The yacht was caught in a vortex that he had to steer out of.

The closest island was Long Island in the Bahamas, and he decided to wait there until the weather got better. His captive was still quiet in the cage, and it was just as well. The cat was the devil himself, taking on a pit pull, as Cagney had said. Rattel told him about this black cat and his eye the cat took from him.

Rattel told it with deep hatred, almost as if the cat was a human and went after him. Syps steered the yacht toward a pier on Long Island's south coast. It looked harmless enough, so he docked the yacht and walked into the beach bar and hit the john for a piss.

Syps tried Rattel again on his cell, but to no avail. The cell phone service was shut, and he would first wait until he got to Cat Island to call him.

Two men sat at the bar, eyeing the yacht through the window. It would be a good mark for a sale on the black market. Maybe they could get two thousand American dollars. The two men sat at the bar and talked for a while but then disappeared onto the beach. Syps paid no attention to them as he sipped his beer.

The tropical storm was almost blown out, and Syps had one more beer before returning to the yacht. He untied the boat and steered it north to Cat Island.

He did not pay attention to his new boarders down below. They would wait until the yacht was well offshore before taking the boat. It was going to be easy, like picking apples, so they thought.

\*   \*   \*

Cat Island gleamed in the sun. It was a perfect hideaway for honeymooners or just people trying to rest their souls. The sea washed onto white beautiful sand with secluded beach coves. This is what Arthur Catt, the pirate, saw when he landed for the first time and called it his home, hence the name of the island.

At the highpoint of the island called Mount Alvernia stands a monastery, the Hermitage. An architect name Jerome Hawkes traveled many of the islands in the Bahamas and designed and built many church structures, but his most famous is on the highest point of the Bahamas in Cat Island. He settled down and became an Anglican priest where he repaired churches throughout the Caribbean. His greatest love was his Hermitage where he carved the Stations of the Cross on the stone steps in the climb up Mount Alvernia to the monastery. He lived there for twenty years and died in the monastery. This was the island of choice for the drug coalition.

It was well beyond five in the afternoon when Simpson docked the boat off Cat Island's south end by the ranch house Tom had bought.

Tom was outside to greet them. The three men got out and Tom led them into the ranch.

Simpson smiled as he entered the plantation type ranch house.

"Hey, where's the drinks, Rattel?"

Rattel smiled back.

"You made it. Here, grab a glass, your choice."

"Any trouble."

"We lost one man to a pesky dog," Simpson said offhandedly as he poured himself a scotch. "He's dead too."

"A dog. Ha ha." Rattel then saw Tony.

"Well, well the killer of Johnny Amisi. And your dog who was my traveling partner coming here is dead, good. Soon all of you fucking people who caused my problems will be dead."

"Where's Libby?" Tony yelled at Rattel.

"She's okay. She's with your friend Gallo in the other building. You will soon be visiting with her for all eternity."

"Who's this?"

"Some fisherman. We took his boat," Simpson snickered.

Rattel motioned to the two men to take them away.

"Your lucky day, fisherman."

Simpson sat on the sofa and smiled.

"So we going to see all the boys soon, what tomorrow?"

"Yes, yes, and it will be great." Tom couldn't wait.

Rattel grabbed his gun, started to twirl it, and sat down.

"So you been leading the Cimbaris on a string, I hope." Rattel smiled.

"Of course. They think I want you dead, but it's them I want out of it."

"And Eduardo, what's his game?" Rattel asked as he sipped his drink.

"I think he's on your side. They want you to still be their head man down here." Simpson lit a cigarette and took a long drag.

"I see, and who is suppose to kill me, and maybe Tom here too?"

"One of Eduardo's guys. I don't know." Simpson was starting to get nervous. Rattel wasn't a stupid person. "I'll help you with the Vallis."

"Really." Rattel stopped twirling the pistol and pointed it toward Simpson.

Tom sat down, intrigued with the conversation.

"Are they mad? My father started this all. It was his baby. They can't just take it all from me."

Simpson looked at Tom.

"Your father, has he called you lately?"

Tom started to get ashen.

"He's out looking for antique cars. He's—"

"Son of a bitch. They didn't. Who did it? Who? I'll kill them all."

Simpson looked at Rattel.

"It was the Vallis and the Cimbaris. They don't want partners in this."

Simpson looked at Rattel.

"You think I'd come here and tell you this if I weren't on your side."

Rattel twirled the pistol in his hand again.

"I don't believe you. You've been too close to the boys. I know them. They offered you fucking big bucks to take me down. It ain't happening."

"The Vallis want both Tom and me out. Less mess that way and, you, you're their guy."

Simpson knew his speech was not convincing. He had to make a move quick. He would drop his cigarette and grab his gun.

Before Simpson could act, Rattel's gun spat twice. Both bullets entered Simpson's heart. He was dead instantly.

"Son of a fucking bitch. He was in on it," Tom yelled.

"Yes, he was, the fuck. Get the boys to bury the body with the other bodies. Tell them to dig a bigger hole. There will be more."

*   *   *

The Great South Bay had many fishing boats at sea early that morning. It was December and the fish were sparse, but these fishermen were there many years before harvesting their catch for sale in the winter.

The water was clear, and the winter sun was crisp. It was about eight in the morning when a fisherman noticed a hawk flying overhead. This wouldn't have been unusual but right behind the hawk at a lower altitude was a gull. They traveled at exactly the same location and speed.

The next sight was more astonishing. A blue jay and then behind him a pigeon flying in the same direction as the hawk. He called his partner on the boat. and they both watched as the blue jay and the pigeon alit nearby on another fishing boat's mast.

After a minute, they both took off in the hawk's direction. This was too fantastic to not follow. The fisherman pulled in his lines since the fish didn't oblige his catch this morning and followed the birds.

As they started the engine, the fisherman noticed the blue jay coming to rest on almost every boat in the bay. He gunned the engine and followed the hawk's direction southeast.

His partner spoke, "Where in the hell are they going, Billy?"

"Don't know, but call the other boats. They got to see this."

Fletcher was getting tired, and he knew Clay was too, but they had to fly to Arthur. What he didn't know was the fishing boats had pulled up anchor and were following them.

Each boat they branched on started to follow.

Clay started to squawk.

"Oh, great condors, how far is this going?"

"I don't know, Clay, just keep flying," Fletcher chirped back.

Clay looked behind him and noticed the boats.

"Oh no, no. They're after us. The humans. They want to kill us."

Fletcher saw the boats following.

"This could be good, one of them might help."

Clay started to answer him but he had no breath left, so he kept gliding as much as possible.

"I must be crazy?" he said to himself.

Princess saw Arthur on a red metal island in the sea. Arthur wasn't moving. Max spotted him too. They flew down to branch on the island.

"Arthur, wake up, it's Max."

The cat didn't stir.

"Oh, I hope he's not—"

"No, he's not," Princess stopped her friend.

"I sense he's weak but not gone."

"Where's Fletch?" Max turned, and he marveled at the blue jay. He was bringing all the fishing boats with him.

"Only Fletch could do this," Max called out. "Bring them on, Fletch."

Fishing boats headed for the buoy, and with Fletcher and Clay in front of the armada.

The two birds alit onto the buoy and were breathing heavily.

"This was a long way, Princess," Fletcher noted. "Is he all right?"

"I think so."

Clay sat on the bottom rung of the buoy.

"He looks dead, but he is breathing."

"How do you know Clay?" Fletcher asked.

"His chest, look at it. It's moving up and down. I learned this from my suns in the park with humans who sleep there."

Fletcher cawed out, "Arthur, Arthur, wake up. It's me, Fletch, Arthur."

The cat didn't move.

"We're dead. Here come the humans," Clay said excitedly.

"That's what I was hoping for." Fletcher was glad.

The boats neared the buoy, and the fishermen were speaking quickly.

"It's a cat. They led us to a cat."

"If you told me this, I wouldn't have believed it. Why would birds save a cat? Anybody have a camera?" Billy yelled to the other boats.

One fisherman stretched out to grab Arthur and carried him onto the boat.

"He's alive. Get on the radio. We need the vet to meet us quick. He's been through a lot."

The fisherman looked at the four birds and marveled once more.

Other fishermen were yelling across the sea about it.

"Well, birds, are you going to follow us?"

"Billy you talking to birds now?"

"Yeah, maybe."

Fletcher was happy. His plan worked.

"Well, Clay, unless you want to fly back, let's branch on this boat back to shore. Unless you like it here?"

"Oh, crow. Very funny, I'm moving, I'm moving."

Both birds alit on the top rail of the boat and sat.

"Billy, you see what I see."

"Yes, and steer the boat to shore. Don't ask questions." Billy shook his head in disbelief.

"Get me a camera quick. Nobody's going to believe this one."

The fishing boat steered to shore, and the gull and the hawk soared high, watching their friends take a ride on a boat. Fletcher looked at Arthur. He was safe now, and the humans would help him.

The gulls saw from the shore that the cat was rescued and Lulu and Coby cryed out to the sea,

"They did it. Fletcher and Eleanor Roosevelt saved the cat"

Clay turned to Fletcher,

"After we land, what are we going to do next, get in their car to their house next and stop in for bird seed? Or maybe we'll stay for Sunday dinner."

"Clay, shut your beak. You're worse then my cousin, the magpie."

Fletcher was glad he and his friends could save Arthur, but as he perched on the top of the boat branch, he wondered about his other friends and what dangers they were in. He wished them safe home.

\*     \*     \*

The yacht steered in the rough waters to the north as Caesar sat in the cat holder trying to free himself of his cage.

Two men heard noises in a nearby compartment and walked toward it. They laughed. It was a cat.

"Hey, maybe this cat is worth something if this guy has it locked up."

The other man laughed.

"Are you fucking stupid? No cat is worth anything. They're stupid and bite everyone. I hate fuckin' cats. Keep your voice down."

"We're far enough out now. Let's take this boat and steer it to Nassau. We'll get a pretty dollar for it there."

The two men didn't see the cat pushing against the holder. One of the latches on the side was old and wasn't snapped in, and the holder moved against the large cat's frame. As Caesar pushed, the holder slid on the tabletop toward the edge, while the yacht's movements in the rough waters slid the cat holder back and forth.

Syps was oblivious to any noises below when the squall went out to sea it left a very upset ocean. Waves were hitting against the sides, and it took his undivided attention to steer the yacht and keep it due north. He never saw the two men when they hit him from behind.

"Got him."

"Take the wheel, Howe. I'll see to him."

Syps wasn't out cold, but groggy.

"Hit you too hard, mate, ha ha ha. We're taking this lovely boat of yours, so stand up."

Howe was laughing as he steered the yacht, half looking back at his partner.

"Keep your fucking eyes where we're going, you jerk."

"Okay, okay, Sid."

Syps was astonished these idiots even had the brains to walk.

"Look. You're taking a boat owned by the drug cartel. You will be killed for this."

Sid slapped Syps down to the deck and kicked him.

"Shut the fuck up."

Howe was laughing so hard he forgot about his course, and the yacht started to veer northeast. There are seven hundred islands in the Bahamas—some large and some very small, with many reefs surrounding portions of them in the area the yacht was cruising.

Howe was now not paying attention to the yacht's destination, but to his friend's beating on Syps.

"Keep your mouth shut, we will do all the talking," Sid yelled as he kicked Syps repeatedly.

Each lurch of the yacht brought the cat holder closer to the table's edge.

Suddenly, the yacht moaned like a person and leered to one side.

Sid yelled at Howe and grabbed the wheel.

"I hope you didn't damage her, you motherfucker. Throw him below."

Howe grabbed Syps and literally threw him down the small steps into the darkness below.

"We have to steer northwest to Nassau. You've got us off course, you fuck."

The cat holder had fallen, and Caesar was free. He sensed danger and walked gingerly, following his whiskers. The man who had placed him in the holder was not moving, yet he was alive. He heard voices beyond. It was those two men earlier who were talking now.

One of the men had a fear of cats. He sensed it. That scent was unmistakably fear, and Caesar could use it.

Syps awoke, and he was in pain. One of his fingers were broken or badly bruised. He must take the yacht back. He remembered his pistol nearby. The two idiots left him alone and probably thought he was dead. Syps crawled easily to his compartment and retrieved his revolver.

He half crawled, half walked to the steps. All the time he was in pain, he heard them arguing.

"Go fuck yourself. What the fuck do you know? You're just a laborer at ship yards."

"I say go north to Cat Island. It's closer. We can dock it there."

"Both of you step to the side." Syps waved the pistol. "You, Howe is it?"

"Yes, yes." Howe had his hands up.

"Steer the yacht north now. You idiot, sit down on the deck."

Sid started to but reached out toward Syps and hit the gun. Sid punched Syps in the mouth and started to grab for the revolver on the deck. Syps was not moving.

As Sid reached a black sinister figure stood in front of the gun. It gave a chill up Sid's back.

"It's that fucking cat. How did he get out?" Howe yelled, turning.

"Howe keep steering the yacht. I'll deal with this."

Caesar didn't move. He sensed the evil in the man and was going to prevent him from getting the gun. Caesar was familiar with what guns can do.

Sid reached for the gun when Caesar opened the human's arm with two swipes of his paws.

Sid yelled in pain, and it gave the opportunity for Syps. Syps regained his composure and jumped the man and both rolled and punched each other on the deck as they reached for the gun. Both men grabbed the gun and wrestled for its trigger pointing it in all directions.

Howe turned to help his friend when a shot rang out entering Howe's neck. Blood oozed out instantly where an artery was hit. He fell dead instantly. The yacht bounced and weaved as it turned and steered itself.

The stormy ocean decided the ship's destination while the two men fought. The yacht reached a large reef off a nearby small island and smashed onto it.

The groan from the boat echoed across the sea as the two men rolled to one side. Water was now entering the yacht, and it was starting to list to the starboard side.

Caesar knew he had to free himself of the boat, and even though he hated water now wasn't the time for sensitivity. He spotted some pieces of the yacht floating not far away, and jumped into the sea. He grabbed with his nails into the homemade raft and lifted himself on. His breathing was fast as he watched the yacht slip as the sea engulfed it. There was no sign of the humans. The ocean started to swallow the yacht as if it was never there. The reef stood proud as a monument to the many wrecked ships.

Caesar spotted an island in the distance, and the ocean's tide was pushing him slowly toward it. Maybe this is Enew's way to his destiny, and his fate with the evil one.

The sun broke out between the clouds and glistened on the ocean's surface as the storm subsided for now.

*     *     *

Dr. Zine climbed the stairs from the basement to the first floor. He heard men talking. It was Tom and that Franks.

He knew where the keys were to the house, and entered the kitchen. House keys were placed in a drawer near the sink. Dr. Zine opened the drawer and grabbed for the keys. As he turned, Rattel hit him on the forehead with his gun.

"Doctor, Doctor. I suspected your loyalties the last time I was here. Tom, get the others up here. It's time."

Tom ordered two of the men to bring up Gallo and the rest to the first floor.

Eduardo Valli and his three men arrived.

"So you got my sister and her fucking cop?"

Rattel dragged Dr. Z into the living room.

"And more."

Tom's two men led Gallo, Tony, and Darby into the room and pushed them onto a sofa. Behind them the two women were escorted into the room.

Eduardo beamed, "Sister, my long traveling sister, Malena. How are you?"

"Go fuck yourself, you pig," Malena spit out.

"That's not nice." Eduardo smiled and grabbed her to his chest.

"You've been very dangerous to me lately, and I'm afraid you'll have to disappear."

Malena slapped his hand, and Eduardo slapped her back harder. She fell to the floor.

Gallo went to her and a rifle butt landed on his hand.

"Stay put, cop."

Malena wiped away the blood from her mouth and helped Gallo up to the sofa.

"One big happy family right Rattel." Eduardo boasted.

"Yeah, yeah. You take your sister. I don't care about her anymore. It's the two boys here and my sweet girl here, Libby, I want to terminate."

Eduardo took out a pack of Newport and lit a cigarette.

"So when does the Cimbaris come?"

"They're probably here. Their boy Simpson met with an unfortunate bullet. Hey Gallo, he had been telling us all your moves. How'd you think I knew where you were all the time. Ha, ha."

Gallo rubbed his head and swore under his breath to kill him.

Tom went over to Rattel and asked where Syps was.

"Don't know. I lost touch with him days ago. He'll be here."

Dr. Z was coming to, and Tony was trying to revive him.

"Hey, Gallo, do you like the sweet setup. Trillions will flow through here. Trillions."

"Someone will miss us and come looking. It's not over, Rattel."

"It's over. Your cat is dead. You're dead. It's over," Rattel yelled into Gallo's face.

Eduardo was aroused. He motioned his men over to the bar as he sat on a barstool.

"Hey, Rattel, does the Mafia know who you are?"

Rattel's back was to Eduardo.

"I think so, because some people told them."

Rattel was about to reach for his pistol when Eduardo's men already had theirs out. Eduardo motioned his man to take Mead's gun.

"You did make a deal with Cimbari?" Rattel smiled that eerie grin as he turned.

"You know it. Trillions is too much to share three ways, no less four."

"Get your hands away from your gun, and you too, Tom. Tell your men too."

The two men raised their hands.

"Hey, Tom, you know who killed your father. The Cimbaris. His Cadillac had a bomb placed in it."

Tom showed some emotion but strangely so, Gallo noted.

"Now"—Eduardo started to walk to Rattel—"we settle it all. We kill everyone, and my coalition and the American Mafia we'll work together on this great fucking deal."

"Not quite, Eduardo," a voice from the door stated.

Alfredo Cimbari was standing at the door with five men pointing guns from every window. Mead reached for a gun, and Cimbari's men fired their guns and killed him.

"Alfredo, what are you doing?" Eduardo's face was scared.

"It's important to note that we will settle everything today, not you. Did you think we needed you to handle our business? We knew about Rattel here and that you hired him. My father has wanted him dead along with the cop for months now. We aren't going to split anything."

One of Eduardo's men decided to take a chance with his gun and the other Colombian's joined in.

Shots rang out, and the three Colombians were dead. Eduardo stood in shock. A bullet had entered his chest.

"No, no. It's impossible." Eduardo fell dead.

Malena screamed.

Alfredo started to sing.

"It's impossible. Tell the world to blah, blah, blah, it's impossible."

He nudged Eduardo's body.

"You know Perry Como?" he asked Eduardo as he fired another bullet into the still body.

"Now"—he motioned to one of his men—"tie them up but leave Rattel to me."

Rattel looked at Alfredo.

"So I'm to get it here too?"

"Yeah, but not by me. Someone else who joined our fold will. We used him for his connections in Southeast Asia. Not these pain in the asses," he said as he kicked Eduardo's body.

Rattel turned; it was Tom holding a pistol at him.

"Nice move. Didn't they kill your father?"

"Yes, they did with my help. Even the Mafia didn't know where he was. I told them. He didn't want to expand, and he held us back. The Cimbaris approached me with a great deal, but they said to ice the package I would have to kill you."

Alfredo smiled.

"You see, Rattel, you were right. All will be settled here. I have to go to Nassau to set up our first station from our Sandcastle restaurant there. That will be the first station off from the Bahamas."

Rattel turned surprised.

"First station? This is the first station."

"Not after five o'clock today which is in about an hour from now. You see, our friend Tom and his men planted enough C-4 here to blow up Grand Central Station. No evidence of anything."

Tom smiled in reassurance.

"Not my life's work, no, no," Dr. Zine yelled.

"Sorry Doc. It was great work, but you will be buried with it."

"So, Rattel, I'll leave two of my men to watch you die along with the others. I have my algae to grow in the sun. Ha ha ha."

Alfredo left with three of his men. As he left, he sang "It's Impossible."

*   *   *

# DESTINY OF TWO SOULS

The piece of the yacht slid over the water, and the waves grabbed it toward the shore. Its passenger leaped into the water and started to swim to the beach.

The undertow was great, and his body was sucked into the deeper part of the beach. He paddled with his paws as fast as he could to no avail.

The water wanted him. It took him down and water invaded his lungs. He climbed despairingly up for air, grabbing a breath, and then it towed him down again. His body was a prisoner of the tide. It took him back and forth under water and threw him sideways.

His legs would hit bottom, and he would push upward against the great force. Again he reached air and gasped for air, and again he was brought down with the force.

He didn't know how long the sea played with him. Time was standing still. Waves took him finally into the beach and washed him onto the sand, hitting his head on a rock buried in the sand. He lay there motionless as the water ran up the sand and back again.

Water poured out of his mouth, and he coughed violently. He was alive.

Enew had saved him again. He thought and thought, and he saw a seagull swoop low near him, and he remembered another bird. It was coming back to him, but slowly. A blue bird or a red cat danced in his head. It was all so mixed up in his brain. The ocean slammed into the beach with a roar as he started to walk down the water's edge. Then he saw a blue bird on a branch nearby that crackled loudly, and it was as if Enew touched him—the past flashed like a sun in front of his eyes.

He remembered Rattel and his mother's death. How Rattel killed her and then he remembered Master Gallo and Mistress Libby. He spat and wretched violently at the thought of the human rat, Rattel alive. He sensed the rat was nearby and somehow knew it was time to end the pestilence's life. Fate had placed him on this island for a purpose. The pestilence must be destroyed now.

Caesar tested his legs and gingerly walked into the trees and sat. His friends Sam, Arthur, and Fletcher must think me dead, he thought. He would have his final vengeance on the human rat and then set out to get home somehow.

The palm trees whispered in the breeze coming off the Atlantic Ocean from the east. A tropical storm was on its way.

*       *       *

Alfredo and his men were gone on their yacht sailing away when the two men tied Dr. Zine to Tony and tied the two women together. Gallo was the last to be tied as he tried to figure a way out of this.

"So, Tom, you mind if I smoke?"

Rattel had his hands out.

"Go ahead. You can smoke two if you like. It's your last hour on earth."

"You really are something. Lead me along all the way. You are a very good actor, and before you tie me up too, can I have a last drink?"

Tom motioned to one of the men to get him a drink.

"Very cool having your own father killed. I'll have a brandy to settle my stomach."

Rattel laughed.

"Aren't you kind of cool for someone who's going to die?" Tom asked.

"It's not me who's going to die, but you." Rattel smiled again.

Tom looked at him strangely.

"You have no chance, Rattel."

"Never say no to me."

A shot rang out from the rear of the room, and Tom fell to the floor. Rattel, falling to the floor, grabbed at his gun on the floor nearby and fired twice into Cimbari's men. The other shooter took out Tom's two men.

"Nice work, Syps."

"You're lucky, I almost bought it back on the sea. Two pirates tried to take the yacht, but I fought them off with a little help. The yacht's gone though."

"Don't worry, I got another boat nearby." Rattel smiled. "Tie up Tom. He's going to get what he had in store for me, the fuck."

Syps went over to Tom.

"He's still alive."

"Good for him. What did you mean you had help on the yacht?"

Syps was tying Tom's hands and feet when he dreaded this answer.

"You didn't kill that black cat. He's still alive. He's the one who stopped those pirates."

Rattel's face went from surprise to rage.

"No fucking way that cat could have lived. I shot him in the head."

Gallo looked at Libby. It was a miracle again.

"It's him, I know it. He stopped a pit bull in Trinidad."

Rattel turned to look out the window. A storm was coming in from the east, and his mind was racing.

"So let's get out of here. Let them all die, and maybe he died when the yacht went down."

Gallo answered, "He's been dead before and came back."

"Shut up, you fuck. He's dead, dead, dead. That reminds me take the Colombian bitch. I have use for her now.

Malena struggled with Syps, but he dragged her out of the house.

"Well, my friends, my revenge is finally going to happen, and that fucking cat is dead."

With that, Rattel grabbed Malena, and Syps followed.

Gallo pulled at the ropes. He tried and managed to cut his wrists. Tony was ready. He had used an old trick he read about in books. When Tom was tying him to the chair, he expanded his chest by breathing in and holding it. This gave him some room to wiggle the chair.

Tony noticed Gallo's attempt and started to try to walk the chair over to him.

"How long do you think we have?" Libby asked.

"It's about four thirty, maybe a half hour."

Tony reached the rear of Gallo's chair and started to tip over his chair. The chair fell to the left and Tony's face was at Gallo's hands. Tony started to chew the ropes as much as possible. They were both working on the ropes when Tom woke up.

"Oh shit. Oh god. Get me out of these."

"We're a little tied up too, genius," Gallo yelled back.

"It's going to blow at five," Tom yelled.

"Shut up, you piece of shit," Tony screamed out as he kept chewing.

Gallo managed between his pulling and Tony's teeth to get one hand free. He ripped off the ropes and freed Libby, Darby, Tony, and Dr. Zine.

"Help. Get me out of here," Tom bellowed again.

"Get the mad bomber out of here. I'm going for Rattel. Get everybody to a safe distance including our friend the bomber."

Gallo grabbed one of the dead men's guns and shoved it into his waistband.

"Call the police if you can. Tell them what's the deal here and inform them of the Cimbaris in Nassau."

Gallo ran into the darkened starlit night as rain started to fall. Wind whipped the trees from the Atlantic. It was coming for the island and it was a storm.

Tony led Libby, Dr. Zine, and Darby to safety about fifty yards away from the house and returned for Tom.

Syps, in his hurry to leave, did not check Tom for more guns. Tom had a small caliber revolver in an ankle holster, and he was inching down as he arched his back trying to reach for the gun.

As Tony reached him, he grabbed for the revolver.

"Easy, boy. I'd kill your ass, but I need you to cut these ropes," Tom said, as he was pointing the gun from the floor up to Tony's body.

"Grab a knife by the bar. Move easy as I speak, or I'll shoot you and get out some other way, if I have to."

Tony moved over to the bar. On the counter was a knife used to cut lemons and limes. It had a small blade but it was sharp. Tony approached Tom, and the gun was pointed at his head.

"Cut them easy, don't slip or you're dead."

Tony cut the ropes and stood back. He stood near one of Eduardo's dead men and a gun was lying on the floor near the corpse's hand. If he could just jump down and . . .

Tom moved and started to get up.

Tony felt he had no choice but to move now. He fell fast to the floor and grabbed the pistol. He didn't notice Tom pointing the gun to his head, but something then suddenly hit Tom from the side.

At first, it didn't register in Tony's mind, but he recognized his savior. It was his dog. Where he came from he didn't care. Sam had Tom's hand in his mouth, and the gun was pointing all over. Tom's finger hit the trigger and a bullet hit the wall. Tony pointed his gun at Tom, waiting for Sam to clear himself. The dog had Tom's hand and bit down hard and Tom screamed in pain. Tom tried to hit the dog but a bullet rang out from Tony's gun opening a hole in Tom's head. Sam looked at the man. He was still.

Tony ran to his dog and hugged him.

"Where in the hell did you come from? Let's get the hell out of here. Run, Sam."

Both man and dog ran toward where Libby, Dr. Zine, and Darby were. Tony motioned her, and the two men to run farther away.

"Go, go, let's get some distance from the house. It's going to go up."

They ran close to shore, and the house exploded behind them in a massive cloud with debris flying everywhere.

Dr. Zine was hit with a strip of wood in his leg and fell to the ground in pain. Libby grabbed him and fell alongside him. Tony hugged Sam and huddled deep into the sand.

A cloud of smoke rose into the wet rainy night as the wind bellowed and whistled through the trees. The rain was starting to come down quicker and harder.

*   *   *

Rattel had jumped into a Ford Explorer that Tom had used many times to visit town. Rattel threw Malena into the rear and hit her across her head. She fell motionless in the rear of the truck. Syps hopped into the passenger side, and Rattel slammed the gas pedal to the floor.

The truck roared and threw gravel everywhere, and Rattel was laughing.

"They think they killed me. The fucks. We'll get to the boat and to Jamaica, and hide there for some months. I'll think up a plan."

Syps had not forgotten Caesar.

"That cat. He's not mortal. He thinks and schemes. I swear he's human. He knows what we say."

"Stop talking about that fucking cat. He's dead. You said the yacht went down. You barely made it." Rattel was steering the Ford through broken paths between the trees.

The rain was fierce and was coming down sideways forced by the wind.

"Goddamn it. This storm is bad, Rattel. Let's hold up in one of the small towns here. They will never suspect us to still be on the island." Syps hoped Rattel went along with his idea.

"You are stupid. When the Cimbaris don't get word from that traitor Tom, they will be looking for me. This island is dangerous," Rattel spit out as lightning hit a nearby palm tree. The tree fell onto the path Rattel was steering toward.

"Fuck," Rattel cursed as he steered off the path.

The truck's tires spun their disapproval, and the truck slid down into a gap caused by an interior stream. Rattel slammed on the gas pedal, and the tires slid again on rocks and low grass. The truck's rear end was caught in a gully on the side of the path, and Rattel gunned the engine several times to escape, but to no avail.

"Shit, we're going to have to walk to the boat."

"What about the bitch?" Syps asked.

"Leave her, we can't take her now, too much of a burden."

Syps stepped out of the truck and checked his gun. He had a full magazine in his pistol.

"Why you checking your gun?" Rattel asked comically. "They're all dead. Didn't you hear the explosion?"

Syps looked nervous.

"I have a feeling something isn't right."

"Stupid. Come on, we can make the boat this way."

As they walked, Syps could hear movement behind them.

"I know there's someone there."

Rattel stopped to listen. The trees were like an umbrella protecting them from the rain; yet, they were getting soaked. All Rattel could hear was the rain.

"You're fucking hearing things. Let's go."

They walked another hundred yards when Rattel heard a noise too.

"That wasn't rain. Sit down, we'll wait."

They could hear someone, maybe fifty yards away. He was following their tracks from the truck. It was Syps who saw him first.

"It's Gallo. I thought he was killed in the house?"

Rattel was pissed.

"Kill him now."

Syps pointed his pistol and fired. Gallo disappeared in the bushes, and the two men heard no noise after that. Rain smashed into Syps face.

"I think I got him." Syps smiled.

"Go check," Rattel ordered Syps.

"Wait, what about you?" Syps asked.

"I'll go start the boat engine. Don't worry, I won't leave without you." Rattel motioned Syps to go as he got up and headed in the opposite direction of Gallo.

"I'll check that bastard." Syps smiled.

Rattel headed northeast as Syps backtracked the path toward Gallo's last position.

Syps ran into the brush he thought Gallo was at, and it was empty. A little blood was on a leaf nearby.

"I got him. I knew it," he laughed.

Syps followed the blood as best he could in the rain. The rain was washing everything away. Then he heard a noise in front of him and fired his pistol into the brush.

"Gotcha, you fuck," Syps laughed.

"Not quite," came a voice from Syps left. Gallo stood up, pointing his pistol at Syps. "Drop the gun, Syps."

Syps figured if he could turn and fire in this heavy rain, he would have a chance. He spun around with his pistol but was unsuccessful. Gallo fired twice, cutting Syps's stomach open. Syps fell to the ground, groaning in pain.

Gallo looked over him.

"Where's Rattel?"

"Ah, he's too smart for all of you. He'll be gone soon." Syps was fading fast.

"Gone? Where? How? Where's Malena?"

"Ha ha. You'll never get him." Syps was gone.

Gallo stood looking at the dead man for a while and decided to follow the same path. He passed the stuck truck but as he did he never saw Malena in the back of the truck.

Rain, thunder, and wind whipped the trees as the path was starting to be a stream that led to the ocean.

\*　　\*　　\*

Dan Harvey and Furness reached Cat Island at Arthur's Town and located the Bahamian police. They listened intently and gathered up two police boats to go inspect the area. As the boats reached the southern end of the island, they could see a man waving his arms at them.

It was Darby, and he was yelling.

"Help, help, come on. We need help."

The police boats docked, and they saw the ranch house in ruins. Furness saw Tony and Libby, and he was happy to see them alive and with Sam too. They exchanged stories, and Furness told them of Caesar and his memory loss.

"Do you think he's alive?" Libby asked.

"He's too lucky to be dead." Furness smiled.

Dr. Zine was taken onto one of the boats to the hospital with Darby. Libby and Tony were given shelter from the rain on the police boat.

Furness was curious about Gallo.

"He went after them and in this rain too. We have to help him. Do you think Sam could track him?"

Tony smiled.

"He could do just about anything now." Tony kissed Libby. "Stay here with the police. I'll lead them to Gallo with Sam."

Libby loved Tony very much.

"Don't be a hero. Come back to me," she said.

"I promise." Tony hugged her, and Furness and two officers followed Tony and Sam north into the trees.

Libby sat and held her head.

"When will this night be over?"

*     *     *

The squall was fierce. Rain and wind tore into Cat Island as Mount Alvernia stood in defiance of the storm. The Father Hawkins' Stations of the Cross stone steps to the Hermitage mountaintop glistened as the rain washed the stones down.

Rattel had reached the footpath to the first stone stop with the first station of the cross engraved in it. He had been turned around from the direction to the east and couldn't see the shore when he heard a frightening call. It was from an animal. A loud meow, like that of a tiger, echoed through the forest. Rattel's spine tingled, and he panicked at the very thought of a ghost coming for him. He slipped on the wet stones and fell.

"You're dead," He yelled out into the dark. "Die already," Rattel screamed and fired three shots from his pistol into the darkness. He laughed as he did so. "Devil or not, I'll put another bullet into you." He fired again twice. All he could hear was the rain on his shoulders. A lightning bolt hit nearby making a crackling sound. He stood motionless to listen. It seemed like an eternity for Rattel. *Syps is wrong, the black cat is dead*, he thought. He stood up to climb the steps.

It was then that he saw Gallo. He fired twice again and ran up the stone steps. Each step was slippery, and he fell as he did. He stopped some ten or twelve steps up and saw Gallo following him. Rattel fired three shots, and was his pistol empty? He ran again in panic up to the top of the mountain.

A small chapel stood with a bell tower. The bell was clanging in the wind loudly, and Rattel ran into the chapel. He searched his pockets for an extra magazine or bullets. He had four bullets left. He loaded the magazine and waited for Gallo.

Gallo reached the top, and the wind whipped at him viciously. The wind was greater up here, he thought as he scanned the area for Rattel. A bell clanged loudly and he noticed a chapel adjacent to it. He saw a flash of light that saved his life. Gallo fell to the ground as a bullet sped over his head, missing him by inches. Gallo crawled toward the chapel and waited and listened.

Rattel opened the chapel door and fell to the ground. He scanned the area but saw no sign of Gallo. The hollowed meow sound came again, this time nearby and closer to Rattel. It was eerie in the storm. The wind carried the sound around the chapel.

Gallo even felt nervous now. The cry of the cat was scary, and he was coming for Rattel. It was Caesar.

Rattel yelled out toward the sky and fired a shot into the brush. It was Gallo's opportunity. He rushed Rattel and hit him with his gun. Rattel had turned in time to avoid Gallo's swing, and he hit Gallo with his fist. They both fell to the ground in the mud and rolled toward the bell tower. Gallo lost his gun in the mud as he punched Rattel in the face, throwing him toward the edge of the cliff.

Rattel fell, and as he did he fired at Gallo. It hit Gallo in the left arm, the same arm Syps shot him. Rattel's shot, however, went through his arm and didn't hit a bone.

"This is it, Gallo. You're finished. You and that cat. I got one bullet left and—"

A cry came out from the chapel like a demon in pain. It echoed and lasted long. It was a cry of vengeance. It distracted Rattel and was just the second Gallo needed. He jumped at him as he punched him full force in the stomach. Rattel let out a gasp, and both of the men rolled over the cliff's edge.

Gallo grabbed at the first thing he could. There was a young tree growing on the side of the cliff, which he latched on to with his right arm. Rattel too had found a handhold with a small bush. The two enemies looked at each other with hate. Gallo couldn't reach him, but he noticed something in Rattel's hand. It was his gun. How he held on to it, he never knew, but Rattel started to point it his way. Gallo had no foothold just his right hand. He just couldn't reach Rattel. The rain punished both men, and Gallo could feel the mud on his hands.

"Ha. Seems we will part from each other finally Gallo. You will have a nice fall to the forest below, say about two hundred feet down. I got one bullet left and it has your name on it." Rattel pointed the gun and was about to pull the trigger when a sound out of hell came from above them.

They looked up into the rain. It was terrifying to Rattel. The cat's golden yellow eyes glared at him, and Caesar let out a loud cry and spit down at Rattel. It chilled even Gallo at the sight. The cat's eyes seemed to be floating in the darkness.

"Die, you fucking devil, die. Go back to hell," Rattel cried out as he fired his last bullet.

What made Caesar move, he didn't know. It was just an instinct or a feeling to move his head. The bullet missed him whistling by his head.

Rattel knew he missed and was terrified.

"Go away, go away, you fucking ghost. You're dead," he yelled.

The cat now stood at the cliff's edge and knew now what Enew had meant. His life was meaningless. Revenge wasn't the answer. It wasn't his petty vendetta that was important. It was Caesar who had to rid the world of this pestilence. It was his destiny. All the hate rolled into one fireball in his mind. Caesar knew what he must do. He must save his master and kill the human rat. Visions of his mother's death and this man's laugh burned in his head. It was time to end this pain.

Gallo saw what the cat was planning and yelled into the wind.

"No, Caesar, no, don't do it"

It was too late. The cat spit and then arched his back and positioned his legs and leaped with all his force at Rattel with claws extended out. The cat hit the man at his face, scratching his neck as he did. Rattel yelled out in pain. The weight of the man and the cat was too much for the small bush Rattel was holding on to. Rattel was trying to get the demon off him with his left hand. The bush root gave way, and both man and cat fell in to the darkness below.

Gallo yelled out but it was useless. Rattel was screaming in fear. The last he could see before they disappeared in the blackness was Caesar with all paws fiercely swiping at the man's face.

Gallo heard nothing below now, just silence. The force of the rain hit him and ran down his back. He never noticed how hard the rain was falling before this. His left arm throbbed in pain. It seemed like hours that he had held on to the small tree when he heard a voice from above. It was Tony with Sam.

The police made a rope from their belts to pull Gallo up easily. Tony looked at Gallo and knew something had happened to Rattel.

Gallo fell in exhaustion to the ground.

"He saved my life again Tony, that brave cat. He came back from where I don't know, but he took Rattel with him."

The men stared down into the darkness below, and Sam understood his friend was gone, and he had his vengeance finally, and now Caesar is at peace.

*   *   *

Morning came over Cat Island quietly. The tropical storm had passed in the night. The sun rose through fluffy white clouds, and the ocean was still.

The white sandy beach was calm except for men searching for bodies along its wooded edge. The police started their search in the early morning light and still hadn't found anything of a man or a cat.

Gallo and Tony with Sam in the lead walked the base of Mount Alvernia with no luck. Gallo had his left arm attended to by the Bahamian police medic. He was lucky both bullets missed bone, but it didn't alleviate the pain. They searched all morning, and Sam was getting anxious. His friend's body would surely have been found by now. It was strange.

A cry came out from the police in the distance.

The two men with the dog in the lead ran toward the cry. The police found an area freshly moved as if someone had been there all night. It was Rattel. It had to be.

"He was here, and he's not dead. How did he survive the fall?"

Dan grabbed at the palm tree leaves on the ground.

"This broke his fall but he had to be in pain, maybe a broken leg or arm."

"Shit. He should be dead. Search the whole island, everywhere. He can't get away," Gallo barked. "Did you call Nassau to pick up the Cimbaris?"

"Yes, they will be apprehended soon," Dan noted.

The police scattered in all directions while Harvey called on the radio to the police chief in Arthur's Town.

"He will not escape."

Gallo and Tony knew Sam might have an edge.

Tony bent down to Sam.

"Boy, you must do this for me. Find that man, Rattel. He's the one that killed Caesar. Let's go, Sam."

Sam understood and pulled on the leash made of rope in a northeast direction. Gallo and Tony followed while Furness stayed with Harvey.

"How is he still alive?" Tony shook his head.

*   *   *

He was walking slowly through the trees toward the boat and moaning. He thought back about last night; when he opened his eyes he felt pain. It was at least a broken rib, and his left arm was broken. He forced himself to stand, and as he did so, the pain hit him hard. He was soaked through, and he needed to wrap his ribs. He used palm leaves as best he could and started to walk. In his fall he had grabbed some ropes put there by rock climbers or from years past. It had saved him. If he could make the boat before the rising sun, he would be home free.

As he walked he looked around him. That fucking cat had to have died in the fall. He kept looking behind him. The cat had cut open gashes on his face and neck, and he was bleeding continuously. Unfortunately, he had lost his gun in the fall. The sun felt good on his face as he neared a clearing, and he could see his boat docked.

A man was fishing off the dock as he approached. He needed no witnesses. Rattel reached for his knife as he got near the fisherman.

"Hello, now . . ." were the last words of the fisherman as Rattel buried his knife in his body. The body fell into the ocean. Rattel, in pain from his ribs, ran to the boat and started to take in the ropes.

"I'll be gone soon, you fucks," he thought to himself.

He boarded the boat in order to start the engines, but then noticed a familiar figure on the beach, wandering and looking for someone. He found his other gun and ran off the dock toward the figure.

"You are coming with me, my dear."

Malena's head still hurt, and she was dazed. She had managed to get out of the truck after she awoke. She walked all morning looking for Gallo, but never even heard him. She was turned around several times and decided to head for the beach, if she could find it.

"Why aren't you dead?"

"Oh no, my destiny is with you, my love, and my real name is Rattel, but you can call me Frank," he said as he winced in pain.

"You fuck, you killed my father and—" She slapped him and he hit her across the face.

"Shut up, get on board." He pointed his gun at her. "No one's coming to save you. You walked destiny's way."

"No. I walked into hell."

They boarded the ship, and Rattel started the engines, never noticing a black figure coming on board the boat, silent and easy. The boarder walked in the rear never making a sound. He was wet and tired but had survived to fulfill Enew's prediction.

*   *   *

Sam found the scent that was odd. It was laced with many strange smells. This area had too many unusual scents that interfered with his tracking, but he followed the odd smell. Tony and Gallo walked briskly when Gallo found one of Malena's hair clips. He knew it from their trip together. It was unusual because it had a bronze cloverleaf on it.

"It's hers, what the fuck!"

They pushed on toward the beach, and they saw the boat speeding away from shore. Rattel had another boat, and Malena was on it. It was too late to swim, and there was no other boat nearby. Tony got on the cell Furness gave him and called for help to stop the boat.

Gallo felt helpless, and Sam was barking toward the water. Sam realized the odd smell. It was Rattel's mixed in with his friend's scent. Caesar was on board. He knew it.

Gallo yelled out, "Get that police boat now."

*   *   *

Rattel was smiling, but his ribs still hurt. It all worked out after all. The cat was dead, and through a lucky break he got Malena. He steered the boat south toward lesser-known islands; from there, he would go to South America to hide out. He had lost the money on the island, but he managed to store one hundred thousand on board. That would give him a good start somewhere, and with the bitch, he would live easy.

He laughed out loud.

"Where's your friend Gallo? Lost, I bet, looking for me. By the time they get their stupid police searching, we will be at Ragged Island and get patched up, then a plane to maybe Aruba. Paradise huh, with me."

"You will never touch me, pig. I will kill you," Malena spat back.

"Fireball. I like that." Rattel's ribs still hurt. "Hey, bitch. Go down below and get the first aid kit."

"No. You fucking get it."

"Go now, or I cut you out of my plans." He pointed his gun at her.

Malena got up and went below, looking for the first aid kit and a weapon. There was only a fire extinguisher and the first aid kit. She walked back up and threw the kit at him.

"Here, die, I hope."

"No, no, my love. We are destined together."

Rattel tied off the steering wheel and started to wrap his ribs. His left arm was either broke or fractured. He wrapped what he could.

They were now approaching Long Island, south of Cat Island—named for its length of eighty miles and only four miles wide at its widest. It is another of the chain of beautiful islands, but this island is noted for its rocky cliffs that reach into the ocean on its east side facing the Atlantic. Rattel's boat was on a direct course for the cliffs.

Rattel never noticed the rocky cliffs ahead because a sound that sent chills up his spine came from on board. It was the cat. That demon from hell came to finish what they had started on Cat Island. Rattel knew in his heart the cat survived the fall like him. He turned to scan the deck. Malena was sitting on the deck as he ordered her to, while the ocean whipped the sides of the boat. Rattel pulled hard at the tied off wheel. As he did, he turned to Malena with an insane look on his face.

"Our friend has returned from the dead. It's time we end it now cat," Rattel yelled down into the cabin holding his gun. "Come out now and face me, demon."

Malena knew of Caesar, but that cry was chilling. She had to escape. If she could only jump off and swim to shore, he'll never notice now. It was maybe a half a mile to the island. She swam that distance before but many years ago.

When Rattel heard the cat, he stopped paying attention to her. He walked below. It was her chance, even at this speed. She ran to the rear of the ship and dove off.

Caesar was near him now. The pestilence scent was all around him. He could see his mother's death from this man's gun and of his Mistress Cathy lying dead. It was burning at his heart, tearing at his soul.

He leaped from his vantage point onto the human rat. As he did so, Rattel screamed in horror climbing the stairs up to the deck. Caesar was scratching with all his strength at the evil one. The ship leered to the right toward Long Island's steep rocky cliffs.

Malena survived her jump and could see the ship from where she was. Rattel was running to the rear of the ship with a black figure at his neck. It was the cat she had heard about. Rattel fired two shots, but Malena couldn't see where they hit. The ship headed for the rocks when Malena gasped. The ship crashed into the steep cliffs and then exploded into a fireball.

Malena never saw either man or cat jump off, or if there was anything alive after the explosion in the water. She floated for a time and swam toward a small island off the coast of the cliffs. Malena reached a rocky beach and collapsed onto the sand.

*Rattel is dead finally, but that brave cat saved me.*

She fell asleep exhausted.

\* \* \*

Gallo and Tony finally got the Bahamian police boat headed south following in Rattel's wake. The police assured him he would not get away. They had put out a total Bahamas Island search for him, and their helicopter was on the way. The police boat made great time toward Long Island but time moved too slow for Gallo. He feared Malena was hurt or killed. Rattel had nothing to lose and Malena was only a burden.

They neared Long Island first, and Gallo could see a figure on an island to the north waving its hands. When the police boat approached nearer, to Gallo's relief it was Malena. She cried out in happiness at the sight of Gallo.

"Mark, Mark."

Gallo jumped down into the shallow waters as they came close to the beach. They both met splashing in knee-deep water and kissed for a long time. Tony was not surprised. They had been through a lot together. Gallo led Malena to the beach, holding on to her waist, and the police came with a rubber lifeboat to take them on board.

"Where's Rattel?" Gallo asked anxiously, scanning the horizon.

Nothing was in view.

"He's dead. The ship crashed into the rocks of the island. It was an explosion. They were fighting each other as they crashed. He saved me."

Malena started to cry. She was talking nervously.

"Who saved you? Who was fighting Rattel?" Gallo asked quickly.

She looked at Gallo and gave a calm answer.

"Your cat. He came on the ship. It was the bravest thing I have ever seen. I don't know how. Rattel went insane when he heard the cat call on the boat. He went crazy and when he heard that cat's call . . ."

Gallo looked at Tony. It was impossible. He saw Caesar fall off the mountain with Rattel. Both had survived the fall and yet what is astonishing is that Caesar followed him onto the boat to kill him.

Gallo sat on the sand, and Tony called the police over.

"Listen, can you search for a cat in the water. I know it sounds crazy but please . . ."

The police looked skeptical at Tony but radioed to the nearby boats.

Dan Harvey, Furness, and Libby were approaching in another police boat and heard the report on the police radio. They landed on the beach to help.

Libby went over to Tony and hugged him.

"It's terrible. Is he really gone?"

Dan looked at the three men and knew what the Bahamian police were thinking.

"There are many sharks in these waters. The chance the cat lived through the crash, the explosion, and then survived the sharks is slim."

Gallo nodded, and Tony looked toward the horizon. He saw Sam on the police boat watching him. Tony then turned his glance toward the rocky cliffs in the distance. The ocean slammed against the rocks, continuously spraying the cliffs up high with water. It was a lot to ask to see Caesar alive again.

Gallo broke the silence.

"He finally got his vengeance. Rattel is dead, and he sacrificed himself again to kill him. It's amazing."

They all entered the lifeboat and rowed to the police boats. A helicopter the police ordered started to circle the tip of Long Island, noting nothing unusual down below.

When the humans boarded the ship, Sam noted Master Tony's sadness. It was about Caesar.

Tony hugged Sam.

"We won't be seeing that brave special cat again, Sam. He took that evil man with him."

Sam had thought Caesar dead before and didn't believe it. The gods wouldn't take him so early in his life, not after what he had done. Sam was at the front of the boat and with his eyes and his nose searched the waters beyond. The boats started to rev up their engines and turned in a southwest direction to go to Stella Maria on Long Island. Stella Maria was the closest port and had doctors to tend to Gallo and Malena. Gallo had been shot twice in the same area of the left arm and needed medical aid. They had to pass the most northern point of the island and travel south to the resort area to get a final report in to headquarters.

They were passing the rocks within two hundred yards when Sam started to bark furiously toward the rocks. Gallo ran to the spot Sam was and looked in Sam's view. He grabbed a pair of binoculars from the police. On a small rock, maybe two feet square, with the ocean whipping him was the cat. He had survived it all and was hanging on for dear life, waiting to be saved. He was having a hard time holding on to the rock.

"I see him. He's alive, my god," Libby screamed

The two policemen lowered the lifeboat, and Gallo and Tony jumped in immediately. It was a dangerous run to the rocks with the sea whipping the boat. It took all four men to make it. The cat was soaked and exhausted and couldn't jump into the boat. Gallo had to get him before he fell into the ocean. Caesar started to slip when Gallo grabbed him.

"I got you. Don't worry you're not going to leave me," Gallo yelled out.

Caesar clung to Gallo's chest as the lifeboat fought the ocean back to the ship.

Caesar was safe, and he thought about Enew and what he had said. Yes, he didn't think about his life. His only thought was to save the humans. Vengeance was finally his, but it wasn't as lasting or satisfying as he thought it would be. The pestilence was dead, and the human world was better for it, and he was alive.

He thanked Enew and all the gods and hung on to Gallo as each human had to give him a pat on the head. All the humans were excited and happy.

"How could he have survived?" were the comments over and over.

Sam was relieved.

"You did it. It's a miracle you're alive," Sam barked from afar.

Caesar was too tired to answer but instead lay down on a blanket on deck and fell fast asleep as the police boat headed to port.

*    *    *

# EPILOGUE

It was Christmas in New York City, and the weather was unusually warm. The city was abuzz of the miracle cat and his companions. When news of the death and the capture of the Cimbari family in Nassau came to the city, it made the headlines. All the television and newspapers and the Internet had pictures of the damaged house on Cat Island and the closing of the Sandcastles Restaurants in Miami and Nassau. News spread fast, and so did the notoriety of the miracle cat. Everybody wanted him.

Dan Harvey and Furness became heroes in Trinidad with pictures of Caesar alongside them.

Tony and Libby and Gallo were anxious to get home since that night and subsequent morning, there was no rest for them. Between the police reports and the news media, they were hounded.

Sam barked his disapproval every time some stranger came close to Caesar.

Caesar took it all in quietly. His soul was at peace. Revenge was the reason for his quest, but he learned vengeance serves nothing but to eat at you from the inside. He was at peace with his life and his surroundings. Enew challenged his very essence, and he survived. Why Enew let him live he didn't know, maybe for some other challenges at a different time or place. Right now though, he just wanted to sleep.

The Cimbaris, especially Alfredo, was in deep trouble. The Bahamian police along with the DEA were going to indict him. The Bahamian police had him in custody and would not let him out on any bail. His father called and threatened, but to no avail. The Bahamian police searched the waters near Long Island's south point for the body of Rattel, but it never turned up. They concluded it was washed out to sea or eaten by the sharks.

Dr. Zine, on the other hand, was arrested but with Gallo and Libby's testimony at the hearing was going to get off with a light sentence. His old boss, NASA, wanted Dr. Zine back, and so did every subway and train manufacturer. Dr. Z had tickled their interest in a new kind of travel.

Gallo was offered a permanent job with the DEA but wanted to relax awhile; they wanted to give him Simpson's position.

Furness and Harvey were leaving, and Furness gave the black cat a big kiss on the head.

"You are one in a million, cat. Come visit Trinidad for Carnavale in February,"

Gallo laughed.

"I think we had enough Caribbean travels for a while."

They all laughed, and Furness and Harvey left.

The police had cleared them to leave the Bahamas, but they would have to return for court dates if necessary—they weren't sure.

Darby, the fisherman, was the local hero, having been kidnapped and almost killed. He gave television interviews and described his ordeal. He was almost the most popular person from Cat Island, except for Sidney Poitier.

Susan Whittier and her father met Caesar before he flew back from the Bahamas, and Susan hugged Caesar all the time she was with him. Whittier was just amazed by the cat and told the press the whole story. He also was going to return to America. He finally realized he must have a home for his daughter, not traveling from one island to another. Whittier promised to come visit Gallo and Caesar as soon as he was settled in the States.

The question bothering Gallo was what about Malena. She now was the sole owner of the ranch and farm in Colombia, and she wanted to go back to right some wrongs and find her father's burial plot. She was torn because she had fallen in love with Gallo, and she knew he was also in love with her. It would be hard to separate after all that had transpired, but she had to go back.

Gallo, for his part, was resigned to the fact she would return to her home. They had enjoyed each other this past week, but there was always this underlying tone that they were not meant to be. He was saddened by this fact.

The morning came she was to fly to Nassau and then on to Bogota, Colombia. They walked out to their terrace and kissed long. He loved the feel of her against him.

She was hesitant to leave, but forced herself. She grabbed her bag and walked down to the hotel lobby and jumped into a taxicab. Malena waved to the three of them and pressed her hand against the glass window. The cab rolled down the drive and onto the road to the airport.

Tony knew Gallo's sadness.

"We invited her to our wedding in April. She said she would come."

Gallo smiled. "Perhaps she will," he said as he walked into the lobby and out to the beach.

The reporters and onlookers numbered in the thousands at JFK Airport when the group arrived with the miracle cat. The papers had Caesar on the front page, knocking off the latest political talking heads and the latest Hollywood noise. Both Jay Leno and David Letterman wanted him on their shows. Paramount and Warner Brothers called to sign him up for a film with Matt Damon, and Friskies wanted him for commercials.

The FBI and DEA gave him awards and citations for bravery. It was hectic, but what made the travelers' day was news out of a Long Island animal hospital and talk of a red cat saved by four birds; this was in the news prior to their entering the scene.

A letter was handed to Libby from a messenger when she arrived home.

It read:

> Your cat, Arthur, is with us. We heard of your Caribbean story
> on the news, and we would like to deliver him to you.
> Signed Dr. Norman Watts, DVM

Libby screamed with happiness, and Tony and Gallo were amazed.

"Look at the old papers. Libby, did you read the story the last two weeks about Arthur? He was saved by birds. They mention it here. One was a peregrine falcon; another a white seagull, a pigeon, and this is the one that sends chills up my spine, a blue jay. You don't suppose it's the same one that always wakes me up outside my window?"

Libby looked at the paper.

"Arthur must have swam to a buoy after Rattel threw him overboard. What a story."

Tony looked outside his window. He didn't see the blue jay, but he knew he was there.

Gallo laughed at Tony.

"You know, after what I've seen Sam and Caesar do these past weeks, nothing surprises me with these guys." Tony couldn't believe it.

Caesar and Sam were ecstatic. Arthur was alive, and that Fletcher saved him was not unusual for the blue jay.

The next day, Arthur arrived, and Libby placed hugs and kisses on him, while Sam and Caesar jumped on him and around him.

"Oh god. I thought you dead for sure," Sam barked.

Arthur was tired but really happy to be home and with his friends. When the three were alone in the living room, Arthur turned to Caesar.

"It was you whom I heard on the water. I never gave up because of you. You saved me, great one."

"Stop calling me that. It was you. You had it in you to save yourself. I just brought it out."

Sam pushed Arthur to go outside. There was a surprise, because on the branches was Fletcher, Clay, Max, and the Princess.

"Well, cat, you made it. I knew it all along," Fletcher chirped out.

"Yeah, I thought you croaked but the blue one here, he never gave up," Clay cooed.

"Thank you, all. We have all become famous, but not as special as Caesar. Enew has blessed us all with you." Arthur smiled.

"Tell them of your adventures, oh great one," Sam laughed.

"Okay, okay, where do we start?"

Caesar began to account the whole tale and his forgetting all of them and then his fight with the dog on the island and finally with the human rat.

Max squawked out, eating a fish bone.

"Is he dead finally?"

Caesar looked up at Max, and his eyes gleamed in the sun. His face appeared radiant in the morning sun. It was finally gone the old feeling since that day his mother was killed.

"I don't know. After the boat hit the rocks I was thrown into the ocean. I never saw him again. The boat was destroyed, and nothing was around."

They all stood silent for a while, and Fletcher broke the silence.

"What is this, a pet cemetery? We should be happy we're all alive and together again."

"You got it, Fletch." Arthur looked up but forgot about the steps; he fell, head first, onto the pavement. He looked up but was not hurt.

His friends all laughed. Life was back to normal again.

Gallo came out on the step and sat next to Caesar. The cat jumped on his lap and made a snuggle point, purring.

Tony and Libby came and sat on the sidewalls of the steps.

"Tony, look, it's those birds, look." Libby was excited. "It has to be them."

"Yeah, yeah. This is scary." Tony shook his head.

The three humans laughed, and Sam barked. Arthur ran to Libby's lap to find her warmth.

Caesar snuggled deeper into Gallo's lap and was at peace with his soul. Life was going to be easier from now on, maybe.

The End

Printed in the United States
206499BV00001B/142/P